MARKING THE OCCASIONS

COLLECTED SHORT STORIES

Andy Botterill

APS Books
Yorkshire

Also By Andy Botterill
An Appointment With God
21 Days In Swansea
A Life In A Day
At Heart A Romantic
Miscellaneous Thoughts
Sick Note & Scrapbook
Welcome Lonely Hearts
Years Spinning By Out Of Control
The Wind Changes Direction
The Sands Of Time
Poems Of The Eighties
Young Punks

APS Books,

The Stables Field Lane, Aberford, West Yorkshire, LS25 3AE

APS Books is a subsidiary of the APS Publications imprint

www.andrewsparke.com

©2025 Andy Botterill

All rights reserved.

First published worldwide by APS Books in 2025

A catalogue record for this book is available from the British Library

CONTENTS

HANGING ON THROUGH THICK AND THIN

You can see it all from here. It's a tiny microcosm of the life outside. They change the sheets twice each day, always at the same time, for those who can't hold their wee in or make it to the bathroom in time. You can watch it happen and watch their embarrassment. You can watch their shame as it trickles down their legs. You can see it all from here. You really can. Each individual aspect of existence is on display to be examined and diagnosed. You can categorise them if you wish. You can separate them off and isolate each sentiment into its component elements.

This ward houses the chronically sick, of whom I'm one. On average we lose about two a week. Sometimes it's more. On occasion it's less. There's no regret. The conveyor belt goes on. It doesn't stop. They wheel in the new ones. Some only last a day or two. Others drag it out. I've dragged it out for six months now. I've been stubborn and awkward. I've interrupted the smooth-running routine. I've hung on, when many would have preferred to see the back of me.

The nurses are polite and efficient. They have their jobs to do. Sometimes they ask if I'm feeling any better. I nod, whether it's true or not. Often, I ask to be moved to the ward for the chronically sick in the head. I deny the physical symptoms and insist mine is a broken heart, a psychological breakdown of the nerves, a temporary relapse and nothing more serious. I try to cut out the pain. I ignore the lumps that appear in my neck and under my arms. I dismiss the hair that falls out in little clumps, the bald patches of a wasted life, and the dark blotches and bruises that stain my skin. I refuse the pills and the medicine. I say I have no need of them.

No one will shake my hand, share the same glass, eat from the same plate or use the same toilet, as if this illness of the heart was somehow contagious. You notice these small things. You notice how they gain significance and meaning. Mostly I use a bedpan. Normally I get to it in time. Occasionally I don't. I ask them when I'll be allowed home. They tell me quite soon. Somehow, I don't believe them.

I feel my energy draining. I'm exhausting myself by continuing this writing as I've always done. It's force of habit. Somehow, you can't reverse the patterns you've set or break the mould and the habits of a lifetime. It would be nice to be able to walk into a shop or go to a pub. Just to stroll down the street or eat a good meal would mean a lot. These

1

simple things remain tantalisingly out of reach. It doesn't matter. It's not important. You can't have everything at once. I think I'd settle for a letter right now, and a little piece and quiet.

IN THE CAGE

The mirror and the man have become as one. Outside the mirror the man doesn't seem to possess a life of his own. The reflected image is his subtle heartbeat. The cold, dull surface is his soft breath. He can't be isolated or ignored or remain unseen. He's given his soul and his entire being to the glass on the wall. His face is only seen in the mirror and can't be seen elsewhere.

I conclude the man isn't happy. It's not that he's so obviously miserable, but he doesn't smile, and he has that look of scarred indifference which seems to fit so comfortably on the expressions of the broken-hearted. He doesn't move much at first. He just stares blankly from his reflection and lets his eyes do all the talking. Then he reaches across the table and takes a can of beer from a pack of four lying in front of him and begins to drink in little gulps, almost like a fish breathing. There's a letter on the table, already opened, and he picks it up and fingers it, whilst simultaneously lighting a cigarette which his other hand, which he inhales on. Only the words at the beginning and end of the neatly written text can be clearly read. *I think if we would be best if we never see each other again, love Christine*, it finishes.

There are other letters on the table, seemingly older ones. He glances through them, as if they have some deeper meaning and then lets them flutter to the floor. There's also a photograph. It carries the face of an attractive, young woman. The man picks it up and pauses, touching its edges, viewing it as if it was almost something important. Once more he inhales from his cigarette, and then quite calmly and deliberately holds the burning end to the unmoved, smiling face in the photograph, which starts to darken, then shrivel, then flare up into a crimson flame. As it nears his holding fingertips, he lets the burning coated paper drop impartially onto the table. The man also burns the letters in the same delicate fashion, as if it doesn't touch or move him. He then sits back almost surprised he could do what he's just done. Quickly, however, his trance is broken, and he reaches for a bottle of vodka in front of him, pouring a glass and drinking from it in large, neat mouthfuls, one after another. Then he picks up his notebook and enters the date. It's December 24th, 1974. He leaves the rest blank.

There's a wash basin in the corner of the room. The man in the mirror gets up and walks over to it with a casual air. There's an old, cut-throat razor on the basin rim which he picks up and opens the blade. Holding his arm under the running tap, the man slowly draws the blade across his pale, shrunken wrist. He watches with impassive eyes as the blood spurts out in scarlet jets like coloured water from a novelty fountain over his hands and onto the white ceramics, before trickling down the plughole, and that's it. He just waits for the end to come.

There's a room with a table and mirror. The furniture's been somewhat rearranged and there's the faint residue of a stubborn, dark stain on the carpet by the basin that hasn't quite been scrubbed out. It looks like someone has tried to remove it, perhaps many times, but has been unable to do so with complete success. Part of the stain always remains as testament to something that occurred there once. The curtains are drawn back and sunlight's able to filter into the room for the first time in many years. It's cold outside and the trees are coated with a thin layer of frost. There's nothing on the table except a copy of *The Daily Telegraph* printed in London and dated December 24th, 1984. A voice, the landlady's, drifts into the room from the passageway beyond.

'You say you saw a young man kill himself? Are you sure it was this room? You must be mistaken. It can't be.'

'But I saw him. I saw his reflection. He was in the mirror. I saw him take hold of the razor,' a second voice, that of a woman, replies.

'But all that happened years ago…'

'Yes, I know. I knew him. I should never have come back here again. Will he never leave me alone?'

'Please don't excite yourself. Here, now you just sit down, and I'll make you a nice cup of tea,' the landlady says soothingly.

'But I saw him…'

'Yes, of course you did my dear.'

The landlady is interrupted by a knock at the door, which she goes to answer.

'Hold on, I won't be a minute. Just sit yourself down nice and quietly whilst I answer that,' she says, before hurrying off down the stairs.

'Mrs Paynter? I understand you might have the person we're looking for. We thought she might come back here.'

3

An ambulanceman stands on the steps with a concerned but understanding expression on his face and several support orderlies standing behind him.

'Thank God you're here. I didn't know what to do. She's upstairs. She's been talking about a dead man or something here in the building,' Mrs Paynter explains.

'That's all right. It's nothing to worry about. It's quite usual and totally expected for someone with her condition,' the ambulanceman says calmly in an attempt to sound reassuring, as if the situation isn't something to get unduly alarmed by.

'Is there anything I can do?' Mrs Paynter asks.

'No, I'm sorry. There's nothing anybody can do for her,' the ambulanceman replies.

With the help of Mrs Paynter and the orderlies he leads the hysterical woman from the house and into the back of the waiting ambulance parked outside. She's seated on a reclining chair and a thick blanket is wrapped around her. The rear doors then shut, and the ambulance pulls slowly away from the kerb and into the road.

ON OPPOSITE SIDES

'So you don't love me anymore? You think I could care? Do you think you were the only one? Do you want to know just how wrong you are?'

The man talking stares into a darkened room, trying to separate the animate objects from the shadows. The lighting is subdued, and the television is off. Only the sound of a radio echoes somewhere in the distance. His voice cuts through the tense atmosphere. A meal lies half eaten at a table. Only one place is set. A woman sits with her back to the man. She doesn't answer him. She allows him to rant on uninterrupted and with complete freedom.

'Oh, there were plenty of them all right. The first was on our honeymoon in fact; a pretty, young waitress. Ah, but it didn't stop there. That was just the start. I did it with some of your friends, when they came round, and you weren't here. And you thought we just sat and talked. Ha! How naïve you were.'

He sounds almost triumphant in his recounting. The woman doesn't even look up, so the man continues.

'Tell me, does it hurt to hear these things? Does it hurt to find out you weren't so very special after all and to know you weren't the only one? Does it hurt you now as much as you've hurt me?'

'Is it true Peter? Did you really do that to me?'

The woman finally speaks, but she doesn't turn her head. She continues to keep her back to the man as part of a quite deliberate and pointed action against him. She doesn't want to have to see his face or have to look into his eyes.

'I thought it worked for a time. Was I so wrong?' she asks.

Only her voice can be heard. Her figure is still immersed in shadow and half light.

'Are you asking me to carry on living this lie? Is that what you want from me? From what you say, I should have ended it much sooner,' she tells him.

And then the full realisation of his admission hits her.

'On our honeymoon? Is that really true? You bastard! What made you do it? I thought we were happy?'

'I thought we were happy too,' Peter replies solemnly.

'How could you?' she demands to know.

'It was easy.'

She finally turns now to face him.

'And Claire, did you sleep with her too?' she asks.

'What do you think Sarah? You know I always liked her. How could you be so stupid? Of course we did it. Is that what you wanted to hear? Does it make you any happier knowing the truth now?' Peter enquires coldly.

'I can't believe this is happening to me. I can't believe you're saying these things. I trusted you. I really did. I wanted it to work. I gave it everything. For five years, I didn't give up,' she announces and then stops, realising further conversation is virtually pointless. 'Look, just take your things and get out. I never want to see you again. Do you understand?'

Peter doesn't move. The expression on his face doesn't change or betray what he's thinking inside.

'Please, it would be better if you just leave,' Sarah continues. 'But before you go, let me just tell you this. You know you were my first.'

Her words hold him back and grab his attention.

'You know I saved myself for you,' she tells him. 'I didn't want to be like all those other girls, sleeping around and getting pregnant at sixteen.

You don't want to be that foolish, I said to myself. You don't want to do things you'll regret. You know I still a virgin when we first met, and now you tell me this. Anyway, I think you've heard enough. Just go!'

'If that's what you want?' Peter asks and Sarah nods. 'It's actually what you've wanted for a long time, isn't it?' he observes. 'Yes, I'll leave all right. I'll collect my things and go. I've got better things to do than waste my time with you anyway.'

'You do that. Just get out! And don't bother with any goodbyes. There's no need for them. I've had enough of your pathetic excuses and lies for a lifetime.'

The front door slams shut as he leaves.

'Claire, there's a woman at reception who says she wants to speak to you. She says it's important.'

Claire looks up.

'Did she give her name?'

'No, I'm sorry, I didn't ask, but she was very insistent. I asked her if it could wait until after work. She said it couldn't,' the receptionist explains.

'OK, I suppose I can break off for a moment,' Claire says reluctantly.

She gets up from her desk and walks from her office to the waiting area. She sees Sarah standing by the door and greets her.

'Hello Sarah, what brings you here out of the blue?' Claire asks.

'Only this,' Sarah replies, reaching into the bag she's carrying and pulling out a gun, a small, medium calibre revolver that fits her hand perfectly like a glove. 'You slept with my husband, didn't you?' Sarah continues.

'Don't be so ridiculous. Of course I didn't,' Claire replies firmly, but with a tangible sense of alarm and rising panic in her voice. "Look, just sit down and we'll talk about this. You can't be well. You're not yourself. I'll get you a doctor. Someone call the police.

'It's too late, too late for you Claire. Goodbye you snake!'

Sarah gently squeezes the trigger. A single shot rings out. Claire clutches her side. Blood spreads across her torn dress where the bullet entered, the red poisoning its elegant whiteness. She staggers back. She still manages to look up. Her face is a picture of tortured disbelief. A second shot passes straight through her heart. She's dead before she hits the ground and the gun slides from Sarah's hand. Sarah makes no attempt to run or disguise what she's done. She waits motionless for someone to take her into custody.

At the prison visiting room, two people sit on opposite sides of a thick, glass screen that separates them. They stare at each other, trying to bridge the enormous physical and metaphorical gulf that keeps them apart and as divided as their stricken emotions, but they never quite manage it. Success and resolution elude their doomed efforts.

'Why did you come here? You needn't have bothered. We have nothing more to say surely,' Sarah announces.

'Oh Sarah, why did you kill her?' Peter enquires forlornly and with a tone of near desperation in his voice.

'Why did I kill her? That's a stupid question. She destroyed my life, didn't she?' Sarah points out.

'Sarah, I don't know how to say this, but I never slept with Claire, or the others. I just said it to make you jealous, because you were leaving me. It wasn't true, not a word of it. There were never any others. There was only you.'

Sarah's face remains frozen as his words slowly sink in and the enormity of them quietly dawns on her. She doesn't reply. There really is nothing more to say now. She gets up quite calmly and without so much as looking at Peter returns to her waiting cell. She knows that it or one very like it will be her home for the next twenty or thirty years at least.

THE HOMECOMING

It's been a long, hard, painful journey and things will never be the same again. Nothing can remain as it was or be seen in the same way. Every connection has been broken. Every fear has found a new home. Every loved one has been taken. Every emotion that can be experienced has been, but not one could move him now. He's been through them all and reached the end of the line. He doesn't know which was worse, the fighting or the waiting. He remains tortured by the knowledge that each new skirmish could be the last, or the first of many more yet to come. He tries to remain optimistic, but it's hard. Perhaps something will change and the biting cold give way to spring and summer. He prays for the crushing burden of war to be lifted, and his soul to be released from its obligations, but it never happens. There are no trees and no flowers, only mud, and death, a lonely friend.

He knew he was going to die eventually, just as his friends had done. That much was certain. He knew there was no way out and it was just a matter of time before he could let go and drift off into a higher kingdom, far away from the place he was in. Then suddenly without warning he was on his way home, out of that hellish pit. He didn't know why or what had happened, whether it was shell shock, a bullet wound or complete mental breakdown. Perhaps he'd simply forgotten or was just too tired to care anymore. But out of the blue they sent him away and unexpectedly he was back here, on familiar shores, alive and a free man.

Now standing as he is on Southampton Docks on a fine, cloudless Tuesday, there are no flags waving. There are no Royal Marine bandsmen to greet him. No red carpets are rolled out. No civic reception in the Town Hall is planned. No Mayor's banquet is prepared, where he is the honorary guest. There is nothing much at all. Everything is still and quiet, with only the sound of seagulls overhead and the lapping motion of waves on shingle in the distance breaking the May silence.

The sky is clear and cloudless, and this is England for the first time in so long. He has a small suitcase with him, all battered and worn at the edges, with just a few personal possessions to cling to that he can call his own. He's starting to remember a few things now. Tiny details are slowly returning to him that he can piece together to make something whole and of meaning. It's funny how it all seems so strangely familiar and dare he think it normal. He wonders how it can possibly be so normal after everything that's happened and everything they've been through. It makes little or no sense to him, but then nothing does. Perhaps no one knew the dark reality of what had gone on over there. Perhaps they just didn't care. Perhaps they'd simply forgotten and refused to remember. Perhaps it was a case of out of sight and out of mind. He can think of no logical explanation to justify the apathy he's seeing.

His mother is the owner of a small grocery store on the edge of the city centre and lives in the rooms above, or she did. He assumes she still does. He's not heard otherwise. One day the shop will be his and he hopes to settle down there and make a wife of his childhood sweetheart and have two kids or more if they can. One will be called Christine, if it's a girl, and the other Simon. He feels sure he'll have at least one boy whomever he marries.

He walks at a leisurely pace, trying to take it all in as it gradually comes back to him, bit by bit. He recalls certain particulars of where people and old acquaintances have lived and died, many in the same row of houses all their lives, born and bred in the only town they knew as home, much like him. He remembers the faces he used to know and the places he used to go to. He wonders if things can really be the same as they appear and as they'd always been after so many years, or if it's just an illusion and under the surface things have in fact changed and moved on, as indeed everything invariably must in the fullness of time.

As the old shop comes into view, he's quietly reassured. It looks just as it should and as he hoped and expected it to. He feels glad his mother has kept it the way he liked it and as he'd always remembered it, the way it had been in his father's lifetime, as the old man would have wanted it, the way it suited them and the way it looked best. There was no great surprise about that. He remembers the old woman's scrawny, ageing face, ravaged with the lines of a lifetime of hard work. He remembers his father's fists, all scarred and creased. He wasn't one to be messed with. He could pack a fair punch when he had to all right. As a boy he used to steal apples from a nearby orchard from time to time and eat them behind a derelict farm building where no one could see him. Occasionally his father would catch him and give him a good beating from the palms of his giant hands. He was a hard, unaffectionate man but he had morals and principles, and he stuck to them.

But that was the past. His son is here now and this is his home, or the last proper home he had. It has a feeling of familiarity which he enjoys and makes him feel warm inside. It beckons to him and calls out his name. It holds a sense of security like a mother's shoulder to cry on or a girlfriend's loving kiss. Something instinctively tells him he belongs here. All his memories and dreams for the future are held here behind this door. It's real and solid to his touch. He won't change it when it's his.

At first he's frightened to knock. He hadn't sent a letter to say he was coming. It had barely sunk in even to himself that he was really coming home. He thought it would never happen, but he was wrong. Here he is, back on home ground, standing outside that familiar, scratched wooden door, like he'd never been away. He wonders if perhaps the army had notified them and given the date he'd be arriving. He cautiously hopes so. He realises it would make it somewhat easier and less startling if they had a little advanced warning of his homecoming.

He touches the door with the back of his hand in an indecisive manner. He pauses, almost as if there is something stopping him continuing. His first knock is so light as to be barely audible. He hits it again, this time a little harder and with his knuckles. He then steps back into the street, where he is half hidden by the shadow of the building and so his mother can't see his face or recognise him too quickly. He wants to surprise her at least a little by his presence, and hopefully in a good way. The door creaks open. In fact, it is he who is surprised. It isn't his mother who confronts him with open arms, but someone strangely unfamiliar. It's a man he doesn't know and has never seen before.

'Oh, excuse me, I'm sorry to bother you but is Mrs Bennett home?'

He coughs with slight embarrassment and shuffles awkwardly. The man looks up. He's middle-aged, unshaven and has a receding hairline.

'Mrs Bennett, the old woman who used to live here? No, sorry squire, she sold up ages ago. She went to live with her sister, I think. Yes, I remember now. She said something about a son, but he wouldn't be needing the place no more. She said he wouldn't be coming back from the war. She hadn't heard anything for so long you see. It was easier just to assume he was lost for good. I guess she didn't want to raise too many false hopes. Well, you know what they say it's like at the front. It's hell all right. I suppose she just couldn't face kidding herself there was any real chance he'd ever be coming back. It was better to accept the inevitable.'

Bennett doesn't respond. He's a little shaken and lost for the words, as the man continues his monologue.

'He was one of the first to go you know. I remember her saying to me. She was quite proud of him in her own way. But they don't last long out there, do they? So many of our boys have gone missing and no one knows what's happened to them. It's hard to say for certain. Then again, if he was shot as a deserter, it would be better not knowing. Perhaps she knew more than she was saying. The truth is I don't really know. I only know she's not here now.'

'Thank you for your trouble. You've told me all I needed to hear,' Bennett says and starts to move away.

The man calls him back.

'Say, why aren't you in the army, fighting at the front with the others your age? A young man like you ought to be doing his bit for King and Country. You should be ashamed of yourself sitting it out back home. I'd give you a white feather if I had one.'

Bennett's completely forgotten he's back in his civilian clothes. He doesn't reply or try to explain. The man can think what he wishes as far as Bennett is concerned. He simply turns and slowly starts to walk away. He hears the man mutter something else under his breath and then the door shuts behind him. Bennett needs a drink but remembers the pubs won't be open yet, not like in France where they're open all the time. He decides to go for a walk to clear his head and think things through. He realises he's truly alone now. He recalls a small public park he used to go to as a child and he finds himself heading there.

Bennett reaches the park gates and pushes them open. He stands for a moment in the entrance, surveying its once familiar grounds. Countless memories come flooding back to him. He can see a young woman in the distance. To his amazement it's Lily. She's waving. Is she beckoning him over? Is it his name she's calling? In his confused state, he thinks it is. He blinks several times to see if he's simply dreaming instead. He suspects his mind is merely playing games and tricks on his tired brain. He stares again. She could almost be real, but he knows it can't be her. He must be mistaken. Surely, it's too good to be true. It's only his imagination, he tells himself, but it doesn't matter. Any reminder of her is better than none. She remains beautiful and always will be to him. From where he is, he accepts the passing moments of watching gratefully and with quiet admiration. He knows them for what they are and is fully aware the likelihood is he's destined for disappointment and nothing more.

Yet wait, perhaps it really is her. It's so hard to tell from where he's standing and with the passage of time. He can only make out the bare outline of her figure against a dazzling background. He realises the years have probably taken a heavy toll on their relationship anyway and they can't just pick up where they were. It's almost certainly too late to save what they had and start again, but for his personal sanity he has to find out. If only he could have written to say he was coming home. She was second on his list to track down after his mum. Perhaps if he'd written he'd be with her already. They'd be together now and could marry and settle down and have those children he so dearly wanted. Or was it all just a forlorn dream and indeed beyond saving?

Bennett pauses briefly to gather his composure. He has to consider what he should say to her. He lifts his head and begins to wander slowly in the direction of Lily, careful not to move too suddenly or too quickly, lest she should notice or be alarmed by his presence, and he should scare her off. He's so close now that if he shouted, she'd surely hear. But no, he decides to wait a little longer until he gets even closer. He's aware he could almost reach out and touch her, if it was his wish to do so. He takes in every last detail of her elegantly defined figure, as he surveys her timeless features, casting his eyes up and down, trying to determine what's different and what's changed about her, if anything has. There's nothing obvious that he can put his finger on. She appears the same as she always was.

He falters momentarily in his step as she throws her head back. She's laughing gaily with obvious pleasure and delight. Her hair iscaught in the gentle breeze and wraps itself round her bright, beaming face. She's content, happy and enjoying herself. It's clear for anyone to see. Perhaps it's not too late after all, Bennett thinks to himself. Perhaps he can still be a part of her life and make her happiness complete. He wishes he could hold her in his arms again, just long enough to express his undying love, to explain the truth, to tell her how he feels and in fact has always felt about her.

Just then she turns. Someone has been standing behind her all this time but obscured from Bennett's view. His mind has been so engrossed by strange thoughts and forgotten feelings from the past, his senses too exhausted by the day's events, even to notice and to make the connection between them. It's another man, older than Bennett and the age of conscription, with greying hair but with a distinguished manner about him. He's handsome in his way and he walks towards Lily with arms outstretched. She takes his hands in hers and throws herself lovingly around his impressively lean torso. They embrace warmly. They're evidently lovers. It's clear for all to see. There can be no doubt. It's all so obvious. She didn't wait. The savage truth stares Bennett in the face at barely an arm's length, and he recoils back.

It's very simple now, he thinks to himself. There's no need for further thought or reflection. She's betrayed his trust and that's that. He stops in his tracks. He knows to go any further would be pointless. Reopening old wounds, dredging up memories from the past and confronting her with them, would serve no purpose. His shallow attempts to invoke her pity, to make her feel sorry for him, to question her choices and how she came by them would in the final analysis look bitter and misguided and fall sadly short of the mark. Better instead to leave what is as it is. He realises she's lost to him forever and they can never return to their previous life. He must make a dignified exit and leave her to her newfound existence.

To the rejected lover, all sorrows look alike. There's nowhere to hide, no place where you can forget, no way you can't be wounded, cut open with a single hurtful word, your inner most feelings exposed, put on full public view and subjected to ridicule. The vanquished have no pride, Bennett reflects with regret. He knows now he has no right to be here at all, to bring back old memories with no future and offer them without dignity as a substitute for real love. There's nothing left for him here. It's all been a terrible mistake. It's so sad but true, and he knows it now. There's only France to go back to. There's only France and the slaughter and the mud. There's only France to return to. It's waiting for him with callous eagerness and death in its clutches.

He knows he will surely die this time, sooner or later, but it doesn't matter. After all, it was what they always wanted. Well, wasn't it? And they'll never know the difference. They'll never know how he bled and went to hell and back to be reunited with them. Serving England and Great Britain again is all that matters now. There will just be a letter on a mantelpiece somewhere and a medal to remember him by, to show to friends and family once in a while from time to time saying he gave his life willingly for King and Country. He won't be entirely forgotten.

PLEASE LOOK AFTER THE FAMILY

'I'm sorry Mr Crosby. It's not my responsibility. I have no authority to just dish out money. That's not how the system works. You'll have to complete all the necessary paperwork, go through the usual procedures and interviews and they'll decide in due course what your entitlements are if any.'

'And just how long will that take?' Crosby asks irritably.

He feels he's going round in circles and getting nowhere. It's been the same for the past half hour at least.

'I can't say for sure, but it shouldn't take more than a month if there are no issues and delays,' Crosby is duly informed.

'A month?' Crosby repeats with incredulity. 'And how am I supposed to manage until then? You realise I have a wife and children to support,' he adds with a note of desperation in his voice.

'Well, you should have thought about that before you gave up your job,' he's told somewhat curtly.

'Look, I was forced to work away from home, and it wasn't working out for anybody. My kids missed me. Do you think I want them growing up without seeing their father every day? My wife missed me badly too. We couldn't stand to be apart. Besides, I could hardly support myself anyway, let alone send much money back for them,' Crosby explains pleadingly.

Subconsciously he realises all too well his pleas are destined to fall on deaf ears.

'I appreciate what you're saying, but as I say it's not up to me,' the young man behind the reception desk reiterates impassively.

He looks a little bored and mildly embarrassed at Crosby's relentless and unending series of questions, which he's already answered more than once. In fact, he's answered them many times in different ways and from a variety of angles and perspectives without fully getting his point across. He has an air of increasing exasperation about him. He's beginning to lose patience with this particular claimant and fidgets a little awkwardly in his seat as he's forced to explain the official position to Crosby yet again.

'I'm sorry. This is just my job. There are rules to be followed. I don't make them. I can't take sides or tell you anything different than I already have done, whatever my personal views on the matter,' he reaffirms.

'No, but you could try to be a bit more understanding,' Crosby pleads.

'Believe me, I do understand, but there's absolutely nothing more I can do. Look, I've tried to explain the situation as best I can. Now as you are aware other people are waiting. You'll just have to wait and see what happens when they process your application.'

The waiting room is indeed full of other anxious people, waiting nervously for their appointments. More are arriving all the time and there are simply insufficient staff and space to accommodate them.

'I've been waiting in this office for three hours myself this morning,' Crosby states indignantly. 'Is that what I'm to do every day?' he asks, with a palpable measure of anger and growing frustration in his tone that he finds hard to disguise.

'In fairness you didn't have an appointment. Other people have. You're lucky to have been seen at all,' the young man points out.

'I see. So I should be grateful? Is that what you're telling me?' Crosby retorts.

'Really, this is ridiculous. Others are waiting for their scheduled appointments. We can't discuss it further now. If you want to come back later when there's less of a queue, perhaps we can talk about it then, but truthfully there's nothing more to say on the matter,' the young man states firmly, in a forlorn effort finally to bring their conversation to a close.

'Don't worry, I'll be back all right and sooner than you think,' Crosby announces, turning on his heels and walking purposefully towards the door.

An hour later, Crosby returns. 'This is my wife. If you look closely, you'll notice her arms and hands have a nasty rash. It's not considered sufficiently urgent, however, for her to see a doctor at present. Never mind. I'm sure there are more pressing cases to be dealt with. And these are the kids. You'll observe their clothes don't quite fit and their faces are a little pale and thin. We can't afford to feed them every day and the clothes they're wearing were the best we could get from *Oxfam*,' he continues.

'And this gun I had from the time I worked on a farm. I was going to sell it. It might have bought us another meal, but perhaps I've found a better use for it after all,' Crosby says coldly and without apparent emotion.

He casually lifts a double-barrelled weapon out of the bag he's carrying and without looking points it in the general direction of the Social Security clerk. He fires once. The young man's face is blown clean off. Crosby then turns the gun on himself.

'Please look after the family,' he mutters as he pulls the trigger.

A child screams. A dull explosion fills the air and then there's silence. Not everyone in the waiting room even seems to notice.

A DIRTY JOB

'Do you mind if we join you?' Mr Anderson enquires jovially

'No, not at all. Please pull up a seat,' is the reply.

'Well, it seems rather silly just four of us dining in the restaurant and not sitting together,' Mr Anderson suggests with a good-natured smile. 'This is my wife, Gillian,' he says, introducing his companion.

'Hello,' their fellow diners reply in unison.

'My name's Anderson. I own a little café just around the corner. We've only just moved in, and I thought we should check out the competition. Perhaps you can tell me what you think of the food here,' Mr Anderson says hopefully.

'Certainly, we'd be very happy to. I'm sorry, I haven't introduced myself. My name's Bob Morley and this is my wife, Sandra. We're on holiday in the area,' Bob explains.

'Yes, it's a lovely part of the country at this time of year,' Mr Anderson agrees.

'That's why we like to come here. It's not our first visit by any means you know,' Bob says. 'You could say we're almost regular visitors or have been in the past at least.'

'Really, that's wonderful to hear. We need all the tourists we can get,' Mr Anderson says, getting up and calling over the waiter. 'Another bottle of wine,' he requests. 'Sparkling if you have it.'

As instructed the waiter brings a bottle of chilled, sparkling white wine and places it on the table.

'I'll do the honours,' Mr Anderson tells him.

'As you wish sir,' the waiter replies and retires quietly with a little bow.

Mr Anderson pulls out the cork with a flamboyant flourish and pours four glasses of the bubbly liquid.

'Ladies and gentlemen, may I propose a toast to the four of us,' he announces.

He holds up his glass and takes a deep gulp of the fragrant wine. Sandra pulls at Bob's arm as if she wishes to say something. Mr Anderson looks a little puzzled, as if his moment as dinner party host is being compromised in small some way.

'Is something wrong?' he enquires.

'No, not at all. I'd just like a quick word with my husband in private if you don't mind,' Sandra explains.

'Why of course not. Go right ahead,' Mr Anderson replies, undaunted by the request.

Bob and Sandra momentarily depart.

16

'I've seen that face before somewhere,' Sandra whispers to Bob with concern in her voice once they're out of earshot. 'I'm sure I have. I know him. I just can't think how.'

'Don't be silly dear. Who would recognise us here?' Bob asks.

'I don't know, but I've got a bad feeling, and I don't think we should stay. I'm sure I recognise him. I think he knows who we are. Why else would he come over? That's not normal behaviour. We can't take the chance. He may be a police officer. He's probably lying about being a café owner and been following us for weeks. It was your idea to escape. You should never have done it. I should never have let you,' Sandra says, with a growing sense of alarm.

'It's all right. Don't worry. Leave it to me. We'll go back quietly and talk to him normally. Try to be pleasant and be careful not to arouse his suspicion. Don't let him think there's something wrong and we're onto him. If you're right and he is who we think he is, there's only one course of action to take,' Bob says.

'What's that?' Sandra wonders, barely daring to hear the answer.

'We'll have to kill him of course,' Bob confirms to his wife's horror.

'You can't commit another murder,' Sandra objects.

'Why not? Once you've done one, what's one more?' Bob says callously. 'What's the matter? Are you getting cold feet or something? You shouldn't have agreed to this in the first place if you are,' Bob tells her.

'I just don't want any more trouble,' Sandra says defiantly.

'Just do everything I say, and it will all be OK,' Bob assures her.

'Promise me, darling. Tell me I can trust you,' Sandra begs.

'Of course, you can always trust me,' Bob insists, squeezing her shoulder as a means of reassurance.

They return to the table together.

'I trust everything's all right?' Mr Anderson asks. 'I was just saying to my wife I thought I recognised you both. I can't think how though.'

'I shouldn't think so,' Bob replies hurriedly.

'That's what Gillian said, but I'm not so sure. You're not a golfing man, are you? I used to play a spot of golf before I messed up my arm,' Mr Anderson explains.

'No, I've never played,' Bob insists. 'Now if you'll excuse us, we must be going.'

'So soon?' Mr Anderson asks with a hint of disappointment.

'Yes, we have a train to catch,' Bob says.

'What, now? From here?' Mr Anderson enquires, looking somewhat confused by their sudden need to depart.

'No, but a little later on,' Bob confirms. 'We have to get to the station first and we don't want to miss it.'

'Well, if you must of course, but what about your wine?' Mr Anderson reminds the couple.

'You have it,' Bob says.

'Well, if you insist,' Mr Anderson reluctantly agrees.

Bob nods.

'I do,' he says.

Bob and Sandra quickly gather their things and leave. They wait just around the corner from the restaurant.

'They'll probably follow us out shortly,' Bob says. 'They'll wait a few minutes and then come after us. They won't want to make it too obvious. Neither will they want us to get too far away.'

Bob's voice tails off, lost in the cold, moist air of late evening.

'I suppose you've got to do it. You have no choice,' Sandra says, with a note of urgency and a grudging acceptance that their options in the situation they find themselves in are limited.

'Yes, it has to be done,' Bob concurs. 'There's nothing else for it. As soon as they come out, we'll do both of them and make it quick.'

'You'll have to find an excuse to get them somewhere quiet,' Sandra suggests.

'It's all right. I have an idea. I'll ask them to show us their café for another time,' Bob says. 'I'll say something like if we're passing again, we'd like to pop in.'

'That should do it,' Sandra agrees.

'Right, this is how we'll go about it,' Bob starts to unveil his murderous plan, and Sandra listens with care and close attention.

Time passes slowly. They wait outside anxiously. Bob lights a cigarette and inhales deeply. Angrily he stubs it out on a wall and begins to pace. Ten minutes become fifteen. The tension mounts palpably.

'Why are they taking so long?' Bob asks.

The lined expression on Sandra's face doesn't alter. Finally, there's some movement at the restaurant door. Mr Anderson emerges first, helping his wife into her coat, as she follows just behind him. He doesn't see Bob and Sandra at first but looks up as Bob begins to walk across to where they're standing.

'You're still here?' Mr Anderson enquires. 'I thought you had a train to catch.'

'Yes, silly me, I got the times wrong,' Bob says, smiling casually and trying to keep Mr Anderson at his ease.

'You could have had that wine after all,' Mr Anderson observes.

'It seems so,' Bob nods. 'But it does mean we've got a bit of time to kill. We thought you might be able to find a moment to show us your new place.'

'Why certainly, it would be a pleasure, though I must confess we have drunk rather a lot with that extra bottle of wine. But it's not far. It's only round the corner, if you'd like to come with us,' Mr Anderson says.

The four of them walk closely together.

'This is the shortcut,' Mr Anderson explains, pointing to a dark alleyway.

Bob senses his opportunity. He and Sandra lag slightly behind.

Suddenly Bob stops. 'Turn around slowly,' he hisses.

Mr Anderson turns, as does his wife, Gillian. Bob has a gun in his hand.

'What's the meaning of this?' Mr Anderson asks, unsure exactly what's taking place. 'Is this some kind of joke? Do you mean to rob us? Believe me, we don't have anything of any great value, and I don't have much left in my wallet.'

'It's not a joke,' Bob tells him.

There's not a hint of a smile on his face. It's beginning to dawn on Mr Anderson it's no joke at all.

'You shouldn't have followed us here,' Bob continues. 'We know who you are.'

'I don't know what you mean,' Mr Anderson protests. 'You're frightening me. Please put the gun away. We can talk about this. It's just a misunderstanding of some sort. I'm sure there's a logical explanation and we can sort it out between us.'

'No, I'm sorry. There's no time for talk. You both have to die I'm afraid,' Bob insists coldly.

There's an ear-splitting detonation in a confined space. Mr Anderson lurches backwards as he takes the full force of the bullet in the stomach. Gillian's mouth drops open as if she's about to scream, but there's no sound, only shock and silence. Bob turns the gun on her and fires into her chest. She drops to the floor.

'Check his wallet, Bob. It will say who he is. You'll see. You had to do it,' Sandra says.

Bob reaches into the bloodied coat pocket and pulls out a wad of papers. He shuffles through them. Suddenly he stops and steps back.

'What is it?' Sandra asks.

'Oh my God! We've got to get out of here,' Bob announces.

'What is it, Bob? Tell me,' Sandra presses him.

'They're his probation papers. I've killed the wrong person. He's a fellow lag. He must have been in prison with me. That's where you saw him. He was another inmate. How stupid I didn't realise myself,' Bob says.

'Drop it!' A voice suddenly from behind.

Bob turns. Armed policemen confront him. One levels a pistol at Bob's chest. Another steps forward with handcuffs.

'You picked the wrong place to do your dirty work this time mate,' he says. 'There's a police station just across the square. How you could think no one would hear a gunshot here.'

Neither Bob nor Sandra reply, as they're led away. They know it's a fair cop and they're in for a very long stretch inside.

ALL OUR YESTERDAYS

She stands in the doorway, her bags in her hands and her coat draped over her arm. She glances around, her eyes gliding over shelves and desktops for that book or record she might have missed and is in danger of leaving behind. Neither angrily nor sadly she says she has everything and mutters a sort of mumbled bye as she leaves. I start to speak.

'How can you do this to me?' I ask.

I remind her of her many promises. I remind her of all the good times. It's no use or doesn't appear to be.

'How did we let it come to this?' I ask.

'It's easy,' she answers. 'I no longer feel the way about you I did. I've tried to make it work. God only know I have, but there's no way it ever will do. It's just the way it is. It's no one's fault. We both just have to accept that and move on with our lives.'

Your first thought is always to kill yourself, go ahead and finally do it. Pull the razor across your shrunken wrist or put your head in the oven and turn on the gas. Your second thought is inevitably one of hate, not for the love you've lost, but the sense of bitterness, rejection and uselessness. You picture her in the future out drinking with friends, the ones who never liked you and always said she was better off without you. You picture her in the arms of other men, and it makes you feel a little sick, but there's nothing you can do to change the reality of the situation you face. You know you still love her underneath. It's just so hard to admit.

You disguise your hurt by cutting yourself from the outside world and distancing yourself from the truth. You picture her ravaged face after a night of too much drink, followed by unplanned sex. You turn on the TV to take your mind off it. You see fragments of her in every gesture and every voice. You see her skin draped over every person, her bones hidden in every limb. You see her unmistakeable expression on every face, and it haunts you still. The flickering screen has no sympathy for your plight and never will. You shout out her name and it bounces off all four walls without reply. The anguish of her silence only serves to muffle your inner world, and you sink into it even further than you already are.

Finally, you reach a decision. You hold the jerrycan of petrol in your hand, remove the cap and start to douse the entire room; walls, floor, furniture and all. When you've finished you cover your entire body too; your head, your feet, your arms, limbs, legs, torso, chest and clothes. You are determined to extinguish all memories forever in one grand gesture no one will ever forget or ignore. You fumble inside a coat pocket for a match. You have a vision in your head of your love burning crimson and then existing no more. You hold the match but at the last lose your nerve and merely carry on as you've always done, alone. It's the only way to keep going.

REACHING FOR THE SUN

The rattle of a lock; slowly the key turns and footsteps echo in the confined space of ceiling and corridor and grow more distant and eventually disappear. An eye peers through the small keyhole and sees nothing but a dark void and emptiness. The blanket of darkness is only broken by a single streak of fine light that cuts through it at one point, dissecting and illuminating the thick dust that floats suspended in the heavy, torrid air like a knife through butter. The sharpness of this one ray of hope contrasts starkly with the anguished gloom it's surrounded with. Where the light comes from is uncertain. Another room perhaps, a skylight or a window to the outside world?

From within a barefoot young man licks his lips and wipes his mouth in dull, feverish repetition. Awkwardly and with sustained determination, he repeats this strange action over and over again. He fidgets incessantly as if in constant turmoil and discomfort. The tiny space he inhabits is all he knows and the limits and extent of his sorry existence and forced confinement. There are a few bare living essentials inside his locked room, including a single bed, a scuffed table, a wobbly shelf containing a few bits and pieces, a lamp powered by a low wattage bulb and not much else. There's a small mirror on the wall, in which he likes to examine himself for changes to his appearance.

He drags his long, jagged nails over his face, until a cut gracefully opens on his fragile skin like a flower, and he draws blood. He's fascinated by the redness. It absorbs him wholly, as he lets the blood drip down his cheek and a drop hits the floor beneath with a pleasing splash like a raindrop. He remains unmoved. He blocks out the stinging pain with ease by sheer will power and concentration of the mind. The intricacy of the delicate operation captivates his entire being and dulls the hurt of torn nerves. He has the skill of a surgeon but isn't one. He stares coldly and impassively at the colour of his own blood and thinks of it as mere paint. It obsesses him fully as if it's an art. The action he performs swallows him totally and spits him out. The control of mind over matter or flesh in this case hypnotises his spirit and is complete. The desire inside him to kill is satisfied momentarily and slowly subsides, as he tries to fathom in vain the reasons for his own insignificance.

His head drops into the palms of his hands. He holds himself in a tight embrace, his long arms slowly wrapping themselves round the entire length of his pitiful, broken body, as he brings his knees up to his chest in something resembling the foetal position. Nothing can loosen his grip. He rocks gently to and fro as if he's playing some kind of game. Faster and faster, he goes. Then he stops. His fingers part momentarily. One eye peers through with the confused and questioning look only a child can have. He wonders incessantly about himself and his predicament. He has many questions to ask, but only the most basic ones at that. Who is he? Where is he from? What is he doing here? Where is he going to?

Finally, his trance is broken, and he lets his hands fall back to his sides. He raises them again within seconds to wave at his mirrored reflection. All his previous actions are instantly forgotten. He's briefly pleased. His reflection is smiling and waving back. Is he happy? He doesn't really know. He doesn't know what happiness is. He doesn't fully understand the concept. He stops, then cautiously starts to move one arm at a time. He does it slowly, with care and complete concentration, as required by a precision act such as this. He doesn't want to frighten his only companion and friend away. It's OK. He needn't have worried or become alarmed. The arm in the reflection moves too. Now for the other one. No sudden movements though. They could prove fatal, and reflections scare easily. Now both hands together at once. Yes, he's still there in one piece. He allows his limbs to gain momentum until they flay wildly and frantically, but with a peculiar sense of rhythm and timing all of their own. His entire body rocks, captivated by this one singular activity. As quickly as it arrives and blossoms, so the inspiration that gives energy to motion dissipates and is gone.

He pauses with slight embarrassment. He covers his head and holds it for a moment, caressing it fleetingly in his soft grip. Recovering his composure, he peers out once more. His hands reach outwards as if in some wretched plea for clemency he'll never have or in a bid to locate the unseen source and cause of his incarceration. He contorts his face in anguish, trying to stretch his bottom lip as far from his body as he possibly can. Madness takes many forms. His eyes squint. He closes them tightly, so it seems as dark as the corridor outside. He remains shut off in his room. The lines in his forehead produced by squinting only deepen and bore into his skin like tiny valleys. His mouth drops open. He pulls a funny face. It amuses him to do so. A belch rises from the depths of his throat, but he stifles it from coming out. He tries to hold his breath. He mustn't let it escape, or his very essence will escape with it.

Outside somewhere far away he can never get to, there's a man. He can picture him clearly in some dark corner of his mind. He's reached the other side. But who is he? There are no clues. Perhaps it's himself in a former or future life? He has no means of knowing. The man's face is hidden. His features are partially obscured by a thick, grey overcoat, pulled up to the top of his neck. He wonders if it is truly himself that he's seeing? He tries to get a better look at the face, but he can't quite penetrate the fine layers of mist that swirl around at the man's feet. The mysterious figure turns slowly and begins to walk off into the distance, leaving the young man frustrated and no wiser. He tries to touch him and hold him back, but he can't. His efforts are futile. If only he could reach him, tug his coat, make him turn his head in some way and hear the tone of his voice for just seconds as they briefly exchange words. It would be enough to confirm his suspicions. If only he could feel the softness of his skin. He yearns to find a glimmer of hope in his expression. He looks for the tell-tale scratches on the side of his face and finds them present and correct. It is me, he realises. I'm alive. I must be and I'd be free if was sane.

Back inside the room, he picks up a forgotten book. He touches its spine and fingers its pages lovingly but without understanding. The sentences and paragraphs have no meaning. They mean nothing to him. Bored, he pushes the book away again. He picks up a toy model aeroplane instead, which he grips tightly in his clenched fist. He plays with it and lets it circle round his head. It comes into land. The undercarriage breaks. He handles the broken pieces, then quite deliberately snaps off the wings. He plucks them out at their roots without mercy, as if plucking the wings of a butterfly from its tiny body. The plane dies quickly. Its mutilated carcass lies still. There are no last twinges of life. A giant foot crushes it, sees off the job and leaves the broken pieces engrained in the threadbare carpet.

Telepathic communication is easy if you know how. Not everyone can master it sadly. Only a few gifted individuals can. He focusses once again on his recurring vision of the outside in his mind and locks onto the slowly walking man with complete concentration. He continues to move in ever widening arcs round a central pivotal point. The circles get wider and wider all the time, as he gets further and further from the centre. Round and round he marches like a faulty clockwork soldier. Overwound, he can't stop or break out. He only gets further from the middle with each stride he takes. With deep mental focus he tries to claw his way back to the centre, but it's no good. Arms are locked and the gears are set. There's no turning back. The direction of motion has been decided. Everything moves forward, getting faster and wider, faster and wider with a self-perpetuating momentum of its own. There's a feeling of confusion. The soldier only knows the fight and not the reasoning behind it.

The young man shakes his head. No, it cannot be. He's the master of his own destiny. It's not really him. He's not as insane as it seems. He can control his movements and that of the clockwork soldier in his brain if he wishes to. It's them. They're the ones, not him. Don't be fooled. Don't be taken in. He's not the one. Please God, don't let it happen. Don't let them prove him wrong. He scratches his head. A look of puzzlement and pain manifests itself in his sad expression. Pent-up agony turns to sudden realisation. The pitiful departure of reality and dignity cuts him down to size. Then just as suddenly the despair and desperation evaporate, to be replaced by mad, surreal, wild oblivion. The here and now has done its bit and duty. It's played its part. In its place comes the sheer ecstasy of something else that isn't real and borders on fantasy and illusion but provides some element of escape and freedom.

He floats in pure abandonment. The soft air cushions him from underneath, gently lifting his tired, fragile limbs to some new plain, providing new energy and vigour where there was none. He feels a sense of joy in the wonderful defiance of gravity, but true wisdom somehow eludes him. The levitation of spirit, both actual and metaphorical, brings new dimensions to the four walls of his room and crazed mind. Captured by the beauty of the dance, he moves through time and space like a god through time. He pretends to swim. He thinks only of the dance and what his body can do to the rhythms of his trapped thoughts. His slow, graceful movements captivate his soul, and he starts laughing aloud. He forgets where he is. His hands reach up and he can almost touch the sun. He can feel its warmth. He forgets it's almost pitch-black outside this room. Almost isn't quite enough. The distance is just too far to bridge, even for someone with his special powers. No matter. Nimbly, he proceeds on headfirst into the dream.

The atmosphere becomes gradually more intense. It merges his senses into one and they coalesce in unison. The beat quickens, the mood thickens, and the air coarsens. He doesn't realise he's hallucinating, or as good as. The cacophony of noises that he hears reverberate like drums inside his tortured ears and he dances to their wild and twisted melodies without restraint. How he dances; the waltz, the tango, the can-can, the twist. Each subtle movement is unlocked within the impenetrable depths of his mind. The wall of sound intensifies to a crescendo. All sense and awareness of distance and nearness is lost in the magic of the moment. His hands cover his soft ears, and he dances on until he achieves a form of weightlessness where time no longer has meaning.

The young man tries to fight it, but outside his alter ego in the overcoat is dancing too. He's turning, twisting round, spiralling upwards, then back down again. He can't control it. He can't resist the immense, hypnotic power of the music either. The pure weight of its overwhelming mental onslaught is too much to resist. There's just the dance. That's all there is. There's only one direction to go in. No other exists. Forwards is the only option. He watches with a bewildered, horrified expression gradually creeping over his face, as his only friend swims through the air, caressing its fine texture and sensing its light moisture. He bows to it gently with the dull acceptance of someone admitting defeat or in inviting a whore to his bedroom as he has no one else. It's all a sad nightmare. Once more his alter ego in the overcoat leaps up and traverses silently beyond despair. There's nothing left. All hope is lost. It can't be, he thinks. It's not me.

The drum cracks. The music stops. The man outside drops. He's just a mound of discarded clothes, piled in a crumpled heap on the floor and nothing more. A finger has scrawled words in a layer of dust. It reads: *I'd be sane if I was free. I'm too insane to be free.* Inside the room he smears the contents of a sachet of strawberry jam he's managed to smuggle in over his naked arms. There is no reason in his action, but he finds it satisfying just the same. Sighing quietly, he smiles to himself in a slightly melancholic fashion. He holds his breath and then lets it out with gentle relief. He repeats the action and then smears more jam from another carton over his neck and face. It feels sticky but tastes nice. He laughs aloud at the repugnant, gluey mess he's made. He rakes his fingers through his hair and admires them after. They're strawberry colour like blood.

With huddled body and head and legs tucked under tightly, he crawls to the safety of the corner of the room using only his arms and hands to shuffle along, scraping the floor as he does so. Even the far wall isn't distant enough to feel safe. There's light in the corridor and he hears a movement at the door. The lock rattles once more with the sound of a key. He knows what it means and instinctively it causes him to scuttle under the bed to hide himself. He peers out of his bolthole with a timid look on his face. A bowl of tepid soup is placed on the table and the intruder departs. At least it's something warm to eat and nourish his tired, confused thoughts. That's it, yet he is troubled by a nagging thought. He realises at last perhaps it wasn't himself he was seeing in his vision after all. Instead, he finally understands the vision carries the face of the man who brings him food and keeps him incarcerated here. They're connected in some way and bear a strong family resemblance, only one is older. That's what confused him and made him think he and the vision were one and the same person. They're not in fact, but they somehow satisfy some mutual need in each other. They're both in it together and that's what keeps him here in this room alone forever.

YOU CAN PICTURE HOW IT HAPPENED

'So you slept with another man? Is that what you're saying? You should have told me before. You know what it means? You have heard about AIDS, haven't you? You know what a high-risk group is, don't you? Have you lost control of your senses? What was all that we agreed about sex within a loving relationship only? Doesn't that apply anymore?'

The questions come thick and fast, fired off one after an another without a pause to allow the recipient time to answer.

'What can I say? I was pissed. You know how it is. You didn't seem overly concerned at the time. You seemed to have found yourself some nice, young guy to talk to. You looked like you were getting on famously with him. I got the impression you wanted me out the way, so I obliged and left you to it. I'm sorry if that wasn't what you wanted.'

'Sorry? You're sorry? Sorry isn't good enough by half. How can you do this to me after all we've been through?'

They two men just sit staring at each other. The tension between them is clear to see. They've had this row before.

'A bit of flirting is one thing, but you didn't have to fuck him, did you?' Gary asks.

His words send a shiver down his spine, as if he realises the full consequences of them. Thoughts of terminal illness, a waiting hospital bed and death enter his head. His hands are clammy with sweat, and he can hardly feel them. His throat is dry and tight. He desperately needs a drink. He knew they were on borrowed time. He'd been waiting for this to happen and now that it finally does, it only seems half real. He feels worried, awkward and uncomfortable in his partner's presence. There's a cup on the table in front of him and he starts to play with it, hardly noticing what his hands are doing. John doesn't look at him, as Gary continues talking.

'So what do you think our chances are then? You know it can take a year or two before symptoms start to show and before we find out if we've got it or not. And what are we meant to do in the meantime? Just wait? Is that it? And what shall I tell my parents, relatives and work colleagues? They already recoil away from me as it is, as if I'm infected with the plague and don't want to shake my hand. I can just imagine them whispering behind our backs and saying buggery is a crime against God, and we just got what we deserved for our obscene, filthy, unnatural behaviour.'

'It isn't only gay men who get AIDS. We were just first on the list,' John points out.

'What, first on God's hit list for instant retribution? Frankly that doesn't comfort me all that much right now,' Gary says. 'I don't know about you, but I can't just sit and around and wait to die. Can't we do something and find out for certain if we've got it or not? We could both take blood tests perhaps?' Gary suggests.

'And see their smug faces when they tell us we're positive. No thanks, I'd rather not know and take my chances,' John insists.

'So we just do nothing? Brilliant! That's a great plan,' Gary announces, before pausing for a moment to collect his thoughts. 'Why did you do it, John?' he eventually asks again. 'I thought you loved me.'

'I do love you, Gary. But you're always flirting with other men and sneaking off with them, making me jealous all the time. I guess I'd just had enough. I was sick of it. I mean, you always look so perfect. Go ahead, just take a glance in the mirror. See for yourself. You're far better looking than me, aren't you? No, don't say it's not true. I wouldn't believe you, and besides I don't need any of your false modesty right now,' John explains, tears almost welling in his eyes.

He pauses momentarily before continuing. 'You know when I first met you, I was just so happy you liked me too. I couldn't believe someone so charismatic and handsome would want me and feel the same way as I did. It seemed too good to be true, and perhaps it was. I was never really good enough, was I? You never stopped letting me know how much others still wanted you. Well in the end it started getting to me and I just couldn't take it anymore. I'd had enough. I thought I could take it and turn a blind eye, but I was wrong. I guess I realised we were just wasting each other's time,' John admits, as much to himself as to Gary.

'Have there been other men?' Gary asks softly, not really wanting to know the answer.

'Some,' John answers. 'Not at first, but later when I stopped feeling so youthful and when I became aware what you were doing. I started to feel I was missing out on something.'

'You bastard! How could you? To think you were doing this behind my back all the time and I never suspected a thing. I must have been mad. Now get out!' Gary barks. 'I never want to see you again.'

'This is my home,' John protests.

'It's my home too, but I wasn't the unfaithful one, remember,' Gary points out.

'And I was. Is that it? Is that what you're telling me? So what? None of us are perfect,' John says. 'You're welcome to stay here with me. I'm not asking you to go. You're the one who wants us to break up, so it's up to you to move out,' John suggests, with a defensive tone in his voice.

'God, you're so proud of yourself,' Gary hisses.

'I'm not proud. I'm just saying it as I see it,' John argues.

'You know, I'd like to kill you for what you've done,' Gary rages with undiluted venom. 'And I haven't really got anything to lose, have I?'

He gets up from the chair he's sitting in and walks towards the lounge door, before slamming it shut behind him. He emerges some five minutes later much more quietly than his grand exit had been. John doesn't see him at first. He's too lost in his own earnest thoughts and anguish. There's a crazed look of hatred on Gary's face. He looks as if he's in some kind of demented trance. A glint of light reflected on sharp, shiny metal reveals he's carrying a knife in his hand and making little attempt to conceal it.

He creeps up behind John, moving stealthily and making only the faintest of noises, as his feet scrape lightly and almost noiselessly over soft carpet. At the very last, John turns to face him. Gary doesn't stop or get distracted from his murderous purpose. He plunges the knife deep into John's plump belly just below the heart. John slips meekly into Gary's arms. Warm, crimson blood runs between them as a dark stain spreads out over John's shirt. For a brief moment, there are indeed blood brothers. John moves to speak but struggles to get his words out. His complexion is a deathly white and his facial expression one of shock.

'I lied,' he stutters. 'I made it all up. It wasn't true. There was no one else. I said it just to make you jealous.'

With these final revelations he goes limp and drops to the floor in a crumpled heap. Gary looks aghast.

'Oh my God, what have I done?' he asks. 'Hold on, John. I didn't mean to. I'll get help. I love you,' he says.

It's too late. John slides uncontrollably into unconsciousness and death. Gary stares in horror and disbelief. He can't quite believe it. His options are limited. There's no way out. This is it. He's brought it all on himself. There's no other action to take. He knows he has no choice. Gary turns the knife on himself and allows his body to fall onto it, instantly piercing his broken heart.

'It's not the first time I've seen this kind of thing happen lately. Sadly, gay lovers fighting over other boyfriends, scared to death one of them will catch AIDS has become all too common,' the doctor comments impassively.

'Have we had the results of the blood tests yet?' the nurse asks.

'Well, they're holding the inquest next week, but initial tests from the post-mortems showed that one was carrying the antibodies. It could have been the reason why they were fighting. You can almost picture how it happened. Perhaps the one told the other he'd contracted HIV. An argument followed. They struggled with the knife. They both received fatal wounds. The rest is history as they say,' the doctor replies, with limited emotion in his voice.

'As a matter of interest, which man was positive?' the nurse enquires.

'Oh, I'm not sure. I'd have to check. I see so many names in this business. I start to forget who is who and what is what,' the doctor admits.

'It might be worth finding out,' the nurse presses. 'It could shed some light on what happened and be useful evidence at the inquest.'

'Let me think. It was Gary something. I don't remember the surname. No matter. It will all come out next week, when I'm sure they'll get to the bottom of it…'

His voice tails off.

At the inquest a week later, a short note is read out to the court. 'In the event of our deaths from that hateful disease, I'm sorry if it was me. Love, Gary.'

BUSINESS AS USUAL

It was an ordinary day at the office for Mr Percival Butler, or Percy to his friends. He got up at precisely 7.30am as he always did, put on his slippers and dressing gown and went to the bathroom to shower, shave and brush his teeth. Returning to the bedroom, he put on his newly pressed, dark grey, flannel suit, with matching waistcoat, and proceeded to comb his hair neatly with an unnaturally high degree of careful precision and attention to detail. He performed this daily routine in such a fashion as best to disguise the small glimpses of bald scalp that were gradually but relentlessly beginning to appear beneath his thinning, light brown locks.

Mr Butler, of *Butler Bathroom Fittings Ltd*, was in his late forties and married. He wasn't a fat man as such but was undeniably portly and like so many of his age would have benefited from losing a few pounds in weight. His tendency to appear somewhat bulkier than he really was in the flesh was a feature of his appearance probably exacerbated by the fact he wasn't a tall man. He was rather short in stature but had a friendly and personable demeanour. Everyone remarked on it. His face had a warm, smiling quality of almost perpetual glee, enhanced perhaps by an over fondness and indulgence for a drop of sherry at the end of each day. This particular vice had given his complexion a disproportionate amount of ruddiness of colour around his cheeks. In conclusion, Mr Butler wasn't a classically handsome man, but he was an amiable fellow and he certainly considered himself to have been at least a modest hit with the ladies in his day and to his own mind still was.

That morning Mr Butler had breakfast with his wife at precisely 8am, as he always did. There was little conversation other than the usual *Any post, darling?* Or *Would you be so kind as to pass the butter, dear?* At one point he said *Could you pour the tea now please?* And finally *I'd better hurry. I mustn't be late for work today. It sets a bad example to the staff.* Mr Butler preferred instead to direct and devote his full attention to his regular morning newspaper, naturally *The Times* of course, which he examined thoughtfully and with deep interest every day of his life. What other paper would a man of his standing and social position take? He felt a degree of natural curiosity and well as a certain obligation to keep informed of events of importance and expand his already not inconsiderable knowledge of world news and affairs. At 8.30am precisely, he kissed his wife goodbye and departed, calling out *I'll be home for supper* as he did so. He closed the front door of his beautiful semi-detached property and drove to work in his brand-new *Ford Fiesta*.

As always, when Mr Butler arrived, his personal secretary was already at her desk opening the day's correspondence and sorting it into piles depending on its level of importance. She looked up and smiled as Mr Butler entered and started to take off his coat. She was prepared. She knew what to expect. She knew the routine and what was required of her. She'd worked for Mr Butler for some considerable time now and she understood what kind of employer and secretary relationship he liked.

'Mrs Brown, would you be kind enough to join me in my office? It will only take a moment,' Mr Butler announced cheerfully.

He took the opportunity to pinch Mrs Brown's shapely bottom as he slid past her. Mrs Brown shrieked with mild surprise, although she wasn't really surprised. It wasn't exactly the first time. Such an invasion of her person had happened before without invitation She composed herself quickly and began to follow him into his office.

'If you do that again, you'll get rather more than you bargained for,' she said firmly.

She spoke with a concentration of purpose and making little effort to disguise a hidden threat and menace in her voice. Mistaking her tone as some kind of attempt at foreplay, Mr Butler was erroneously encouraged to repeat his daring act. Mrs Brown didn't waste any time or pull any punches. He'd had his warning after all. She bent down and reached into her handbag which was positioned by the side of her desk, from which she produced a very small pistol, which she motioned towards Mr Butler, and he mistook for a toy not a loaded weapon.

'So you want to play games, do you Mrs Brown? Well, that's fine by me,' he said, his eyes positively lighting up with obvious pleasure and delight at the thrill of the chase, as he tried to touch her rear again.

Fatally misjudging the situation and Mrs Brown's mood, it was a foolhardy move to make on his part. Mrs Brown didn't warn him again. At that moment she gently squeezed the trigger. There was only one shot. The bullet hit Mr Butler between the eyes, and he was dead before he struck the ground. Strangely, his expression didn't change. It was the same in death as it had been in life. He looked remarkably contented and at peace. He was almost handsome in a strange way.

Mrs Brown dragged his body into the company safe. Fortunately, Mr Butler had entrusted her with the combination, and it seemed a fitting place to bury him where he kept the money that he'd spent a lifetime accumulating, although she now removed that for herself. Having completed the sightly distasteful operation of disposing of his body, she returned to her desk and began typing. She had some correspondence to finish. She knew Mr Butler would be cross if she didn't get them done in time to catch the last post. You could set a watch by him, she always said.

It was an ordinary day for Mrs Brown. She finished work at 5pm on the dot, just as she always did. Closing the office door behind her, she proceeded to make her way to her bus stop, where she'd catch the 5.15 bus as always and be home shortly after. *I think I'll have pork chops for tea*, she thought to herself as she went. It was most unlike Mr Butler to be working late, she considered, with a wry smile spreading across her lips.

AT YOUR WITS' END

The scene is one of neglect and social deprivation. A child barely eight months old lies whining and sniffling in the corner of the room. Damp clings to the wall in patches and runs down in places, making it the perfect habitat for spores to breed and lung infections to develop. The baby's mother is a young girl still in her teens herself. She lights another cigarette, her tenth of the day, and her hands tremble visibly. She'd rather buy cigarettes and alcohol than food anyway.

A man quietly leaves. He's had his brief respite of physical pleasure from her and that was enough. He shuts the door behind without him words, saying nothing at all; not even thank you or see you again. She holds the grubby notes tightly in her greasy palm, as she waits for the next customer, wondering what he'll be like, and her emotions churn inside. Her hair remains unwashed after days. She reapplies some lipstick and powder and readjusts her dress to at least appear vaguely presentable and attractive. The child starts to cry again. It misses its mother's affection and love. It's largely neglected and will remain so. The young mum tries to muffle her baby's sobbing. She tries to stifle it at source by some brief rocking, whilst holding back her growing anger inside. The phone rings. She puts her baby down and moves to answer it. It's another wrong number. She must get the number changed, she thinks. Moments later there's a knock at the door. She opens it. A young man fidgets awkwardly at the entrance. He's ill at ease and struggles to disguise it.

'Come in,' she says, trying to seem calm and casually relaxed herself, even if she isn't. She's anything but in truth.

'How much do you charge?' he asks at last, with a slight stutter in his voice.

'It depends on what you want,' is the reply.

'I want to lose my virginity,' he explains firmly and with a determination that implies his mind his made up and he fully intends to go through with it whatever the consequences. 'The other kids all laugh at me. I feel it's time I started doing it too,' he adds by means of explanation.

It's clear he doesn't want to be persuaded otherwise or challenged in any way over his reasons for being there. He doesn't wish to be deflected from his sole purpose by this young woman or anyone else for that matter. She has no intention of dissuading him any anyway. She needs the business and money.

'Then you've come to the right place,' she says quickly. 'It's me you want. Don't be shy. Slip out of your clothes. Here, let me help you.'

'It's OK. I can do it myself,' he says.

'You watch me first then,' the young woman tells him.

She slips out of her dress. She reclines back on the bed in a vague attempt to look seductive. Her arms and legs are thin. Her breasts are only slight. She is bruised here and there. The young man looks at her with a mixture of pity and sadness.

'Did they do this to you?' he asks gently.

'Some of them like to,' she answers. 'It's all right. You can do anything you want to me. It's all part of the service. Is there anything particular you wanted? Some like me to dress up. Some like to lick my boots or touch my feet. Others like to watch me smoke. Some like to hit me. Others like me to hit them. Don't worry, I'm used to it. I believe in giving the customer what they want.'

'No, I only wanted straight sex. But it doesn't matter. I can't. I've got to get out,' the young man says, suddenly getting cold feet at the thought and beginning to panic.

He turns to leave.

'Don't go. Please come back,' she calls after him, but it's too late.

The door shuts. The young woman pulls her dress back over her head and hugs it tightly to her thin body. A tear rolls down her cheek but quickly disappears and dries up. The baby cries. The light dims outside.

'Shut up!' the girl screams. 'Just shut up for a moment and give me some peace and quiet.

The baby doesn't understand. She squeezes its arms and pinches its red, puckered skin, deliberately to inflict discomfort and suffering on the infant. She slaps it none too lightly around the face, but it continues to bawl without stopping. She shakes it with rage like a rag doll and bangs its tiny head against the sides of its cot to no avail. She tries to smother its cries by covering its mouth with her hand. Suddenly she stops, as the full realisation of the madness and cruelty of her actions finally takes hold.

'My God! What am I doing?' she asks herself. 'Oh baby, I'm so sorry. I don't know what to say. Please forgive me.'

She gently lifts the child out of its cot and holds it tightly to her chest. She rocks it back and forth and strokes its fair hair. She lightly touches the places where she's hurt it, trying to nurse it back together and brush away the pain she's inflicted, but somehow is always failing and will only fail again.

'I'm so sorry,' she repeats. 'I don't know what I've done.'

The baby doesn't listen to her empty apologies or understand them. It starts to cry again. They're a world apart. In pure frustration and anger, she punches its defenceless body, and its face contorts in ugly torment.

'Shut up!' she shouts. 'Please shut up. Can't you see you're killing me doing this? Shut up just for one minute. I just need a break. I just need some rest.'

The four walls seem to close in. She dreams of home and the mother and father she left behind to make her own way in the world. Yes, the father who hit her and the mother who ceased to care long before she finished school. Fleetingly she actually misses them, although she can't imagine why for the life of her. Hers was a broken home anyway. She recalls how her parents had split up and remembers how deep the fallout had cut. She is reminded how it felt to be caught in the middle of their ceaseless rows and arguments. Of course, neither one of them had wanted her when they eventually separated after years of toxicity, at least not with a kid on the way. Her dad had another woman by then and her mum was at her wits' end, drugged to the eyeballs on antidepressants and Valium. That's how she came to leave them both behind. One day she just walked out through the door. She didn't look back and that was that. She doubted they even noticed she'd gone. That was how she came here, to face crumbling oblivion, feeling so cold and lonely on her own in a cold and lonely town, with just a room and barely a life of any description, paid for five times daily at least.

The boyfriend didn't stick around of course once he found she was pregnant. He was quick to run off and make himself scarce once he got what he wanted. It was pretty much all she could expect from someone so useless. They'd always said he was no good, and they were right naturally enough, but she didn't know, blinded by love as she was. She was so young and full of hope once, even against the odds of a difficult upbringing. She believed eventually everything would come good. She hadn't bargained for his type. He never saw how sad he made her, but it wasn't his nature to care. They were meant to be moving into a decent flat together. It never happened. He took what little money and jewellery she had when he left and the modest savings she'd built up. That's how she wound up here, doing this. She still kept a picture of him, sentimental fool that she was. She looks at it occasionally and even shares a tear or two. She was always too soppy by half. She only ever wanted to be loved. It just didn't work out.

She waits for another knock. Sometimes they wake her when she's fallen asleep. She recognises different people and sorts by the way they make their entrance. Some knocks are soft. Some are loud. Some scrape the door with their knuckles. Some enter unannounced, usually the most dangerous ones. She entertains all kinds of clients; the wild and untamed, the awkward and ill at ease, the vain, the arrogant, the scared and frightened, the aloof, the wayward husbands, the ageing and near decrepit, the mildly disabled, the plain mad or bordering on it. She knows them all and treats them the same. She gives them what they want where she can. All of them have taken and used her for what she is; a shameless, worthless, teenage whore.

She hears new footsteps outside. Her mind locks onto them. They ring like bells inside her head, reverberating through each strand of thought and sounding a warning. She feels her pulse quicken as the man slips quietly into the room, his face half hidden by shadow and two weeks' growth of stubble on his chin. He frightens her with his sheer size, his physical presence and powerful stature. He doesn't speak. He just places his large hands on her breasts and grips them tightly, squeezing them in the palms of his hands like oranges. He pulls her head back suddenly and roughly and she feels the air rush out of her lungs. He moves closer, thrusting his tongue down her throat and pushing her onto the bed, where he pins her down with his full weight now upon her. He rips off her dress in one swift movement and she hears the release of his belt and his trousers unzip. He manoeuvres himself into position on top, sliding his fingers between her legs, making room for his penis to ease its way into the tightness of her shrunken vagina. His free arm wraps itself around her throat. She tries to shout but nothing will come out. He slaps her across the face with the palm of his hand and a trickle of blood dribbles from her nose. The fear makes the hairs on her neck stand up. For fifteen minutes he continues his assault. His appetite eventually satisfied and his hunger abated, he gets up. He allows several notes to slip from his hand onto the bed. He says nothing, not a single word throughout. As she moves to pick up the money and put it in her purse, once more his fists lash out.

'Filthy slut,' he finally speaks, as he closes the door behind him, leaving a deceptive stillness and false calm, almost as if he'd never been there at all.

It's only then she hears her baby's cries and tears. She hadn't noticed them before when he'd been fucking her. Fear had shut the noise out, but no more. How they grow now and absorb her very person, drowning each faculty with a dull, insistent precision. They hurt as if they were her own. How they parody everything that has happened to her, like a distorted reflection of herself in the mirror or clear, running water exposing some savage truth. It's so painful, but so obvious. She prays the noise will stop, but it doesn't. She's no longer sure if it's real or just locked inside her head. She throws a shoe at her baby's cot, then an ashtray, a mug, a book and finally a jar of food. She gets up and goes over. Still, it cries. She finds her hands round its soft neck and squeezes its throat without release until the crying finally stops. Gently the baby is sucked into the still vacuum of death. Quiet now, its complexion is a purple blue. A grotesque expression of disbelief hangs on its face as it stares accusingly into the eyes of its murderous mother, who stands back, shocked at what's just taken place.

She looks at her hands, the weapons and instruments of torture that have taken life and she feels quite sick. She can't cry. She can't move or avert her gaze. The final, tragic instalment of her baby's short existence has unfolded, and the reality of the situation hits her like a sledgehammer. It knocks her backwards and sideways with its full force and harsh, unrelenting impact, bowling her over and to the floor. It electrifies every emotion, amplifying each one, and they tear her apart as she realises and understands what she's done. She holds the baby close to her bosom, encouraging it to wake up and feed. She wills it to draw breath and to be coaxed back to life, but there's no response. All visible signs of movement have been extinguished. She shakes its limp, wretched body, and strokes it soft head, but it won't wake. Somehow every effort is just too little and too late.

Moments after she'll cease to remember anything herself. All will be swallowed up and absorbed into nothing. No more sitting alone, waiting for the men to come, wondering what will become of her sorry life. She can just lean back and drift into the welcoming abyss. She holds the glass in her trembling hands. It contains whisky with a dash of water, spilling over the overfilled sides. Her dead baby lies in the corner of the room, for once quiet. On the bed is an assortment of pills she's tipped out from various bottles and containers she keeps. She takes a handful and crams them into her mouth. She swallows them down with the whisky. The dash of water helps to conceal the bitter taste. She takes another and another until she slides silently into the waiting arms of death. Her baby is expecting her and awaits her arrival eagerly.

PORTRAIT

I wonder how it is he ended up here, in this place, at this precise moment in time and nowhere else. I contemplate the separate instances of pain that gouged each deep line on his face with care. I wonder who he is, what he's done with his life and what might have been if fortune had shone kindlier on him.

Sitting on a park bench outside the local Civic Centre buildings, a favourite spot, he sups from a can of cheap lager, rolling the sour beer over his furred tongue before swallowing it. His complexion is a rusty shade of red, spending every day exposed to the elements as he is. His eyes are tired and melted. His head gently lolls from side to side, as if he's in some kind of trance. He isn't. He lights a cigarette, which hangs from his mouth and absorbs him briefly. Above all he's still and silent.

He sees everything yet knows nothing at the same time. He only takes snippets in. He has no sense of pride, purpose or belonging. He experiences only emptiness and the slow passing of the minutes, hours and days. He feels but has no feelings. He weeps but there are no tears. There are no visible signs of emotion. He only has one fixed, unchanging expression. He knows the outside and surface exterior of buildings, of people, of houses and homes. He never ventures inside a single one. There's no open invitation for the likes of such as he. Doors are closed to him. Passages are barred and keys withheld. There's an unseen yet ever-present perimeter fence around his person. A total exclusion zone surrounds him. It bears the metaphorical words *Do not enter!* He's cut himself off from the outside world by choice. He keeps his emotions in check and under wraps. He maintains his distance and observes at a distance that is safe. Children don't look at him. Parents tell them not to. They don't want to attract the strange man's attention.

I wonder if he was ever married. Do the fading tattoos on his arms and hands bear the names of past lovers and brief encounters? Were they women or men or perhaps both even? Perhaps he never had anyone. Was he a soldier? Was he a sailor? Daddy, what did you do in the war? I wonder how well he fought? Did he do his bit? Did he surrender everything for king and country? If he did, for what? Perhaps he never worked. Perhaps he did something entirely different in his working life. I have no means of knowing, except by asking. But I'm merely an observer of life myself.

Did he live alone? Did he have a wife and children? There are so many unanswered questions. Did he leave someone behind? Were they killed by a German bomb? Is that what afflicts him? Did she leave him? The questions continue to spin unabated in my head, as I investigate each thread of evidence and probe each vague suspicion in search of truth. I'll never be quite certain if I've found it, or I'm still guessing and it continues to elude me. I wonder if he wished he was dead too. At the risk of being wrong again, I begin to suspect so. It's not much of a life is it, sitting drinking day after day at this park bench? Then again everyone sees things differently. Perhaps he remembers himself as a great thinker, a scholar, a writer or a politician. Perhaps he was once a successful businessman, a millionaire even, but lost it all and fell on hard times. Perhaps he chose to leave his successful job and his luxury home behind him. Whereas I just see a vagrant before me, going nowhere and sliding slowly towards death. Everyone sees things differently of course.

He's noticed I'm watching him, and he motions me towards him with a beckoning hand. Something holds me back, unsure if I actually want to enter his world. I prefer to observe. I imagine he's only after money anyhow. He bears a scar down his right cheek. Perhaps it's the result of some ugly pub fight or long forgotten fencing duel. He's a troubadour. He's a voyeur and I'm one too. He's everyone's sins and troubles combined, yet he has no solutions, no messages to deliver and no advice for the future. He's just a symptom and not the disease itself. Yet they never disappear, like a strange sore or an unexplained rash. How they spread, weaving into each dark corner and through every opening pore. They are the perfect cancer.

VANISHING TRICK

The time is 8.45am. A letter arrives. It's pushed through the letter box and falls gently onto the mat beneath. There's no address or stamp on the envelope. It bears a name only, which is Michael. It's evidently been delivered by hand and the deliverer presumably either didn't wish to disturb Michael at such an early hour or wished to avoid meeting him.

By 9.15am Michael is up and sitting at his study desk with the letter in his hand. He's dressed but hasn't showered or shaved or eaten breakfast. He's wearing a pair of faded denims and a dark grey sports jacket, a little too large for him and probably obtained from a friend or relative. It's certainly seen better days, but it serves the purpose for which it was acquired. Michael seems unconcerned with his appearance. He knows it will suffice for his needs.

There are a number of items on the desk, including several files, some pens and pencils, writing paper and a ruler, which he pushes to one side. He presumably also has a fondness for alcohol, as there's several bottles of claret, one of which is opened, and a partially consumed bottle of navy rum in front of him, which he uses to supplement his daily calory intake. There's also a glass, some cigarettes, an overflowing ashtray that he's forgotten to empty, a novel by Maupassant and a record sleeve. There's music playing. It's Leonard Cohen. His voice is cold, bitter and searching. He's singing about the death of love.

Michael opens the letter with a paper knife. At first he thinks it's empty and is confused, but it's not. He tips out the contents onto the desk. There's just a small ring. No note or explanation is enclosed. There's just a ring and nothing else. Michael stares at it, weighing up its significance. He almost stares through it. His eyes are transfixed as if staring at the wall behind. There's nothing there that could hold his attention in this manner. He remains entranced and motionless for several moments.

Then suddenly his trance is broken, and he seems triggered into an explosive change of mood, as if the ring holds some special meaning to him. He becomes visibly angry. His face reddens and screws up in mounting annoyance and frustration. He clenches his fists until his knuckles turn white. He raises them slowly before bringing them crashing down on his desk, making some of the items on it jump. He holds his head in his hands and begins to rock, gently to and fro, like a child abandoned by its parents. He tries to find some comfort in the swaying motion of his body, but there's little comfort to be had. And yet his temper vanishes as quickly as it arrived. In its place emerge feelings of loss, and loneliness, which seem to rear up and submerge his identity and will to live under a blanket of deceit, confusion, bitterness and resentment. He tries to be still, so he can think, but he struggles to concentrate. His mind is cloudy. His judgement is impaired. His pulse is racing. He is overwhelmed by an air of bewilderment. He can't make any sense of the situation that has overtaken him without warning.

Michael reaches for a pen and paper. He starts to write the words *Dear Joanna*, then pauses, as if searching for words that somehow elude him. He finds the focus of his eyes drift upwards towards the ceiling, but there are no answers to be had there. Still his mind remains vacant and in state of hesitation. He seems to change his mind over his planned course of action and pushes the paper away in irritation. He gets up and strides towards the door, but without a true understanding what he's doing or where he's going. He opens the door with a violent jolt of his arm and passes into the outside passageway, kicking the door shut loudly behind him. He picks up a telephone and dials a number. There's no answer. He becomes impatient and anxious. He passes his hands urgently through his hair and rubs the back of his neck, which is coated with a thin layer of sweat. The phone is still ringing at the other end of the line, but no one picks it up. He slams it down in disgust and returns to the other room. The time is 9.30am.

Michael settles back in his chair and lifts the opened bottle of claret from its position on the desk. He pours a glass and gulps it down in one go. He spills a little on his jacket as he does so, which he wipes off irritably, before pouring another glass. He lights a cigarette, which he inhales deeply on, distressed at the thought of having to sit and count the minutes pass. He coughs slightly and scratches his head. Little flakes of dandruff fall on his collar, which he brushes absentmindedly onto the floor. He slides down further into his chair and begins to wait for he knows not what and watches the ashtray slowly mount up.

At 11.15am Michael gets up again and returns to the phone to redial the number. As before there's no answer. He slams down the phone in exasperation and shakes his head. He wonders how anyone could do this to him. He wonders how the sweetest girl in the world could have become the cruellest. He wonders just what it was that changed her mind. He holds himself gently in his own arms, trying to imagine it's Joanna instead, but she isn't there and he can't touch her, however much he may wish to. He's alone. He's fully aware if there's still no answer the next time he rings, he'll surely go insane.

Michael remains in his study and begins to pace up and down. He stops to pick up a large tumbler, which he fills with rum and tops up with cola, until the liquid is spilling over the sides. He begins to drink, swallowing it down in large mouthfuls, one after another. The taste is bitter and makes him cough, so he pushes the tumbler away in disgust. He stares at his hands and the solitary ring on the desk. He tries to calm himself and hold back the tears he knows will surely come if he lets his emotions relax for a single moment. He has little doubt they'll get the better of him if he does. Instead, he continues to drink and lights another cigarette, which slowly burns itself out.

At 3.15pm Michael returns to the phone and rings the number once more. He knows there will be no answer, but he must try anyway. All his worst fears are realised. There's no reply. He slides down the wall utterly dejected and defeated and lets the phone slip from his grasp into his lap. He holds his head in his hands and begins to sob in bitter, uncontrollable spasms that shake his body to the very core, as he gradually sinks into the last, final depths of despair. The phone continues to ring at the other end of the line, but no one lifts the receiver.

Michael sits at his desk in solemn silence. He has the ring in his hand and examines it impassively. He'd liked it well enough in the shop the day she chose it, but he hates it now with a passion. It seems such a trivial thing to make a grown man cry, but it does, and he can't help himself. He stares at the ring and feels every emotion inside him being engulfed by a torturous sensation of torment and self-pity. Suddenly he picks up the ring, clasping it tightly in his clenched fist, before putting it carefully in his pocket. He picks up his scarf and overcoat and leaves the house via the front door. He walks slowly but purposefully. A bridge crosses a river near his home. It separates the town in two. He remembers it. He knows it well. They used to go there when he was a kid and walk along its banks, feeding bread to the swans and ducks. He recalls the drop from the centre of the bridge is high and the current is fast in winter and the waters deep. He'll have to climb to the very top. He knows it will be quick.

There's a police car in the road. It's parked immediately outside Michael's house. Several policemen are standing about chatting and smoking cigarettes. The front door is open. More policemen are inside. One, a Chief Inspector, with a grey raincoat and matching hat, screws the lid on the empty bottle of rum and flicks his way through the pages of the novel by Maupassant. He looks at the haunting face of Leonard Cohen on the record sleeve. He could almost be saying *There was just nowhere else to go and no other option to take.* Just then the phone finally rings. One of the policemen moves to answer it. It's the voice of a young woman on the other end of the line.

'Michael, I'm sorry,' she says. 'The ring, it wasn't me. It was my mother. She took it when I was sleeping. I would never have done such a thing.'

The voice breaks off. Only silence follows.

BACKED THE WRONG HORSE

It was a cold, wet, winter evening in November 1931 and the Berlin sky was blackened by a thick, impenetrable belt of brooding cloud, that cast its ugly shadow over the empty streets. It brought with it that strange sense of emotional gloom and despondency that always seems to go hand in hand with the ceaseless, monotonous regularity of dull, unyielding drizzle falling from the skies. It had that ability to tire and make weary even the most hardy and optimistic person, with its capacity to soak through any number of outer layers of clothing. Targeting the vulnerable, it reached every last corner of the human body and soul, sapping reserves of strength and consuming every last ounce of energy, drive and enthusiasm until there was little or none left.

The eerie stillness of night-time was only broken when a butcher's van, matt green in colour, emerged cautiously from a side street and accelerated into the main highway, travelling east towards the Jewish sector of the city. It was driven by a young man, with short, brown hair and sharp, pointed, somewhat exaggerated features, that gave him a slightly haunted, grotesque air. His face was thin and gaunt. His cheekbones were harsh and prominent. His nose was lean and compact, his jawbone dominant and obtrusive. His eyes had a savage, penetrating quality, and he possessed a frenzied, hypnotic look that hinted at near obsession, bordering on insanity and madness. His overall appearance was vaguely irregular and lopsided, and he gave the impression of a loner with few friends of consequence or closeness.

His pale, white skin seemed to stretch over his haggard, bony framework with the characteristic texture of a taut drum. He had the suggestion of a man who'd suffered some great, indefinable tragedy in his past that he'd never quite recovered from. There was something enormously sad about his eyes, yet also something ruthless, cruel and unforgiving. There was an unreal and inhumane quality about his manner, as if he had or was about to commit some great wrong. Such were his glazed, wild looks, he could have been in a trance or state of shock. Perhaps if the right person had clicked their fingers, he would have woken up. He might even have wondered whose life he was really living and whether in fact it was his. As it was, his attention remained firmly fixed on the driving wheel and the road ahead, which continued unabated into the distance. There was clearly a purpose to his actions, which he had no intention of being deflected from, though it wasn't clear what those intentions were.

The man's name was Klaus Muller. He was 27 years old and still hadn't found a permanent job or occupation he could remain in any way committed to for more than a month or two. He had great hopes, dreams and aspirations inside him, but they never seemed to come to fruition. They remained dampened and unfulfilled, and his disillusionment about his situation was only growing. Of course, he wasn't the only unemployed German in Berlin. There were many others just like him, waiting on street corners and dark alleyways, in the dockyards and red-light districts, in the gambling halls and ale houses, on underground platforms, on benches in parks and city subways, in cheap, seedy hotels and single rooms overlooking Jewish businesses. They waited for the call to arms and their time to come, as it surely would, but in the meantime they could only wait, listen and watch out.

There had been the great stock market crash and the depression that followed. It had hit everyone hard. It had made the city streets stink with hardship and disenchantment. There had been no escape. It had latched hold and taken root like cancer, eating away at the very fabric of society. It had become a sad reality of life, lingering like a bad odour and infecting all it came into contact with. Savings had been wiped out overnight. Inflation made sure of that. Money was no longer worth the paper it was printed on. Jobs were like gold dust. There were no jobs to be had. No one was taking anyone on. Business was stuck in a rut and couldn't find its way out. There was no investment, as there was no money to spend. It had been rendered worthless. Only physical goods retained value, to be swapped and bartered with for basics and essentials like food.

Muller found himself at the bottom of the heap, the lowest of the low. He had no house, no warm bed, no fireside by which to warm his feet, no wife to cook for him and go home to at night, no one to make him breakfast on cold, winter mornings, no one to hold him tight and make him feel wanted. He had none of that. He'd almost forgotten what it meant to eat a hot meal even. He slept on park benches and in shop doorways mostly, occasionally on other people's floors when he could. He scrounged most of what he ate and the clothes he wore. He made the best of what little was going and came his way. Yet today was different. Today he felt important. Finally, he was somebody and could hold his head up high. He could stand up and be counted as a man of substance with the cream of them. For once in his life, he could shout out and let it be known that he, Klaus Muller, was going somewhere and was no longer a good-for-nothing vagrant with no job and no identity.

It seemed that after years of searching he'd discovered his true vocation and found what he was looking for and had been missing in his insipid, lonely existence. The Party had saved him. It had fed him, bought him new clothes, even put a little money in his pocket. It had given him back his sense of pride and self-worth. He'd begun to shrug off the feelings of futility, negativity and desperation that had shackled him and hung round his shoulders like an albatross for far too long. Adolf Hitler had shown him a way out and he was determined to take it and grab it with both hands. He wanted that more than anything else in the world. He was determined to grasp the opportunity that had presented itself while he could. There was no going back. This was it. He was a winner in the new order of things or soon would be. He

45

wanted to hold that trophy high above his head. He'd let too much of his life drift by in dull, pointless obscurity. All that would change now. It was time to stop the rot and halt it dead in its tracks.

That was why tonight he knew he must get it right. There could be no mistakes. He couldn't afford them. Everything had to go to plan. He'd let nothing go wrong. He'd waited too long for this. It was his chance to prove himself and he wasn't about to blow it. He knew what he had to do, and he'd do it exactly as he'd been told to, down to every last detail. It was as simple as that. He had it all worked out. He was master of his own destiny, just as Hitler was leader and master of the party that gave his life meaning where before it had none.

As Muller drove he became increasingly consumed by feelings of both tension and excitement and began to sweat with nervous anticipation. His clothes stuck to his back and a thin layer of perspiration coated his forehead. He'd increased speed and was taking the corners faster and faster with each one that approached, driving into them and letting the brakes screech their angry opposition to his relentless, uncompromising assault on the van's suspension. As he drove out of the tight corners, the wheels of the van sent silvery jets of road spray splashing over the stone pavement. Luckily, few other vehicles were about, as Muller drove like a man possessed, with thoughts only for his destination. Eventually the van pulled into a vacant space outside a row of small shops and stopped. They'd arrived and Muller got out. He went to the back of the van and opened it. Three men jumped down into the street to stand beside him. They wore brown uniforms, with armbands of red, white and black swastikas proudly displayed on them.

'This is it boys,' he hissed, as if he was giving the orders.

Muller reached inside his overcoat and produced two pairs of stockings, which he distributed among his companions, keeping one for himself.

'Put these on, so no one can recognise us afterwards,' he said, pulling his tightly over his face to obscure the identity he'd only so recently acquired.

He told one of the men to wait by the van and gestured to the other two to follow him. They moved as silently as hunters in the night, onto the other side of the street, ducking furtively in and out of the shadows, to approach the corner shop. It was dark, but a glowing streetlamp illuminated the shopfront, making the inscription above the window easier to read. It said simply *Albert Steiner – Grocer.*

Muller had brought with him an old army rucksack from the back of the van. He now opened it, taking out several bricks, which he passed around, keeping one for himself. He crept stealthily up the to the shopfront and hurled his brick through the elegant frontage. It collapsed inwards in an instant, shattering into a silvery assortment of tiny fragments and jagged edges of glass and scattering far and wide in a piercing eruption of crashing, high-pitched noise that splintered the very stillness of the night.

Muller then attempted to kick down the front door, but it wouldn't yield. He drew himself to his full height and launched himself at the wooden door, connecting with the full weight of his shoulder. It sprung open, causing him to slip onto the floor, carried by his own momentum. He quickly dragged himself back to his feet, using the door handle as support. He then proceeded to pull over a number of shelves, letting the various cans of food crash onto the tiled surface below. One of the shelves cracked and splintered as it fell, enabling Muller to break off a piece of wood, which he swung viciously around his head, breaking everything that it came into contact with. He pulled cupboards off walls, scattering the contents and demolishing all that came in his way without pause or respite. He hurled all kinds of foods and packages to the ground in a fit of pure, wild demolition and abandonment. He laughed aloud, as they exploded in a thickening, congealing mess that covered walls, ceiling and floor alike.

Eventually Muller decided his work was complete and he stepped back to survey the scene of destruction and chaos he'd caused. One of his companions continued to wreak havoc inside the shop. Another opened a tin of blue paint and proceeded to daub a hideously distorted Star of David over what was left of the front door, like an obscene, metaphorical branding, as if to say those within were unclean. It had become the standard way of identification for the city's Jewish brethren. Antisemitism was rife and celebrated among a high proportion of the population.

At that moment, a slight man, probably in his mid-fifties, appeared at the back of the shop, presumably anxious to know what all the noise and commotion was. He may well have been in bed asleep, preparing for another early start in the shop, and been woken by the demolition taking place beneath him. For it was the owner, Mr Steiner. He was a short and skinny man. He'd been a weakly child and was neither strong nor healthy, owing to frequent episodes of bronchitis and now angina in older age. His face carried the classic features of his proud race, chiselled out by centuries of persecution, that had now caught up with him on this day and at this point in time.

He'd lost most of his greying hair and his eyesight was deteriorating. He also carried a small stick, resulting from a slight disfigurement of his left leg, a minor deformity he'd carried since birth that had prevented him doing much in the way of sport and other physical activity. He certainly wasn't a perfect example of humanity and mankind in strictly Nazi terms, but he was honest and hard-working, a good husband to his wife and a good father to his children. Mr Steiner struggled to the door.

He was met by the thuggish brute Muller, who dragged him out into the road, kicking away his stick in the process and forcing him to his knees. Muller drew back his boot and launched it into Steiner's face. Mr Steiner wasn't a man of violence. He fell backwards, rolling over onto his stomach and lying face down in the mud and dirt of road and pavement. Muller hauled him roughly back to his feet, punching him in the chest and head, before letting him slip from his firm grasp once more, to leave Steiner gasping for air on the wet and slippery ground.

'You Jewish bastard!' Muller screamed in a demented, high-pitched shout, as he continued his relentless assault on the older man. 'Get down in the gutters where you belong, you Jew scum!' he yelled, as he lashed out a boot again.

It caught Steiner full on the nose, which cracked in an instant, collapsing inwards in a bloody mess of flesh and bone. Blood flowed freely down his cheek and chin, splashing onto the roadside where it became diluted by the evening's dull rainfall. As Steiner fell and his head hit the curb, warm tentacles of crimson blood continued to leak and spread from his face, forming little, dark puddles that grew outwards under the thick, black cloud of the night sky. Again Muller kicked the huddled body, this time in the kidneys and stomach and then finally in the head once more for good measure.

Mr Steiner didn't move. He didn't shriek in agony. He didn't cry out. He lay still in a quiet heap in the road, blood oozing from mutilated nostrils and mouth, to form a deepening pool of redness, congealing around his head. He was clearly dead. Muller stood back to admire his handiwork. The body possessed a strange, morbid fascination for Muller. He found its distorted ugliness almost appealing, and it was hard for him to avert his gaze from it. To be able to stand over his victim and bear witness to such a violent death as this and by his own hands somehow uplifted his spirits and made him feel good about himself inside. His adrenalin was still pumping furiously. He felt a warm glow of pride and intense feelings of power and strength within that he wanted to preserve forever. He was briefly ecstatic.

Finally, he turned away and breathed deeply several times, hoping the cold air would help him to recover his composure and manner of authority as before. In the heat of the moment his emotions had got the better of him. Now he was calm and collected again. One of his accomplices had painted a second Star of David on the dead body. The other was carefully filling a milk bottle with petrol. Muller stood and watched as his companion pulled a handkerchief from his pocket and stuffed it into the end to use as a wick. He soaked it a little with more petrol, before striking a match to ignite it, until it produced a bright, licking flame that spiralled upwards, a thing of beauty illuminating the night's darkness, that contrasted sharpy with its deadly intention and purpose.

Almost as if in slow motion he drew back his arm and sent the bottle hurtling through the shop doorway, before the flame had a chance to work its way through to the gasoline. When it hit the ground, the glass shattered instantly. The fuel quickly spread its blue, steamy fingers across the floor and into every corner of the room, igniting rapidly and sending long, orange flames soaring up towards the roof, scorching the ceiling and curdling and stripping paint from the walls with the intense heat it generated. It was a terrifying but magnificent sight. Muller was both beguiled and mesmerised at once. Gradually the whole house became enveloped in thick, acrid smoke, as both the interior and exterior were ravaged by fire. Outside Muller could clearly discern the cracking and splintering of wood, as the flames reached higher, eating through floorboards, furniture, joists and supports. A cruel, callous smile spread across Muller's lips and his skin tingled with sadistic pleasure.

There was something peculiarly hypnotic about the flickering, weaving columns of smoke and flame that coiled their way up into the dark night sky, giving new light to this strange, dour, urban landscape of miserable homes and shops, crammed into tight, ugly lines, rows and alleys. Muller felt his face flush with excitement and a vague tickling sensation prickled the back of his hands, as he stared into the hot, iridescent warmth of the fire's central cauldron, from which flames continued to leap out. He never saw the sleek, black Mercedes that slid to a standstill just behind him. The noise from the burning shop had cloaked the sound of the smooth-running, finely tuned engine.

Two men got out. They wore cream mackintoshes, matching felt hats and expensive trousers and shoes, that were in sharp contrast to those Muller was wearing. In the faded light of the late evening shadows, they could have been wealthy businessman, but it was reasonable to assume they weren't that, but something else. The purpose of their mission and presence was almost certainly something far more sinister. They approached Muller as silently as cats. One of them rested an arm on Muller's shoulder.

'Come with us. We need to talk,' he hissed.

Muller suddenly felt confused and less sure of himself. He wasn't certain what was wanted of him and what was his best course of action. Surely, he'd done nothing wrong. Surely, they'd only come to praise him, but he didn't care for the harsh tone he'd been spoken to in or the expressions on their serious faces. Their looks were ones of foreboding.

'Where are you taking me?' he eventually asked after a lengthy pause.

He tried to convince himself he was to be rewarded for a good night's work and the successful completion of a difficult job, but somehow he had his doubts.

'No questions now, you'll find out soon enough,' he was told curtly.

The two men led Muller to the waiting car and hustled him roughly into the backseat, where he sat somewhat uncomfortably, almost as if he was at gunpoint or under arrest. One of the men walked round the vehicle to get in the front. The other got in the back, where he could keep an eye on Muller in case he made any attempt to escape. The driver started up the engine and the car pulled out, accelerating smoothly into the cold, wet drizzle of the November night. After some miles the eerie silence was broken by a voice.

'Are you sure you told us everything and missed nothing out?' Muller was asked. 'There was nothing else you should have told us that you can think of? Are you absolutely sure of that?'

'Who are you?' Muller demanded to know.

'It doesn't matter who we are. Just answer the questions. It's who you are that we're trying to find out,' he was informed sharply.

'I don't know what you mean,' Muller protested.

The interrogator ignored Muller's response and persisted with his line of questioning.

'I repeat, did you tell us everything? Because we're not sure you did.'

'Yes, I think so,' Muller insisted.

'What do you mean you think so? Did you or didn't you?' he was asked again.

'I think so,' Muller repeated. 'What is the meaning of this? I've done everything you asked like the loyal Party member I am, haven't I?'

Muller couldn't fail to be aware of the intensity and seriousness of the situation he unwittingly and unexpectedly found himself in. A look of growing concern and alarm began to spread across his face. He felt a mixture of fear and anguish. He didn't like the questions he was being asked, or the manner in which they were directed at him.

'You're only making it harder for yourself,' he was informed. 'If you won't answer the questions, I'll have to answer them for you. You didn't tell us everything, did you?'

His unnamed, anonymous inquisitor paused momentarily for an answer that didn't come. Muller remained silent.

'So where shall we start then?' his interrogator continued. 'Tell us about your grandmother for instance.'

'I have no grandmother,' Muller cried, suddenly aware his palms were sweating, and a small bead of perspiration ran down the side of head, followed quickly by another.

'Liar!' screamed his backseat interrogator, slapping Muller across the face with such force and power that his head seemed to roll freely on his shoulders for a moment.

It appeared fleetingly in danger of leaving his body. It didn't, however.

'Your grandmother was Rebecca Rosinsky. She was a Polish Jew,' the menacing man in the mackintosh declared. 'I think you know the rest.'

'It's not true,' Muller maintained, becoming ever more agitated and unnerved.

The driver just stared ahead, keeping his eyes firmly on the road in front of him. He played no active part in the questioning and interrogation taking place in the back of the car. By this time the Mercedes had passed the outer suburbs of the city and was heading north. There were no other vehicles on the highway. Muller looked at his watch. It was now almost midnight, and the small hours were approaching fast. Everything had happened so quickly. It was difficult to recall the exact course of events as they'd unfolded. He couldn't think clearly. It was all so confusing. Who were these men? Who had sent them? Where were they taking him? They were obviously fully acquainted with his mission and indeed his personal life, even more so than he was himself.

Muller tried to unravel it all in his mind and put back together the various pieces of the jigsaw as best he could, but it still made no sense. He could picture the face of the dead Jew, Steiner. He recalled how it was repellent, yet almost beautiful at the same time. He could remember the crimson flames soaring high above the shop, and how they delighted him. Yes, there had been a fire. He and his accomplices had started one after ransacking the shop. Of that much, he was sure. At least one Jew, Steiner, had died at his hands. Perhaps more had perished in the fire. They'd painted the Star of David on the front door and over the dead man, and it had been fun. Yes, it had been a laugh and made him feel renewed, bold and satisfied. Muller had expected some kind of reward at the end of it; a pat on the back at least, not this. A little further on, the car pulled off the main road onto a narrow, deserted track that didn't appear to lead anywhere. The Mercedes continued for another fifty yards and then stopped.

'Get out!' the man in the back snapped at Muller.

He pulled a gun from his pocket, and he used it to prod Muller sharply in the ribs. The driver got out and went to the back of the vehicle to open the rear door and drag Muller to his feet. Muller could feel his legs faltering on the wet ground and go weak under his own weight. It was hard to find a grip on the dirt track that had muddy, grass clumps protruding out of it at irregular intervals. Muller could sense the light rain brushing against his clammy skin. He wanted to run, but there was nowhere to run to. He considered an escape attempt and making a wild bid for freedom, but realised he would be cut down before he could take a handful of steps. The situation seemed hopeless, and he began to mumble in desperation to himself.

'I've always been a good Party member,' he complained. 'I did what I was asked to do without argument or complaint. I asked no questions of my superiors at any point. I followed orders without hesitation. What exactly have I done wrong? I thought this was just the start of something big for me. I thought it was an opportunity to better myself. Please don't kill me. Give me another chance to prove myself. I can do it. I'll do anything you say. I killed one, didn't I? I can kill more Jewish scum if you only let me,' Muller pleaded.

'Shut up, we're not going to shoot you. We don't want your body on our hands. It would be more trouble than it's worth. Go now, while you can, but we never want to see your ugly face in Berlin again,' Muller was told.

'You mean I'm free to go? What can I say? Thank you, thank you very much,' Muller enthused, with feelings of light headedness, euphoria and relief.

'Go quickly before we change our minds. Remember, we're letting you off lightly this time, you hear,' Muller was informed in no uncertain terms.

'Yes, of course, certainly,' Muller agreed gleefully. 'I'm sorry.'

Muller had taken about five paces when the stillness of the night was shattered by the ear-splitting detonation of a gun being fired. The bullet struck Muller in the back of his head with such force that his body was thrown forwards. The top part of his skull was blown clean off by the impact of lead on flesh and bone. He managed to stumble on blindly for another yard or so, before a second shot followed. He was dead long before his body hit the soft, muddy turf beneath him.

'You didn't really think we were going to let you get away with it, did you?' his assailant said, as he calmly returned his gun to his pocket.

The two me got back in the car and drove off, leaving Muller's body where it had fell.

ALL THERE IS TO SAY

You've seen it all before. You stop at the off-licence to pick up some beer. You pause at the door before going on up. You can hear your own nervous breath. The room is hushed, still and silent. A record has just finished playing. She doesn't look at you when you move to kiss her. She carefully applies her make-up. Textured brush strokes are her quiet amnesia and pleasure. Her long, blonde hair is tamed now, but later it will be a different story. She knows all the right moves. There's nothing you can teach her. You just haven't got a clue. If only you hadn't told her how much you were in love with her. Ah but you did and now it's too late to take it back. The cat's out of the bag.

You've seen on her face all there is to be said. It's a look that holds no more and no less that can be viewed on the bare surface. If only you could make her love you as you love her, but you know you never will do. What a fool you were to imagine for one single moment the feelings could ever be reciprocated. It's all a bad joke. Hopelessly you trip and stutter over every word. There are never enough to say what you truly mean. You're such an absurd failure when it really matters. You're the master of your own indignity. Sadly, she knows you for what you are. She can see straight through every single letter of your bankrupt vocabulary. Talk is cheap. The words spill out but find no meaning. The scene is all too familiar and always equally embarrassing. You can hardly bear to face her now. Her layered eyeliner that you've seen run with tears, her false, penetrating laughter, her relentless anger and her vile deceit, all act like a barrier. You don't know quite what to tell her.

'I'm sorry I'm early. I just had to see you,' is your poor, ill-considered, eventual opening gambit.

'I'm sorry too,' she says blankly and without emotion.

Her monotone reply has a cutting edge that plunges deep into the sad, bottomless pit that is your heart. The sound of your voice isn't enough to capture her interest, to break her concentration and take it away from what she's doing, to deflect her attention away from the mirror and the picture she's painting on her flawless skin for a single moment. A look of slight irritation twitches at the corner of her mouth. The first cut isn't always the deepest. There's murder in her eyes, and she moves gracefully in for the kill.

'I don't know what you mean,' you foolishly reply, as you're a mere pawn to her in a game where she is queen.

Your worst fears are soon confirmed.

'Yes, I think you do. It was just a bit of fun. It wasn't meant to go this far. You weren't meant to care,' she says.

She pauses momentarily for effect, before delivering the punchline with a strange sense of power and triumph.

'Besides, I've found someone else,' she adds, almost as a casual afterthought.

'It isn't true,' you protest in vain. 'I don't believe you. How could you? Tell me it isn't so. I want it to work out between us. Please don't do this to me now.'

A feeling of total despair pours through your limp, tired body and you want to cry out. You want to give verbal expression to your private agony.

'I'm sorry. I just don't want that kind of relationship with you. Can't you see that? It was just something to amuse me for a while and nothing more. It didn't mean anything. I don't think we should see each other again,' she says.

'So that's it then? I thought I meant something to you. I thought what we had was special. I thought it was different for us. Well, wasn't it? You were always telling me it was,' you plead, but your pleas fall on deaf ears.

'No, you were just like the rest. There's nothing more to say. I'm sorry but you must go now,' she announces coldly.

As you leave you realise you haven't even opened any of your beers. You resolve to drink them later to drown your sorrows as best you can.

That was the last time. You never got hurt again. You swore it to yourself that there would be no repeat, and largely there hasn't been. But things never work out quite as you intend. Sometimes you just can't help yourself getting sucked in, only to pull back at the last. It's a sad but inevitable process. Your thoughts turn to her every now and then and from time to time. You remember her voice. It comes back to you on occasion when you least expect it to. You remember your once smart appearance and how you let it go to seed and to waste. You remember the softness of your face, and the stubble you let grow in its place. You were never quite as tough as you pretended to be.

In retrospect the lies you hid behind were a little too transparent and obvious to be believed by anyone. Drinking yourself into an early grave was surely a bad mistake and a senseless course of action by any standards. It was a reckless decision to take at your tender age, but you did your best to achieve exactly that regardless of the consequences. What a fool you were. You meant nothing to her. Did she have to mean that much to you? You tell yourself she didn't do but are fully aware it isn't true.

It's been ten years now. It's no wonder she doesn't recognise you. Who would? The transformation from good to bad has been quite dramatic. There are only glimpses left of the handsome man you were then. Life has taken its toll and exacted a heavy price for your errors of judgement, of which there have been many. It hasn't stopped you. Of late you've taken to watching her every day from a safe distance across the street. You saw her one day by chance and decided to follow her. Now it's become a habit. You couldn't resist the temptation to watch and observe and savour small aspects of her new life. Now you know it almost by heart. Catching brief moments and episodes here and there has allowed you to build up a picture that is more or less whole and complete. You know where she lives and where she works. You know she has two kids. You never thought she had it in her. You presumed her to be too selfish ever to be a mother. You were wrong on that score. Perhaps you are wrong about other things and assumptions you've made too. You see her once treasured beauty is fading, just as your good looks have done over time. Perhaps that's not the only thing you have in common.

You watch her routine and know it almost like your own. She lives with her new family on the top floor of an apartment block near the centre of town. It's not overly spacious but it's a palace compared to the humble single room in a run-down, shared house you have. Well, she always had a taste for the high life. You see her laughing sometimes. More often you see her crying. You make an educated guess that despite appearances it hasn't all worked out quite as she hoped, but then nothing is as perfect as it seems. Your life is far from it. Your life is as far from perfect as it can possibly be.

You watch her at every chance and opportunity you get. You know when she goes out and when she comes back. You know when she eats her meals. You've followed her to a nearby park, where you've seen her feeding bread to the pigeons and observed her sometimes with her head in her hands. You wonder what she truly feels inside. You want to get close enough to touch her. You want to speak, but you know she won't answer. You wait for her to call you over, but she never does. You remain the unseen observer. You keep your distance always.

It pains you to see her start to cry again. You will her not to, not alone, with you so near, yet so far away at the same time. Just one word from her and you'd be there. You're not beyond reach. A simple word of encouragement would be enough to break the ice. One day you see her huddled on a park bench, a suitcase by her side and her children nowhere in sight. It's too much for you not to act and try to help at least. You cautiously walk over and sit down beside her. You start to speak. She clearly doesn't remember you or know who you are.

'There, there, dry your tears. There's no need to cry. Try not to be so unhappy,' you say soothingly, as if your words alone could wipe away her tears.

She continues to sob quietly.

'It's my husband, you see,' she explains. 'He's found another woman, after nearly ten years of marriage. He just came out with it one morning over breakfast. He said she was moving in with him and the kids. He told me to take my things and leave. He's more or less kicked me out into the street, and I have nowhere else to go. I don't know how anyone could do such a thing.'

'And I can't let you do that to me again,' you mutter under your breath.

'I'm sorry, what did you say?' she asks, unsure if she's heard you correctly and not quite understanding the meaning of your words anyway.

'It was nothing,' you tell her, attempting a smile of reassurance.

'Do you mind putting your arm around me?' she enquires pleadingly. 'I really feel in need of some human contact and moral support right now. I don't know quite where I'm going to go or what to do with myself.'

'You don't remember me, do you?' you venture to guess, but you already know the answer to that before she attempts any form of reply.

Why would she remember when you meant nothing to her? The last time you spoke she couldn't get rid of you quickly enough.

'No, have we met before? I can't quite place the face,' she says.

'Yes, we have, but it doesn't matter. It's not important,' you tell her, as you get up and move to leave.

'Where are you going?' she wonders, with slight alarm in her voice.

'Nowhere special, but I always have places to be and things waiting elsewhere for me,' you reply neither truthfully nor wholly dishonestly.

'Do you have to go?' she asks. 'Will you take me with you?'

'I'd like to, but I can't forgive or forget the past, not now or ever,' you tell her.

'What do you mean?' she wonders, with a confused expression on her face.

'I mean you shouldn't ask. It's not fair and it would be wrong of me to accept your company after all that's happened between us. If only you'd asked me ten years ago, I'd have accepted without hesitation. Now it's too late and I can't undo what's already been said and done. But don't worry, you won't be on you own for long. Give it time and he'll come back to you. They always do once the novelty of someone new wears off,' you assure her. 'And if not, many other men would be glad of your companionship and proud to have you as their partner, even me perhaps one day.'

'But I still don't know who you are,' she says.

'You will when I've gone,' you tell her. 'You'll remember then, but I must leave you now. There's nothing more I can do for you.'

With that you walk off into the distance and out of her life forever. It feels satisfying finally to be able to let her go once and for all. Perhaps you'll even have a shave and stop drinking when you get back to your room. You may even finally move on with your life after a decade in little more than limbo and find a degree of meaning and motivation, where for so long there has been nothing.

THE LONG ARM OF THE LAW

It was a cold, wet, miserable evening in early February. To a tourist on his first visit to this world-famous, historic city, London would surely have been a disappointment, with its grand and magnificent buildings obscured by a fine mist of rain and adorning fog, and the Thames shrouded by thick, dark layers of cloud. Simon Davies had never seen London before, but for him the inclement weather didn't spoil his early impressions. His mood was dark anyway. Indeed, if anything it only served to enhance and intensify his general feelings of depression, sadness and despondency. It was now eight months since he'd left university with a degree in history. During that time, despite his best efforts he'd neither found gainful employment of any sort nor a permanent place to live. For a while he'd stayed with his parents, but it hadn't taken long for their patience to wear thin. Eventually they'd told him it was time for him to move out and learn to stand on his own two feet. Their message had been clear enough. They couldn't wait to see the back of him in truth. He had to make it on his own and sink or swim, they said. So like many before him, he'd made his way to London, to seek his fortune and a sense of purpose and direction in his life. So far, he'd found none.

Simon Davies wasn't large or tall man. In fact, he was rather short and slight in stature. He lacked both physical strength and a build that was in any sense imposing or impressive or suggested he could look after himself should the need arise. He was of a polite but rather timid and uncertain disposition. He kept his light brown hair cut short and wore small-rimmed NHS glasses, as his eyesight was poor and he struggled to afford better ones. He shuffled about rather awkwardly, hiding himself inside a thick, grey overcoat. He walked cautiously along the largely empty street, fearful of what he might encounter and with his hair plastered to his forehead by the rain. It continued to fall, but he had ceased to notice, as it slowly soaked through his coat to his pullover and shirt beneath. He was aware his shoes and trousers were also wet.

Davies could hear the sound of music and voices drifting from the other side of the road. It was a pub and there were people inside. He knew they'd be laughing and joking as they drank, with contented smiles on their faces. They'd be relaxed and enjoying themselves, as they forgot the problems of their lives for several hours at least. Davies stood and stared, pausing for a few minutes under the illuminating light of a streetlamp, watching people come and go and trying to pluck up the courage to join them. He knew theirs was a very different existence to the one he endured in stoic solitude.

He looked at his watch. It was eight-thirty. The pub was getting busier. More were entering than leaving. Davies ventured a little closer and wondered to himself if he could go in and order a drink like any other normal person. He was still assessing the various permutations and possibilities, when a taxi drew up outside the pub and three men got out. They were young, loud, confident and energetic and enticing to a man like Davies, who had no one and was alone. Davies felt compelled to follow them in. He stumbled across the road but hesitated at the entrance for a moment before going inside. It was a big step to take for someone as insecure and lacking in self-belief as he was.

Eventually with huge effort he crossed the threshold and found himself propped up somewhat awkwardly against the bar, where he ordered half a pint of bitter. He sipped it quietly, his eyes darting about, trying to take in as much of his surroundings as he could. He could see the young men who'd come in just before him. They were sitting at a table almost directly in front of him. One of them brought over a tray of drinks to share with his companions and placed it down. Davies found himself drawn to one man in particular with blonde, curly, shoulder-length hair. He had sharply defined yet delicate features like finest porcelain. His nose was proud and prominent. His cheekbones were high, his face narrow and his eyes strangely penetrating. All in all, he was an attractive man and Davies felt oddly drawn to him. He felt he already knew him. He wanted to reach out and touch him. It stirred some silent yearning within Davies. He watched him out of the corner of his eye, without tilting his head, like he was watching an old friend come home.

Moments passed and became minutes, even hours. Davies was no longer counting. He didn't move. He stayed where he was, barely touching his drink. He'd forgotten all about it. He just continued to stare at what to him was an almost godlike creature. To Davies he was watching the epitome of masculine beauty, as it sat before him in all its impressive splendour. One of the blonde young man's companions seemed to notice the undue amount of attention Davies was giving his friend, and he furtively motioned towards Davies with his arm, to make his companion quietly aware of the situation. Davies turned away hurriedly, his face crimson with embarrassment. The three men suddenly finished their drinks and got up and left. Davies rose to his feet too, gripped by an uncontrollable urge to follow them out into the street. It was still raining and evening was slowly turning to nighttime. To the surprise and discomfort of Davies, the three men were waiting in the street for him.

'What's your game, mate?' one of the men demanded to know. 'Why did you keep staring at us, and why are you following us now? Are you gay or something? Have you got the hots for us?'

He didn't wait for an answer. Instead, he gripped Davies by the coat lapels and threw him roughly to the ground. His glasses fell from his face and bounced on the pavement. The blonde young man saw his opportunity and crushed them under his foot, laughing loudly as he heard the glass and plastic of lenses and frames crack and splinter. He drew back his boot and launched it viciously into the exposed body of Davies, who doubled up in agony. One of his companions held the blonde Adonis back, as he prepared to swing another boot and angle a kick into his helpless victim's midriff. They could see Davies had taken enough punishment and was in no position to fight back. All three left quickly before an alarm could be raised or the police called.

Davies fumbled myopically round on the ground for his glasses. One of the lenses was shattered completely. The other was cracked. One side of the frames had broken clean off. The other was hanging on for dear life. Having located what was left of his glasses, Davies did his best to place them back in position on the end of his nose. He peered through them rather uncomfortably, trying to regain some sense of vision and balance. He shook his head once or twice to recover his senses, before hauling himself to his feet. His stomach ached and he had a graze down the right side of the face, where he'd hit the ground. The wafer-thin skin had been scraped off and blood was starting to rise to the surface. He felt vaguely concussed.

Davies knew he must find a public convenience, where he could clean himself up and make his appearance at least vaguely respectable. He recalled spotting one on the other side of the street, not long before going into the pub. Once there he stumbled somewhat clumsily down the steps. He walked over to the hand basin and splashed his cut face with water. It stung painfully. Suddenly he became aware of a shadow hovering over him that in his urgency he hadn't noticed. He turned around.

'Are you all right?' a man's voice enquired.

He was about forty and was wearing an expensive sports jacket and gleaming brown shoes. They gave him an air of both wealth and respectability. Davies would never be able to afford clothes like that, he realised with a tinge of regret. The man had a fine, black moustache, which curled elegantly round his upper lip. His hair was neatly trimmed and combed back, held in position by hair lacquer of some sort. He had the appearance of a film star of the silent movie days. He was proud and dignified but had a manner which was strangely comforting at the same time.

'Yes, I'm all right,' Davies stammered at last.

'No, I can see you're not, young man. I tell you what, I don't live far away. Why don't you come back with me and clean up there? I could make you coffee and give you a good meal. I could put you up for the night, just to see you're all right, and give you breakfast to help you on your way,' the older man suggested.

'I don't know,' Davies began to mumble.

He was slightly confused and didn't know quite what to say, but there was something about the man's voice that suggested it all made perfect sense.

'Of course you do,' the man insisted. 'You can't go home like that, can you?'

The man seemed so assured that Davies didn't want to argue or admit that the only home he had to go to was an unassuming room in a YMCA hostel. So feebly he grasped at the opportunity.

'Well, I suppose I could if you don't mind and if it doesn't put you out too much. That would be very nice,' Davies said meekly.

'Of course, there are one or two favours I may ask in return, if you know what I mean, to help keep an old man company,' the man said.

Davies wasn't quite sure what he was talking about but nodded. He was just thinking of somewhere near to rest his weary head.

61

'Right Officer, you can come out now. I trust you got all that down,' the smart, older gentleman announced triumphantly.

Almost on cue one of the cubicle doors unlocked and a young Constable emerged in a shiny, black police uniform. He awaited his instructions as Davies was read his rights, which he'd heard many times on television crime series and programmes.

'You can take him away now. You'd better handcuff him though. He may be dangerous. He's been in one fight already tonight by the look of it,' the plain clothes officer said

'But I don't understand,' Davies protested. 'On what charge am I being arrested?'

'The usual one, soliciting in a public place,' he was told curtly.

'But I never did anything. It was you. You approached me,' Davies complained.

'Sorry son, that's as maybe, but we've got to keep your type off the streets, haven't we? Honest citizens don't like it you see. It makes them feel uneasy about going out at night. It creates the wrong impression of our wonderful city and it's not good for the tourist industry. We get a lot of complaints about men approaching other men in this neck of the woods, and we're going to put a stop to it any way we can,' he explained. 'Anyway, now I can get out of these ridiculous clothes.'

He peeled off the black moustache and put it away in his pocket.

'But you set me up,' Davies complained with shock and incredulity.

'There's no denying that. You've been had my son. You've been framed and taken for a ride in no uncertain fashion, but it's two witnesses against one, so be a good boy and take it on the chin. There's no chance of you getting off this time.'

THERE IT IS

I didn't believe you'd do it, but there it is. You have and that's it. There's not much more to be said on the matter. You sit before me, idly playing with your hair. You don't allow your eyes to catch mine. You sit uncomfortably on the end of your bed and avoid my shrunken stare as best you can. I still feel the necessity to demand some kind of explanation, although I hardly need one. You say the words quickly again in case something should stop you in midstream. A telephone ringing downstairs perhaps, a doorbell echoing in a confined space or a car pulling up outside. Any one of these could interrupt the flow of your voice or break your train of thought. I wish they would, but they don't alas.

'I'm sorry. I just don't feel it's right anymore. I need a break and time to sort myself out,' you insist.

The problem is we don't have time my dear.

'You shouldn't have said you'd marry me,' I point out, not unreasonably in the circumstances.

'I thought I wanted that, but things change sometimes. We don't always know why. You know I'll always love you,' you feel it fit to tell me.

'Is that right?' I ask rhetorically, without really expecting an answer. 'But it's not enough, is it? It never is.'

It hasn't been enough in a while in truth. It wasn't enough to phone once while we were briefly apart. I received no word from you in four or five weeks. How do you think that makes me feel? Do you really care so little? Apparently so I'm left to conclude. I admit I wasn't always the perfect lover and partner, but surely after two years of living together, I deserve something more than this. I'm shattered by your contempt. Your disrespect makes me shudder and shakes me to the core. Can't you see the impact your disdainful abandonment of our love has exacted on me? I'm mournful to the point of emotional collapse. I'm so choked up I can hardly speak. I can't find the words to express the depths of my resentment. My hatred runs so deep, it arches every bone in my body and makes every moment ache. I used to think we could be happy, but it appears my confidence was misplaced, and I misread all the tell-tale signs badly. I got it hopelessly wrong in the end.

I look around at my things. They still lie scattered on the floor where you threw them down in a fit of temper the last time we argued. I breathe in the foul air, hanging thick and spent as our affection. I can make no impression on the tone of your voice. I fail to dent your defences. I can see no hint of emotion in your expression and the cold, stony features that mould your face. The awkward silence submerges all traces of the tenderness that used to fill me with such happiness. I find myself wishing you were dead. I hate you with a passion. I feel so betrayed by the way you lied. I can hardly comprehend the cold, callous insensitivity of your deceit. I can barely believe this is happening to me, but it must be. The evidence is before my very eyes. I'm here. You're there. The gulf between us is unbridgeable. The words roll off your lips as if laced with poison. They're poisoning me. How they maim and cause me to succumb and break down.

In my head I look for an answer and a way out. I imagine drawing a blade across my whitened wrists as a quick and easy exit. I wish to see the redness of blood mixed with my sweat and tears. It could be a momentary affirmation that I'm still alive and breathing, as my life gradually drains away. Sadly, you have no suitable blade for me to use. You wouldn't hand it to me if you did. You wouldn't want my death on your hands. You wouldn't grant me the mercy of release even if you could I suspect.

How has it come to this? It's a sorry state of affairs indeed. My unrelenting sadness is both savage and stale in equal measures. How the minutes pass and slowly become months and hatch years. They fill me with such deep despair that I can't ever escape from the situation I find myself in. I can no longer answer your irrelevant line of questioning or you mine. I can't offer logical explanation for the things that have happened. It's up to you to liberate me from this burden that weighs me down. I can't do it for you. Only you have the power to tell me to go. All I know is I shall see you with some other new lover at a later date in the future as yet to be decided, and it will simply be too much to bear.

MARKING THE OCCASIONS
(A Movie)

SCENE ONE

The sun gently sets over distant, rolling hills, casting long, red shadows on the surrounding countryside. A man in military uniform stands in the foreground. The camera focuses on the back of his silhouette. The redness of the sun carves out the shape of an officer's cap. He looks ahead into the distance. Poppies dance at his feet in the gentle breeze; one for every friend and comrade he's seen killed. Without glancing over his shoulder, he walks slowly away until he becomes barely visible. The camera remains still. The angle of the lens doesn't alter.

SCENE TWO

Zooming in on a motorway bridge, the sky above is a pale blue, punctuated with thin lines of cirrus cloud. There's a sound of cars approaching and then disappearing into the distance. A shot from the air shows an intersection of lanes passing, crossing, converging and diverging, symbolising the past, present and future.

SCENE THREE

At a disused railway station, the platform is slightly crumbling and overgrown with vegetation. The lines are mostly dug up and the once busy waiting room is an empty hollow, with its roof long since collapsed in places and exposing the floor beneath to the elements. The camera pans to the plaque recalling the name of the stop. One of the letters is missing and ivy has entwined itself round the metal pole that keeps it standing in place, though many years have now passed since its closure.

SCENE FOUR

In a sparsely furnished room with just the bare essentials of desk, bed and wardrobe, a man stands in a green, long-sleeved, buttoned vest and military lightweights with no shoes. He seems tense and nervous. His eyes are somewhat glazed, and his body visibly shakes with fear. His fringe is in need of cutting and it falls into his eyes at regular intervals. He brushes it away with an automatic movement of his arm. It only temporarily removes the annoyance, and the hair swiftly returns to its familiar place. He holds his head up high, standing to attention and saluting as if he's on parade. His head drops suddenly as if he's been shot and a bullet has passed through him. He collapses to the ground, motionless.

SCENE FIVE

He now sits at his desk. A revolver lies on the dull, wooden surface in front of him. He stares at it without blinking for what seems like an age, before picking it up, holding it and passing his fingertips lightly over the shiny, metal exterior. He examines every detail of its design, weighing it in each hand and checking the action, before finally satisfying himself everything's in working order. He loads one bullet into the chamber and snaps it shut. With the slightest touch of his hand, he sends the revolving cylinder into a steady spin. He stops it randomly at the place he thinks best. He presses the gun to the side of his head. He knuckles turn white with the mounting pressure on the trigger. There is a click, but no bullet. He sighs with relief. Lines of cold sweat trickle down his creased forehead. He fires again. For a second time there's just a dull click. The odds are slowly shortening. His face contorts with visible signs of stress and rising pressure, as for a third time he squeezes the metal trigger with his finger. Once for each time he fled from danger, he tells himself.

SCENE SIX

A television switches to a scene from the film *The Deer Hunter*. Blood spurts from the hole in the side of Christoher Walken's head, as Robert De Niro tries in vain to piece him back together. The clip repeats itself over and over again. A young man in a T-shirt and jeans watches the screen impassively from his reclining chair with unmoved indifference. The camera focuses on his face. He changes channel, to a cartoon, then the news, then a sitcom and back to *The Deer Hunter*. Bored, he switches the television off. He sits in the darkened room. Barely any light filters in. He's almost asleep now. He's surrounded by emptiness. His shelves are almost devoid of books and other possessions. There are no records, or games or musical instruments to hold his interest. There's just a chair and a TV. His boredom dissolves him slowly.

SCENE SEVEN

The young soldier still holds the revolver in his outstretched palm. It's still pressed to his skull as before, but he won't shoot and risk spilling his lifeblood. He's lost his nerve to fire again. Despairingly, he flings the gun to the floor. It doesn't go off. There's just another dull click. He's little more than a boy and he holds his head softly in his hands, rocking gently back and forth. He slowly lets his hands slide from his face and he gradually rises to his feet. He runs his fingers through his greasy hair. He removes his vest and rubs his bare shoulders and chest. He lets his arms fall to his sides. He holds out his hands pleadingly. They are scarred and empty, as if he's saying *This is me and this is all I have to give*. His head drops. He kneels. His neck is bent forward as if awaiting the executioner's axe. Perhaps in his mind he is. He holds a full-size Union Jack against his pale face and buries himself in its soft material to muffle his quiet sobbing. He curls up, smothered by the giant flag, and dreams of dying.

SCENE EIGHT

The television screen flickers into life. The youth, slumped in his chair, watches disinterestedly as he swigs from a can of weak, yellow

66

lager. Cigarette ash fills his lap. His face betrays his general air of contempt. The bitter irony is so obvious. More than ever his thoughts should turn to those who gave their lives, so he could sit all day in this chair, supping from a can of lager, staring at the same four walls seven days a week, talking to himself if anyone at all, taking what little there is to take in, but with no job, no girlfriend, no father, no mother, no brother, no sister and nowhere of meaning to call home. The routine is suffocating. Yet, for this those who came before him died. He himself lost several grandparents. How foolish they must have been. He considers ending it himself from time to time. He even holds the knife sometimes to get the feel, but something always stops him before the blade sinks too deep into his soft, white skin. His wrists still bear the scars and mark the occasions that ended in failure. Eventually, however, he opts just to change channels instead. It's a lot easier than death.

SCENE NINE

Evening slowly settles and the sun falls silently over the scenic hills and fields. The captain stands, petering on the edge of a high ledge, looking downwards. Poppies entangle themselves inconveniently round his feet. He thinks of his dead comrades and how he may have failed them as he lets himself slip and plummets towards earth.

SCENE TEN

A camera traverses along the bare walls of a room. A solitary candle glows on a low desk. It flickers for a moment and almost dies in the gentle breeze. A naked body lies huddled on the floor. Hoarse breathing fills the air. The flag is still draped over the young soldier's shoulders. He survived the war, but only just. Years later he'll still refuse to be in a room alone, and can you blame him?

THAT'S MY STORY

Well, I guess that's it. That's all I can tell you. That's my story and I'm sticking to it. There's nothing else to say. You can take it or leave it. It's all there is. There's nothing to add or take away. It's the truth and nothing more and nothing less. I needn't have worried after all. You're the ones who will be left to face the music, if you need reminding of that.

I had dinner with the chief warden, and it shows on my face. Six darling kids back at home. If they could see me now sharing roast with a prince, for that's what he is to us. It was good to eat a decent meal for once. The diner we've got in this place isn't up to much. I ate dinner at the White House once. I ran for Congress back in the old days and that dream palace we had in Pennsylvania won't gather any dust. I must get the motor changed though, and then there's the insurance. I never could get a break on that wretched business. I thought they'd give me a Governorship, but I'd settle for the money right now. It's nice to know there's still something to go back to.

I've started the redevelopment programme. It's not much, but the annual yield will be good. I'll leave my son in charge for a year or two if I can. He'll do a great job if we can keep him off the booze and women. He always had a problem with drinking. You should have seen the bottles he went through after he split with Jan. It nearly broke me that did, but it's just getting him to see it that's hard. He's a good kid though, and I know he won't let me down.

The love I found in Bess was always one of the highlights of my life. She made a good wife, bless her. If you could only have seen her in her wedding dress. She made quite a picture. And the month we spent in Paris after. A warm summer evening outside Notre-Dame, strolling the cafés and luxury shops of the Champs-Elysees, a boat trip on the River Seine, a visit to the Versailles of Louis XIV, were just some of the memories. They greeted me like a king, and I began to feel like one. I'll never forget that day or any of them.

I'd just got the new business moving and all that. It took a long time to get it off the ground, and it was worth it in the end, but nothing meant more than the kids. I could have wept when we had our first. Her dumb, smiling face reduced me to tears. I'd have given any of those warehouses for her soft kiss. They were always something to go back to after a long day at work. She was always first to greet me. She never forgot my face, even when I'd been away. *Daddy, I wanna look just like you*, she said. I could never say no to anything to that silly kid, but then I guess I never really had to.

Looking back, I remember the place more than anything. I loved all that open ground we had. The endless space stretching off into the distance, with scattered trees and wildflowers, was always a joy to me. With all that, it was easy to get lost, and they never could get me to cut the grass lawns at the back even down to the last time they tried. Sorry ma that it ended up like this. It wasn't what I intended and had in mind. I never truly did get to know you. You turned up on our launch day though. I kidded you it would cost us the election, but I knew it never would do. There's always next time I said, and the Presidency isn't so very far off. I just needed that bit of luck. But what does it matter now?

They'll be coming in an hour or two. Waiting on Death Row, what really hurts, what makes me choke is despite the conviction and what they said in court I never killed that guy. It was a miscarriage of justice of the highest degree. No one believed me, not even at the appeal. The circumstantial evidence was overwhelming after all, and they were gunning for a big name like mine. I'm finally resigned and reconciled to it, but I'll miss home and everything I've built up. I'll miss the kids, each one of them, of course. But oh dearest Bess, it's you whom I'll miss most.

FUNNY FARM

It wasn't long before the neighbours began to talk. I'd been keeping this unnatural beast in the backyard for several months, and it had become hard to hide the truth. The neighbours interest all started with just a few polite enquiries and then it quickly escalated. What was the noise? Was I keeping pets or even livestock? The questioning soon became worse and more persistent. Perhaps they'd got a glimpse of her pink porker's flesh. It had always been a nice neighbourhood, they said. There had never been any trouble before and they weren't about to let it start. They didn't want a resident who was going to rock the boat and let standards slip.

What was it that I had in the backyard anyway, that was disturbing their peace and quiet? People were aware of a sort of snorting, as they tried to relax in their gardens or enjoy a leisurely lunch. It was making them ill at ease and putting them off their food, they said. Yet they couldn't actually see what it was behind that tall fence that was making that strange noise. It was a problem they couldn't quite resolve, but the loud grunts were keeping them awake at night. They lay in bed listening and speculating. Then there was the smell. She had to be swilled out at least once each day. House prices would be affected. The local property market would inevitably slump. It was bad news all round. They hadn't slaved for thirty years just to watch the results of all their endeavours and hard work go down the toilet. Something must be done about it.

For the most part I ignored the talk. What else could I do? I was infatuated. Her front was that of a beautiful woman, her rear was that of a fully grown hog. I'd found her one day sitting in my backyard. I got back from work, and there she was. I never once questioned what had caused her anatomical abnormality or how her very existence questioned the fundamental laws of nature. I simply accepted her for what she was, and in return she accepted me. I fell in love with her blonde, straw-like hair in an instant. I marvelled at her fine figure, from her woman's head and shoulders to her nicely formed breasts, down to her pig's back and trotters. I didn't ask about her past or what brought her here. It somehow seemed unfair. I just tried to make the best of what we had. She had a strong command of English and pig language and was equally fluent in both. She told me her name was Kate. She refused to be kept inside. She said it was against her animal nature. I just sat and talked to her from the porch, where I fed her titbits and leftovers. Work started to suffer. I told her about my divorce and the kids I never saw. She was a good listener. She had a kindly, understanding face. I didn't ask her age, and she didn't ask mine.

Gradually as time went on, we grew closer, and one day I kissed her. I couldn't help myself. She responded with a passion I'd rarely known in a human being. We tried making love there and then out in the backyard, but it was difficult. She said perhaps we should wait. Reluctantly I agreed. Every night I couldn't wait to get home just to see Kate, my fabulous half woman, half beast. To all intents and purposes, it was the perfect relationship. Why did the neighbours have to stick their noses in and try to spoil our happiness? She said perhaps she should leave. I refused. I wouldn't hear of it or entertain a suggestion of such an unwelcome sort. I said nobody was going to force her out, and I certainly wasn't going to throw her into the street just because of what a few busybodies thought.

The polite neighbourly enquiries, as we passed in the road or as our eyes met as we headed for our cars on the way to work, became more direct. They were getting increasingly concerned. I said it must be rats or put the noises down to faults in the plumbing system. One man, a Mr Vincent, refused to be put off. He called by one evening and said enough was enough. I made more excuses and told him to mind his own business. In the end I was forced to slam the door in his face. Even the police were called to find out what was going on. I had to let them in. I told Kate to make herself scarce. She did what she was told, and they went away empty-handed. The local environmental health inspectors phoned. They asked when it would be convenient to inspect the premises to see if any laws were being broken. I said I was very busy but arranged a date and time. I made a mental note, however, not to be in.

Meanwhile my love for Kate was only growing. The troubles we were having only served to bring us closer together. She even started coming into the house from time to time to watch a little television or do a spot of cooking with me. I offered her my bed, but she preferred to sleep outside at night. I suggested marriage, but she said it wouldn't be right. There had never been a legal union between her species and mine. I offered to move away and take her too, but she wouldn't hear of any such thing. She said she only wished to see me happy, and she hated all the upset it was causing me. I told her not to worry. It was their problem not ours, I said. We were in love and that was all that mattered. My reassurances put her mind at rest, at least for the moment.

The friction with the neighbours was getting worse by the day, as relationships with them continued to deteriorate and was now virtually non-existent. They'd decided rational argument was pointless. They reasoned I wouldn't be persuaded by logical talk, and they were right. When I passed them now in the street, they just turned away. Yet, they couldn't hide the contempt and hatred in their eyes. It was plain to see, but I tried not to let it get to me. I refused to be blackmailed in this way by their relentless animosity. It would be all right in time, I somehow convinced myself, and more importantly tried to convince Kate, but I didn't really believe it. She put on a brave face throughout. She was my rock. She may only have been half woman, but she was more of a woman that I'd ever previously met. She kept me sane and made me whole.

The neighbours were getting crafty. They were spying on the backyard now. They were taking photographs with high resolution cameras and getting out their long lens binoculars. They were searching for traces and looking for proof that would stand up in a court of law. They had no doubts about the validity and righteousness of their efforts and arguments. They wouldn't be put off. They formed a residents' committee and met every night. They formulated plans of action. They took time off work to keep up their daily vigil. They hired a private detective to snoop about and collect further evidence. It was hard to keep them off our trail. I was forced to keep Kate inside and out of sight more often now. I didn't dare let her be seen in daylight, although she remained cheerful in the midst of our ordeal. She tried not to let it get her down.

I convinced her of my true love and enduring affection that would last forever. By now our sex life was the best I'd ever had. We'd got over our initial difficulties in that department, and I was to discover Kate had an insatiable appetite for making love. On one occasion as we reached the height of passion, I caught sight of a neighbour staring in at the window at us. He'd crawled across the garden on his hands and knees to catch a glimpse of what was going on. I tried to ignore him and hope he'd go away, but he didn't. He remained transfixed where he was like he'd seen a ghost. Eventually he'd seen enough and ran off. I've kept the curtains closed at all times since then.

Things continued to worsen, with no end in sight to the growing tension and sense of being under siege that engulfed us. I found food laced with rat poison thrown into the backyard. Luckily, Kate didn't eat it. If she had, she would surely have died. Each escape was narrower than the last. I could sense something was brewing. I found a bullet wedged in a brick at the back of the house. Someone had taken a potshot at Kate as she relaxed in the backyard. I could no longer go to work. I had to stay home to make sure she was all right. We were getting afraid. They even tried to burn her out. A primitive petrol bomb was lobbed over the garden fence, sending a weaving snake of orange flame across the backyard, as the glass bottle smashed and the fiery petroleum contents were released. Luckily, I got to her in time and dowsed the flames, but one night it happened. About twenty of them armed with shotguns and other weapons beat down the front door. They found Kate in my arms.

'You were right,' one said to another. 'It's half pig. How disgusting! And he's holding it whilst they watch television together!'

They shot her in the head where she sat by my side. Her blood and brains splattered over my face and clothes and the wall behind. It was all over in seconds. I broke down and wept, cradling Kate's lifeless body in mine. It was murder, I screamed, but was it? She was half hog and probably devoid of legal rights and representation. The laws of the land didn't apply to her kind. They said nothing and simply left without any hint of remorse or compassion for my loss.

I buried her in the backyard she'd come to regard as home. I laid a stone with an inscription in gold lettering. It read *To my dearest Kate, they may have slain you, but we'll never be apart.* Afterwards, once the dust had settled, I started going to work again. The neighbours remained silent and never mentioned the episode. It was quiet for some time, and then I started noticing little things not quite right. I heard people screaming in the middle of the night, followed by deathly silence. Lawns weren't being mowed, and gardens went untended. More than once, I was woken by cars being driven off at high speed. What were they doing? Where were they going? Milk, bread and newspapers arrived on doorsteps, but were no longer being taken in. Yet the consumption of alcohol went up. I noticed one or two of the neighbours drunk in broad daylight. I saw them slumped over the wheels of their cars or spread out flat on their backs on their patios and flowerbeds.

It didn't matter what they did, they couldn't forget what they'd seen. It haunted their waking moments and embedded itself in their daily thoughts and routines. A woman's face and chest, but the rest of her pig, was a challenge to the natural order of things. I'd known not to ask questions. They hadn't. They couldn't get to grips with what they'd witnessed or make any sense of it. They might have blasted Kate to kingdom come, but they couldn't erase her face from their minds. How could a beautiful woman be half hog? It was unnatural and obscene. Was it radiation or genetic engineering gone wrong? Was it the sorry result of some perverse act with a beast? They just didn't understand.

The first went by driving his car straight over a cliff into the great abyss. Another threw himself off a bridge. A third died with a single shot in the middle of the night. He was found with his head blown clean off and his little toe wrapped round the trigger of the rifle he must have pressed into his own mouth. Others just broke down and became pitiful, gibbering wrecks of their former selves and the people they used to be. The white vans with men in white coats arrived one after another and drove them away. By the end of the year, I was the only one left. I sold up too. New people moved in. There was something strangely familiar about them. They asked about the grave. I explained it was that of my late wife, but I preferred to leave the past behind. Out of respect, they promised to look after it for me. Only Kate stayed. They'd never get her out now. She would remain for good. The new people even erected their own memorial to her and changed the inscription on the headstone. It said simply *To a loving wife and daughter, we'll always remember.* That was enough.

A CHANGE OF ADDRESS

It was good to be back on British soil. The holiday had been fun, a welcome break for everyone, but it felt gratifying now to be going home. As they drove off the boat and hit the main road, Frank turned to his wife, Jill, and smiled. She hadn't seen him smile like that for many months. Work had been getting on top of him of late. The holiday had been a chance to relax, and they'd grabbed it with enthusiastic, eager hands, even with the kids, who were now sitting on the back seat asleep. Suzie had an innocent expression on her sleeping face. Mark had his back turned.

The family made good time, as it was evening and the roads were comparatively quiet. Soon Frank could see the lights of their hometown approaching. The two weeks had gone so quickly. It only seemed a matter of a few days since they'd been setting off, with strange, mixed feelings of relief and promise, yet some trepidation for all that. It was the first time abroad for the two kids. Now it was all over, and they were back. It had been two weeks well spent. The weather had been good, and nothing had gone wrong for a change. They'd got over the language barrier without any major misunderstanding. Now Frank could go back to work, feeling refreshed and eager to get at it. He found himself whistling a tune, as he pulled the car into the drive. He was first out. His opening of the door woke the children up.

'We're home!' Jill announced.

'Good,' a weary Suzie replied.

'Let's get in and put the tele on,' said Mark, who spent most of his waking moments sat glued in front of a television, movie or games console screen.

'It's too late to put the television on,' his mother told him. 'Let's just get our stuff in and go to bed. You can watch television in the morning.'

'There will be nothing worth watching then,' Mark complained.

'Stop moaning and do as your mother says,' Frank interrupted. 'We've had a lovely holiday, so don't do anything to spoil it now.'

'OK,' Mark reluctantly conceded, as Frank went round to the back of the car to open the boot.

'Right, if you two can help your mother get everything out, I'll go and unlock the house.'

Frank walked up to the front door. He paused for a moment to admire his paintwork, before opening it. He pushed the key into the lock and turned. The key had gone in all right, but it wouldn't release the lock and open the door. He tried to turn it again, but it was stuck fast. He took the key out and examined it. It looked all right and intact not bent. He pushed it back in and turned again, but with the same result. Frank looked perplexed. He cursed and shook his head. He couldn't have locked it from the inside, he thought. He tried once more, before giving up and deciding to go round to the back of the house. He couldn't quite believe it, as the same thing was repeated. He wondered if his keys had in some way been damaged whist they'd been away. They both went into their respective locks OK but then wouldn't turn. It didn't make any sense, at least not to him. Frank returned to the front of the house, mystified more than anything and somewhat irritated by this unexpected inconvenience.

'You won't believe it, but I can't get in,' he said to his wife.

'What do you mean, you can't get in?' Jill asked in a confused and sightly startled voice. 'You've got a key, haven't you?'

'Of course I have, but it won't open the door. Neither will the one at the back. It's really strange. The keys go in all right, but they won't turn,' he explained.

Jill looked dumbfounded.

'If this is some kind of joke, it's not funny,' she said. 'It's late and I'm not in the mood for it.'

'Jill, it's no joke. I can't get in. You try,' he suggested.

Jill recognised by the tone of Frank's voice that it was indeed no joke or prank he was playing. They were shut out of their own house.

'Mummy, I want to go to bed,' Suzie whined.

'Not now dear,' Jill said to her daughter, feeling a little concerned at the unfolding situation and their apparent and unexpected plight. 'What shall we do?' she asked, turning to her husband.

'I don't know,' he replied. 'One thing's certain, we can't stand around like this all night.'

As they stood looking up at their property, trying to assess their disappearing options, a light surprisingly went on inside. They couldn't quite believe it and what they were seeing.

'What on earth…' Frank started to say, moving swiftly forwards towards the house.

Before he knew it, he was rushing up to the door and ringing the bell furiously.

'I'm going to get to the bottom of this,' he announced.

He rang long and hard, until he could hear noises coming from inside. It sounded like people muttering and reluctantly getting out of bed. Frank continued ringing. He saw a head poke round from behind closed curtains in the bedroom, and eventually someone came to see what was going on. The front door opened a fraction, and Frank was confronted by a dimly lit face lurking behind a thick, metal chain that prevented the door from being opened further. Funny, they'd never had a chain like that on the door, Frank thought to himself.

'What's all this about? Don't you know it's past midnight?' a gruff male voice demanded to know.

Frank could vaguely make out the shape of the person talking. It was indeed another man, and he was in their home with at least one other person.

'What's all this about?' Frank repeated. 'What the hell do you think?' he asked incredulously. 'What are you doing in our house? That's what I want to know. Get out at once!'

'Your house? What do you mean, your house? Are you mad? I built this house with my own two hands,' the man insisted, slowly waking up. 'You can ask my wife if you like.'

Frank was vaguely aware someone else was hovering in the background behind the man.

'What's happening, Joe? What do they want?' she asked in a tired but vaguely alarmed voice.

'It's all right. I'll deal with this. You go back to bed. It's nothing to worry about,' said the man, turning to his wife in an effort to reassure her.

He then turned back to Frank.

'Now you lot, hop it! You've woken up my wife and I won't stand for that, so I suggest you leave before someone gets hurt,' Joe said.

Despite all his impetuousness and bravado Frank wasn't a brave man at heart, and he found himself backing off.

'You haven't heard the last of this. I'm going to the police,' he promised, whilst sounding not fully sure of himself.

'You do that, and I'll tell them about all the trouble you've been causing in what's normally a nice, quiet neighbourhood,' Joe said. 'Now sling your hook or else!'

With that he slammed the door in Frank's face. The downstairs light went out just a few seconds after, as Joe and his wife trudged wearily back to bed.

'Come on!' Frank shouted to the other shocked members of his family, as he jumped back into the car.

'Where are we going?' Jill asked, too tired to move.

'To the police station of course,' Frank replied.

'This is stupid. What's going on, Frank?' Jill wondered.

'That's what I want to find out,' Frank responded. 'Now come on kids, do as your father says.'

'Who was that strange me, daddy?' Suzie asked.

'He needs a good thumping,' Mark observed.

'It's nothing to worry about children. The police will soon sort it out,' Frank said with complete confidence, as he reversed the car out of the drive.

There was a slight screech of wheel tyre as they sped off. They got to the end of the road when the car suddenly vanished in a flash of pink and white light and was no more. All that remained was thin air and emptiness and nothing to show they'd ever existed or been there. The flash of light momentarily illuminated the darkness of Joe's bedroom, whilst his wife fell asleep beside him. He nodded knowingly to himself, and a wry smile spread across his lips, as he rolled over and went to sleep himself.

THE COLOUR THAT IS GREYNESS

It was a boring, somewhat meaningless existence being employed as a bank clerk, and living in a semi-detached, suburban house like he was. Simpson had come to terms with his position in the grand scheme of things over the years. Well, what other choice did he have? But that was as far as it went. He wasn't obliged to like it, and indeed he didn't very much. Although for the most part he pretended at least with a degree of conviction, enough to fool his wife for most of the time if not all of it. Simpson was cut out to be a bank clerk. He had to admit that, even if at times it hurt to do so. He looked the part and was of a naturally cautious, honest and reliable disposition, as was required of him in his work. Of that there was no doubt, and he acted it out quite well for as many as 51 of the 52 weeks of the year, without causing so much as a raised eyebrow.

Simpson wasn't depressed as such. In fact, he wasn't particularly dissatisfied with his lot. He'd done all right for himself. He was just tired, very tired. After twenty years of moderately happy marriage, he just felt there should be a little more to life. It wasn't that he could really complain. His wife, Margaret, was pleasant enough. He'd secured quite a respectable, well-paid and secure job in the circumstances, considering his somewhat limited abilities. Well, he'd never exactly pushed himself forward. Unlike some of his peers he hadn't been earmarked for success at an early age, and his appearance didn't especially inspire confidence. He was tall, thin and rather awkward looking, as if he wasn't in complete control of his limbs and movements. He had a slowly receding hairline and a slightly monotone voice that betrayed his innate lack of self-belief and nervousness. He had a tendency to hunch his shoulders, as if he carried the weight of the world's troubles on them. Or else he just wanted the ground to open up and swallow him, because of some perpetual, underlying embarrassment that he felt, and seemed to have afflicted him for the greater part of his adult life.

Margaret was understanding most of the time. She'd learnt not to expect too much of him. Sometimes in the past she had, but it had only ended in disappointment for both parties. It was she who kept the house going. True, Simpson provided the higher proportion of the money they jointly brought in, but Margaret did most of the daily nitty-gritty that was required to ensure their bills were paid and there was food on the table. Without her the house would probably have fallen down around their ears. She had a flare for organisation, and it was probably only down to her care and diligence that Simpson got to the bank on time every morning. She had a part-time job in an office but had reduced it to only a few hours a week now. Her real place was in the home, and that's where she stayed for the majority of the day. She didn't go out very much, except to do the shopping, or perhaps to go to the occasional coffee morning.

They had an established routine, and most weeks were more or less the same. A clock could be set by the Simpsons and what they were doing. Spontaneity, impulsiveness and imagination were distinctly lacking from their humble existence, but this week would be different, although there was nothing to indicate that to be the case when Simpson set off for work at the usual time that Monday morning. Neither was anything very different when he got home. He returned to find his evening meal being presented to him at the precise second he stepped into the dining room, as indeed it always was.

Margaret would wait to hear his key being pushed into the front door lock and turned. That would be her cue to remove his piping hot dinner from the oven, so it could be laid down before him at the exact moment he sat down at the table. To her it was a matter of pride and daily proof of her unshakeable efficiency, and woe betide any interruption that caused her not to have his food ready on time. Simpson himself was less bothered about when he ate, but he duly always emptied his plate with relish to please his wife, before helping her to wash up.

Often Margaret would already have eaten before Simpson got home, but would still join him, perhaps for a cup of tea or something, while he recounted the highlights of the day, what there were of them. It normally involved mildly rebuking the younger members of the banking team for their general tardiness, impropriety and weaknesses. Both Margaret and Simpson himself leaned towards a prudish outlook and demeanour on sexual matters, although probably neither would have cared to admit it. Simpson prided himself on not being the focus or subject of office gossip, although a small part of him yearned to be caught lying across a desk with a semi-dressed female cashier in some compromising position or other. There was little chance of it actually happening, however, and it was best to confine such dangerous thoughts to the back of his mind, or even better, if possible, forget them altogether. No good would ever come of it. Of that Simpson was sure. It was best to keep on the straight and narrow, as was his nature to do so and as he always had done in his humdrum life to date.

After they'd eaten and cleared everything away, Simpson and his wife would usually spend the rest of the evening quietly watching television. They went to bed quite early, generally after watching the news headlines at 10pm. Margaret was always keen for Simpson to get a good night's sleep, so he was fresh and ready for work in the morning. She didn't like him going out, not that he had anywhere to go, and certainly wouldn't have tolerated him going to the pub or indulging in any drinking. Simpson always felt he had to be on his best behaviour and couldn't ever really let his hair down. Tonight was no exception. 10.10pm came and Margaret reminded him it was time to go to bed. They still slept together, side by side under the same sheets. That was something, although there was little actual physical contact between them. After they'd finished their ritual fifteen minutes of reading, as they always did, they put down their books on their respective bedside tables, one at either side of the bed. Simpson reached up and turned off the light and they began to nod off. They fell soundly asleep and several hours passed.

It was a hushed, still night. The air outside was cold and there was little to break the dark, brooding silence. Then it happened, sometime after midnight it must have been, as the small hours came into their own. Simpson didn't hear it at first. Neither did his wife. They were sound asleep, wrapped up in the warmth and comfort of their dreaming, but it was unmistakeable. First a step on the patio at the back of the house, then a knock and a trip over a discarded item, followed by the dropping of something and the utterance of an exclamation. Then it was all quiet again for a moment, before the muted crack of glass. There was no crash of splinters afterwards as one would have expected. Whoever was outside evidently knew what they were about and had some previous experience in this line of *work*.

Surprisingly perhaps the Simpsons had never had any anti-burglary devices or intruder alarm systems fitted and were not in the least prepared for what was about to happen. They had always felt they had nothing of any real value worth protecting or worth taking for that matter. The house and monthly outgoings that went with it stretched them to the financial limit, and there wasn't much left after that. Of course, a prospective thief wouldn't have known that, and on this occasion didn't. He thought he was onto a good thing and a big haul of luxury loot, as he crept in through the kitchen, after breaking a small section of glass just below the door lock.

He hadn't bothered to conceal his face. Well, he wasn't planning to get caught. He was a thickset man in his mid-thirties, bordering on the plump side. He sported a crewcut and wore big, military style boots. The casual observer could easily have mistaken him for a skinhead, as he had that kind of look, which seemed to combine both aggression with the suggestion of a lack of formal education. Unlike some burglars, he wasn't after money to buy drugs. In fact, like many others, he just had a family to feed. He couldn't get a job, so he'd turned to petty crime. Mostly he lifted stereos, televisions, home entertainment systems and other electrical devices, as well as collectibles and valuables from their unsuspecting owners. He took anything he could lay his hands on really and then flogged them wherever he could at whatever price he could get for them. It wasn't the life he would have chosen, but it was one from which he could just about scrape a living and keep his family going.

Having broken in, he was rather disappointed. There was nothing much in the kitchen worth stealing. He noticed an old transistor radio, but that wouldn't fetch much. It was hardly worth the trouble of carrying. He decided to venture further into the home. He went into the lounge and shut the door behind him. He turned on a light, hoping there was no one about. This was a bit more like it. There was at least a stereo system and a television to take, although not much in the way of antiques, ornaments, silver or precious metal, or anything like that of real worth.

It was as he was adding up the estimated value of his haul in his head that he made a crucial mistake. Because of his size, he had the unfortunate tendency of being a slightly clumsy man, despite his best efforts to the contrary, but usually that only served to make him extra careful when on an important job like this one. As he ventured further into the room, his trailing arm caught a vase resting on a small table that he hadn't noticed on entry, and he knocked it off. It hit the ground with a huge crash. How could he have been so stupid? It wasn't really like him. He normally got in and out with the minimum of fuss and no issues or problems, but not this time. He'd already tripped outside, and now he'd compounded his mistake. Should he finish what he was doing, he wondered, or just get out and make good his escape?

The sound of breaking porcelain caused Simpson to leap up in bed. Even in his state of semi-wakefulness, there could be no doubt what he'd heard. Someone was in the house. There was no question about it. Simpson got up and started to pull on his dressing gown. He was determined to go downstairs to investigate, whatever the perils and personal danger to himself a potential intruder might pose. He was vaguely aware of his wife muttering *What is it?* or something of the sort. She obviously hadn't heard the loud crash that had woken him. He didn't want to worry her unduly, so he said he was just going down to get a glass of water. Simpson wasn't a brave man. Indeed, he was of a somewhat timid and nervous disposition, but this was his home, and he was prepared to defend it if he had to, even at bodily risk to himself. In his eagerness to discover just who was in his house, he bounded down the stairs and sprang into the lounge to confront the trespasser. The would-be burglar was still standing rooted to the spot by the smashed vase, pondering his next move.

'Oh shit!' he muttered.

His first thought was to get out, but Simpson was blocking the doorway. There was nothing for it. He'd have to go through Simpson. He ducked his head down like a bull and prepared to charge. Just as he started to gather momentum, he lost his footing in the jumble of broken crockery. He fell to the floor with a tremendous thump. Simpson could hardly believe what was happening or what he was seeing. He stared down at the writhing form of this bullish intruder, who was clutching at an ankle that was clearly badly twisted. The sharp edges of the smashed vase had encountered no difficulty tearing through the fabric of the denim jeans the intruder wore, inflicting several deep cuts to his shins and knees. Simpson stood where he was for a moment, as he waited to see if the man was going to get up and run at him again. It was clear he wasn't and was in no physical state to do so. He was evidently in some pain and having significant difficulty standing or even hauling himself into a sitting position. There was nothing for it, but bizarre as it was, it was apparent Simpson would have to go to his assistance. Simpson held out a hand and the man took it.

'Cheers, mate!' he said.

Simpson managed to get him resting with a degree of comfort against the side of an armchair, whilst he wondered what his best course of action was in these strange and unexpected circumstances in which he suddenly found himself.

'Do you think it's broken?' he asked.

'No, I think it's only twisted,' the man replied.

Simpson then went into the kitchen to get some water to bathe the cuts and some bandages and plasters from the bathroom to cover them. His wife called down to ask what was happening.

'Nothing, I'll be up soon,' Simpson assured her, as he returned to the lounge to begin dressing the intruder's cuts.

'What's your name?' he asked, as he got to work.

'Bob,' the man replied.

'I suppose I should ask what you were doing in my house,' Simpson said almost with an air of indifference.

'Well, I think you can guess,' Bob said. 'It's just as it seems I have to admit. I thought I might find a few things I could sell on, like electricals or a television or stereo, anything of value really. It's what I do, although

I'm not proud of it. I have a family to feed, and it's hard without a job and no mistake. I can tell you that.'

He paused for a moment.

'Are you going to call the police?' he eventually asked, with a solemn tone in his voice.

'I don't think that will be necessary if you leave quietly,' Simpson told him. 'And if you want the television, have it, it's yours!' he added. 'Take it. I don't want it. It will save me having to watch the blasted thing with my wife every evening,' Simpson said. 'Perhaps we'll be able to go to the pub for a change with that damned thing gone.'

'That's very good of you, mate,' Bob said. 'I'll come back here again if I always get this kind of reception.'

'Just knock next time,' Simpson suggested.

They carried on chatting for a while, until Bob felt he was sufficiently recovered to get to his feet.

'Would you have hurt me if you hadn't fallen over?' Simpson asked, as he showed Bob, who was carrying the television in his arms and limping, to the door.

'I've never hurt anyone in my life, and I wasn't about to start,' Bob said. 'I was just trying to get past you and out. I don't normally make such a mess of things. I'm just having a bad night I suppose. When I get it right, you'd barely notice I'd even been in your house.'

Simpson laughed.

'Is the television enough? Is there anything else you want while you're here?' Simpson enquired. 'A drink? New curtains? A nice tablecloth? Some furniture? My wife perhaps?'

The last offer wasn't entirely a serious one.

'No, I'm all right, thanks,' Bob replied, stepping back out into the chill night air. 'You've been kind enough as it is.'

Just as Simpson was waving him off, a police car with flashing lights drew up outside the house and a policeman stepped out into the road, whilst his fellow officer remained in the car.

'We heard you've had a bit of bother here,' the policeman announced. 'A neighbour reported hearing a loud crash at your place. Is everything all right?'

'Certainly, officer, there's nothing to report here. Just an old friend, Bob, popped round to collect a television we're getting rid of.'

The police officer looked Bob up and down in a suspicious fashion.

'It's a bit late to be collecting televisions, isn't it?' he commented with a frown.

'He's just finished a late shift at work, and I said he could,' Simpson explained. 'I waited up for him.'

'Why are his trousers all ripped and torn?' the police officer continued, his natural policeman's instinct telling him something wasn't right.

'Fashion, I suppose,' Simpson answered, trying to remain as calm and casual as possible.

'Isn't he bleeding?' the officer enquired further.

'Oh, it's nothing. He just tripped in the dark, but I've cleaned him up. He'll be all right,' Simpson assured the officer.

'He doesn't look like he comes from round here,' the officer continued, still less than wholly convinced of Bob's good character and honest intentions.

Simpson didn't bother to answer. He just nodded goodbye to Bob and stepped back inside the house, closing the front door behind him and eager to make his way to bed once again.

'By the way officer, which way are you going? I don't suppose you could give me a lift if we're going in the same direction,' Bob enquired hopefully.

He was in no condition to drive himself and would have to return for his transport another night.

The policeman sighed.

'I suppose so. Go on, get in. The back door is open,' he said.

His fellow officer must have wondered exactly what they were doing but chose to say nothing. Bob didn't need a second invitation and quickly jumped in. The television was an expensive and heavy one. They dropped him off at the end of his road, and still carrying the television, he limped the remaining few yards to his home. By that time Simpson was fast asleep again, the excitement of the evening already forgotten.

GRENOGYN THE GNOME

Grenogyn the gnome lived on the outskirts of town by himself. He owned a little cottage, and he was happy most of the time. He didn't need anybody else in his life. He tended his garden, and he sold beautiful flowerpots, usually to rich, middle-class housewives from the suburbs.

Grenogyn filled his pots lovingly himself with dark earth that couldn't be found anywhere else, completing his products with a glittering array of rare plants and colourful flowers. He had that special, magical touch that couldn't be taught or learned. It was enough for him to make a modest living and get by. Over the years he'd built up a hardcore of loyal customers, whose respect for him was such that even the word *genius* would occasionally fall from their enchanted lips when he presented them with his latest creation. They loved to show off his work. His pots and plants crammed every corner of the houses of this elite, little band of dedicated followers. They rested on coffee tables, televisions, dressers, sideboards and cabinets, you name it. Grenogyn's masterpieces invariably provided the finishing touch to any perfectly arranged room.

The only downside was Grenogyn didn't have the land to expand his successful operation. Word had never quite got around as much as he wanted, and the special earth that made his plants and flowers blossom like they did could only be found in this one unlikely spot. Grenogyn guessed it was something to do with the cottage and its past, but it didn't pay to ask too many questions. You don't question miracles, Grenogyn thought to himself.

One day something snapped inside Grenogyn's head. For some reason his failure to really hit the horticultural big time started to prey on his mind. Sure, he was doing all right, but he wanted more than that. He became frustrated. He started to drink heavily and smoke. After finishing a day's work, he'd settle down with a six-pack of beer and drink until he dropped. Standing at a mere three foot nothing, Grenogyn got drunk more easily than the average person. He started to put on weight and got too big for his little, green, felt suits. He started to hatch strange plans, which increasingly occupied his daily thoughts. He started to think about sex and money. In short one day Grenogyn just got greedy.

He stopped filling his pots with beautiful flowers and exotic plants. Instead, he opted to fill them with the strange, ugly cactus that occupied the far corner of his greenhouse that he understood to be peyote, but which he personally had always steered well clear of before. He'd just left the unassuming cactus to its own devices and slowly over time it had grown and multiplied. Still Grenogyn had never bothered to harvest them, until now. This time he did. Nothing much happened at first. He just noticed one or two confused and disappointed looks from some of his regulars, when he handed over his latest prize work, an ugly, sad-looking plant. But they trusted Grenogyn. After all, he knew what he was doing, didn't he? For a while sales remained steady, but then orders started to drop off and decline at an alarming rate. Business wasn't good. Every time someone came in for a special pot, all they got was this weird peyote cactus in its place. But then all of a sudden and for no apparent reason, business suddenly started to pick up again.

Grenogyn first noticed things were beginning to turn around when one of his oldest and most valued customers called by. She seemed distant and distracted. She asked about the peyote and said she needed more of the *stuff*. It was strange. Grenogyn had never heard her use an expression like that before, and she was acting differently, calling Grenogyn things like *man* rather than his name as she usually did. What would her husband think? What would he say if he heard her speak like this? Still, who was Grenogyn to ask questions or challenge the choices of his customers? What they wanted and how they spoke was their business. So Grenogyn just handed the peyote across as requested.

The elderly lady turned out to be just the first of many. They all wanted the same thing, more peyote. Business continued to improve. Grenogyn started to increase the price as demand went up. He could afford proper cigars now, and even bought himself several new, handmade suits that better fitted his portlier size. He started dating women, taking them out to expensive restaurants, lavishing luxury gifts on them and sometimes bedding the more obvious and sexually available ones. Life was good. Grenogyn had no complaints. He grew a moustache, which made him look more sophisticated, he thought. He started getting a taste for extravagance and the finer things. He bought caviar and quail eggs, and ordered elegant hampers filled with all sorts.

Meanwhile, every day the ladies continued to arrive at his cottage. Some of them had begun to lose weight, and their hair went unwashed and was lank. They no longer wore a different outfit for each visit, but they wore the same one as last time and the time before that, even though it had become tarnished with grime and dirt. They no longer seemed to care or notice. It was peculiar how they were changing before Grenogyn's very eyes, and yet their appetite for the peyote plant just seemed to grow and grow at an ever-increasing rate. Grenogyn struggled to keep pace. By now he'd turned the whole garden over to this one line of production. He wondered just what they did with it. He'd had to bring in extra staff to cope. He'd always worked by himself in the past, but it was no longer enough. Not that he was concerned or cared that much. He didn't. he was getting rich.

One day Grenogyn's curiosity got the better of him. He simply had to find out what was going on. After the visit of one regular, a Mrs Kennedy, Grenogyn decided to follow her home. She drove so fast, he had trouble just keeping up. With effort he managed to tail her to her house. She got out of her car and rushed up the garden path. Grenogyn had never seen a middle-aged woman run so fast. She seemed like a person possessed. She ran inside eagerly clutching the two peyote plants she'd just bought from him and slammed the door shut firmly behind her. Grenogyn went to the window to watch the bizarre events that unfolded. Mrs Kennedy sat down at a coffee table and feverishly unwrapped one of the pots. She started to rip away at the cactus leaves, thrusting huge chunks down her throat and swallowing them.

She didn't stop until she'd eaten the whole thing. She even began to suck away at the earth that had surrounded the soft, spineless plant, in case it held any remaining juice or nourishment. Finally finished, she sat exhausted, with smears of mud all across her face. Then she picked up the empty pot and hurled it at the floor. It smashed into a dozen broken pieces. Mrs Kennedy stood up and let out a wild shriek. It was then that Grenogyn first noticed she was beginning to look like a giant peyote cactus. Her arms had a sort of blue-green sheen to them, and little bumps and nodules were beginning to coat her face where her skin had been pale and smooth. Grenogyn turned on his heels and fled in panic.

The peyote was beginning to run out. Those drug-crazed, insane women had eaten the lot. Some had even started to inject a resin solution extracted from the plant. Grenogyn was having to ration what little was left. The price had gone up considerably as a result. Televisions, record players, home entertainment systems, washing machines, mobile phones, jewellery and other valuables accepted in part exchange crammed every room of the cottage. All kinds of vehicles, caravans and even boats sat outside. Some of the women had even resorted to selling their bodies to meet the cost. Many no longer even bothered to go home now. They just lay around dazed and vacant, growing green shells around their skins, as they waited for their next shot. It was a horrifying sight.

Grenogyn had to keep the remaining peyote plants locked away safely inside. When it came time to feed, he just opened the door a small crack and placed a plant outside. The women descended on it and ripped it apart in seconds. It was like an animal feeding frenzy. Grenogyn was beginning to get afraid. The women had lost all sense of reason, and more and more of them were beginning to camp outside his home. He watched them from the window. He saw them on all fours, scratching around in the dirt where the peyote had once grown. Some of them were screaming. Others were laughing out of their minds.

One day the inevitable happened. The last plant was devoured. There were none left. Grenogyn could feel the tension growing outside and the sense of mounting unease. He turned away in disgust, as he watched Mrs Kennedy being torn apart by the mob. They'd taken to cannibalism and eating their own. In all respects Mrs Kennedy had come to resemble a huge peyote plant. It was an easy mistake to make in their drugged state. Those fools could no longer tell the difference. Perhaps if Grenogyn could hold out long enough, they would eat themselves, every one, until there were none left, and he'd be able to walk out a free gnome. It was a long shot, but it might just work. It was his own fault. He should never have got so damn greedy. If only he could turn back the clock. He'd been happy the way he was. Now he was in a worse mess than he could ever have dreamt of.

To keep them out, Grenogyn had to bar all the doors and windows up. He was running out of food and the telephone lines had been cut. There was no escape. His days were running short. Somehow, word got out there was more peyote inside. If only he could convince them otherwise, but sadly he could not. He could no longer keep them at bay. The sheer weight of their numbers and their slow transformation into huge, powerful plants was more than the door could withstand. On the third night after the peyote had run out, they broke it down in desperation. They found Grenogyn sitting in his lounge, casually reading a book. He'd given up. He knew his fate. Mistaking his gnome's green, felt clothing for the outer bark of a plant, they ripped him apart where he sat. His little limbs flew in all directions. After stripping each branch of its soft flesh, the mob headed north in search of more food.

FOR YOUR SINS

It was a dark, rain-filled night. There wasn't so much as a chink of light to break the thick, grey cloud overhead. Jess stood outside the pub, exhausted by his tiring journey. He'd come a long way and now it was time to rest and recover his strength, before continuing again the next day. The place looked anything but salubrious, but Jess was in no position to be choosy, standing there as he did in a long, torn overcoat, marked by dirt and spilt food. His grimy trousers had a rip in the knee on one side, and his shoes were heavily scuffed and marked, testimony to the many miles he'd walked. His journey hadn't given him the opportunity to shave as he would have liked, and his face now displayed a thick, shaggy beard, and his hair cascaded down his neck at the back. It had a makeshift centre parting at the front, where he'd pushed it to either side to keep it out of his eyes. It was near black in colour and enjoyed gentle waves, which helped partially to conceal a tiny row of scars on his forehead, presumably suffered during some fight or drunken argument.

Jess stood outside for a moment longer, deciding whether to go in or not. It may not have looked very nice or welcoming, but it was worth taking a chance on he decided, to get out of the rain. It was busy inside, with grubby looking men and women laughing together at scruffy, broken tables, as they drank themselves into oblivion. The entrance of Jess was greeted with complete indifference and went barely noticed, as he made his way to the bar and put his bag down. It took him several minutes to catch the innkeeper's attention, but eventually Jess managed to do so.

'What can I get you?' he asked rather curtly, as if irritated by the unnecessary interruption.

'You can get me a beer, and I'll need a room for the night, if you've got one spare,' Jess replied.

'Well, as you can see, we're pretty busy tonight, but I can probably find you something if you don't mind sleeping on a bed of straw,' the innkeeper offered, his gruff manner starting to thaw a little as he began to warm to Jess.

He was an old man, with a balding head, whom Jess presumed to be the owner of the establishment, although he couldn't be certain of that fact. There was also a younger woman working behind the bar, whom he guessed was the old man's daughter.

'I'm so tired I'll sleep on anything,' Jess conceded. 'I've come a long way, and I can't go any further tonight. I've got to rest somewhere. I'll take whatever you've got.'

Jess had a natural way with people and was effortlessly able to charm them and put them at their ease most of the time. The innkeeper was no exception.

'I'll sort something out for you,' he promised. 'Don't you worry, mister. We'll see you all right.'

With that Jess took his drink and went to sit down at one of the few empty tables. He told the innkeeper he'd settle up when he left. After a fleeting moment of indecision and perhaps concern he might not get his money, the old man cautiously agreed, deciding Jess was one to be trusted in a world where there was generally little trust given or received. For Jess it was a relief to be able to sit back and relax, however uncomfortable the seat was. He took a long sip of his beer and let out a deep sigh. If he thought he was going to be left alone in peace and quiet, to enjoy his own thoughts and company, he wasn't. A scrawny, middle-aged man from another table approached him and asked if he had a spare cigarette.

'Hold on a minute. I'll see if I can find you one,' Jess answered.

He reached inside his coat pocket and took out a couple of sheets of dried paper, which he rolled up and passed over.

'Say, I didn't see you put any tobacco in that. Are you having me on?' the scrawny man asked suspiciously.

'Smoke it and see for yourself. You won't get a better one,' Jess assured him.

The scrawny man then struck a match and lit the end of the roll-up. He inhaled deeply and let out a cloud of smoke. His face positively beamed, and he seemed satisfied enough.

'You're right,' he agreed merrily. 'Cheers mate and thanks,' he said, turning back to his friends and leaving Jess to enjoy his pint.

His quiet contemplation was short-lived. A boisterous young woman with fiery, red hair and flashing, hazel eyes soon joined him. She had a low-cut, slightly stained dress on, which would have benefited from a wash and an iron. When she smiled, she displayed a row of rather brown and tarnished teeth that were in need of urgent dental attention.

'Hey, would you like to buy this girl a drink?' she enquired, viewing herself perhaps as more appealing than she actually was.

'I don't see why not,' Jess responded, not wishing to cause offence by declining her request.

Rather than go to the bar to get her a drink, he reached across to another table and picked up what appeared to be a jug of water and a glass and brought them across. He then proceeded to fill the glass with the clear liquid, before handing it to the young woman. She looked surprised.

'That's not a real drink,' she observed. 'It's just water, isn't it?'

'Wait a minute,' Jess replied.

He then reached into his pocket and produced a small packet of powder, which he tipped into the water. It quickly changed colour to a deep red.

'Have a taste,' he suggested, which on his instruction she did.

'It tastes like wine,' she commented with amazement.

'No, it's better than wine,' Jess told her.

'Have you got a cigarette as well?' she asked.

Not wishing to disappoint, Jess reached into his coat pocket again and pulled out a pale sheet of paper which he expertly rolled up. He then lit it and passed it across to the redhead. The young woman took a puff, and an expression of approval spread across her face. Jess hadn't been looking for company or conversation, but he was a polite person and was happy enough to talk. He'd been a long time out on the road alone. Besides, it made a welcome change to talk to someone and a young woman at that, not that he was one to look for casual encounters with the opposite sex.

'I'd better show you to your room,' she said at last, after they'd been drinking and chatting together some time.

'Whatever you say,' Jess consented, getting up from his seat.

He finished his drink and followed the young, red-haired woman, who was evidently employed there in some kind of hospitality capacity, as she walked across the bar floor and out through a side door. She guided him to what appeared to be a shed behind and separated from the main building. She stood at the entrance as he went in. Jess assumed she was going to retire, having shown him to his quarters, but instead she continued in after him. It was a sparse room. There was no bed or furniture. There was just a huge pile of straw and nothing much more. Jess tried to make himself as comfortable as possible in the circumstances. The young woman stood looking at him, still not departing.

'I can spend the night with you if you want me to,' she announced, without the slightest hint of embarrassment or awkwardness. 'But the old man will insist you pay me,' she added.

She then paused for a few moments before continuing.

'Have you got any money?' she asked.

'Enough for my needs,' Jess replied.

He produced a small pouch from his coat and threw it across to the young woman. She loosened the thin string that kept it closed and peered inside.

'They're just stones,' she said aghast.

'Tip them out and look again,' Jess suggested.

He seemed to hold some strange power over her. She did as he said and tipped the contents of the pouch onto the floor. Her sight must have been deceived by the dim light, as lying before her now weren't stones but a small pile of glittering, gold coins.

'How did you do that? I could have sworn they were just stones,' she said, evidently perplexed and unsure if she'd made a mistake or if some clever trick had been played on her.

'It's easy,' Jess answered. 'You see what you want to see, and things are what you want them to be.'

'Does that mean you want me?' the young woman wondered.

'Maybe,' Jess replied, without committing himself either way.

He watched in silence as she stood in the corner of the room and loosened her dress, until it fell down to reveal her breasts. She shook out her red hair and started to walk over to him. Jess understood what to expect next.

'Can't we just talk for a moment?' he said.

'If you like,' she agreed. 'What do you want to talk about?' she asked, pulling her dress back up.

'Your teeth, are you happy with how they look?' Jess enquired.

'You noticed their colour,' she said, looking downcast and downwards at her feet to hide her self-consciousness. 'No, I don't like them, but what can I do about it? Do they spoil my face?' she asked.

Jess didn't answer.

'Come here,' he said simply instead.

She did as she was told and sat down beside him.

'Open your mouth,' he demanded.

She did and he touched her stained, brown teeth with his finger.

'Now they are white,' he told her.

'Don't be silly. You're just teasing me,' the young woman protested.

'If you believe it, then they are white and perfect,' Jess insisted.

'I need to see for myself. Have you got a mirror?' she asked.

'You don't need a mirror. Just trust in me,' Jess said. 'And how about your hair and your figure? How do you feel about them?'

'They're OK. They could be worse, but they could also be better,' she admitted. 'I don't really like my red hair if I'm honest. I've always wanted to be blonde.'

'If that's what you want, so be it,' Jess said, running his fingers through her bright, red hair.

Instantly it responded to his touch and changed colour.

'Now you are blonde,' he told her.

'But how can I believe you?' she objected. 'I can't see. I think you're just making fun of me,'

'Am I?' Jess asked. 'You got what you wanted. Isn't that enough? Do I really have to explain myself? Just accept what is in fact is.'

With that Jess kissed the young woman lightly on her cheek and they fell back into an embrace. He realised they hadn't even exchanged names yet, but somehow it seemed unimportant. He was happy enough to accept her company. His plans, however, didn't extend to taking intimate advantage of her.

'If you can do all this for me, why do you carry those scars on your head?' she asked. 'Get rid of them and you'd be a handsome man.'

'That isn't for me to do,' Jess replied. 'Only you can do that for me.'

'What do you mean? I can do nothing. I have no special powers,' she told him.

'Oh yes you do, but only you can find them,' Jess declared. 'I can't do it for you, and it wouldn't be my place to do so.'

With that Jess kissed her again and they fell back into each other's arms until morning. The next day Jess decided to set off early. He still had a long way to go before his journey was complete and he could rest in peace, knowing his work was done. The powerful sun shone in through the cracks in the shed's scant walls, as he started to collect his things. It must have finally stopped raining, he realised. That at least was something. He shook bits of loose straw out of his hair and nudged the young woman next to him to wake. She let out a sleepy murmur and slowly opened her eyes. She seemed surprised to see Jess fully dressed and apparently ready to leave.

Her hair was still an alluring ash blonde, which somehow seemed to capture the sun's golden rays and reflect them back. In the early morning light, she looked truly beautiful, Jess had to admit, as he admired his own handiwork. And it was no cheap trick, or the result of some fake dye that had been applied. It was a miracle indeed. Her hair truly was blonde. Jess watched as she put on her dress. She then followed him out of the shed and back into the bar. The old man, who Jess had taken to be the innkeeper, was already up with his daughter and clearing away the scattered remnants of the previous night's drinking and general revelries, in preparation for opening again. A pungent smell of spilt beer still filled the air.

'Mary, what have you done to your hair?' the old man asked, looking quite puzzled.

'Do you like it?' she replied, pointedly failing to give him a proper answer or explanation for her sudden transformation.

'And your teeth...' he started to say.

'Yes?' she interrupted, cutting his sentence short and almost daring him to remind her that only a day earlier they'd been heavily tarnished.

'Our guest is leaving and wants to pay his bill,' Mary explained.

With that Jess reached into his pocket and threw a pouch of coins over. The old man gleefully snatched them off the floor, but already the attention of Jess had turned elsewhere.

'Why does that boy stand as he does?' he asked, gesturing to a figure in the corner with his back turned and a bucket and mop in his hand.

'He's no boy, sir. He's a midget, hunchbacked from birth. He doesn't like to show his face,' Mary explained.

'Is that right?' Jess said. 'You in the corner, don't be afraid. Stand up straight! You don't have the weight of the world on your shoulders. That burden is for me to bear alone.'

With that the midget stood up straight, gaining at least two and a half feet in height. After what had already taken place, Mary ceased to be amazed and took the further demonstration of the incredible powers Jess possessed in her stride and almost as if they were in some way to be expected. They weren't of course. They were anything but normal. They were remarkable in every way imaginable. Meanwhile the innkeeper had gone out into the street to take some rubbish out. He returned with the news that a drunk had apparently passed out on the step and banged his head.

'He's lying in a pool of his own blood. It looks like he's been there all night. I'm not sure if he's dead or alive,' the innkeeper said to anyone who cared to listen.

'I'll have a look at him,' Jess offered, as he prepared to leave.

They all went outside to examine the gruesome sight of a vagrant lying in a puddle of his own blood and vomit. A white stick lay by his side. Presumably he was blind or of limited sight, which probably

94

explained why he'd come to trip and fall in an intoxicated state. The only other explanation was that he'd been mugged, but he hardly looked like he had anything worth taking. He was certainly in a bad state and his clothes were soaking wet from the rain of the previous night. Jess bend down and touched the vagrant lightly on the head. He wiped away the blood and with it apparently the cut that had caused the bleeding in the first place, as no wound or mark was still visible on the blind man's flesh. Jess helped him to his feet, at which point the vagrant seemed to return to full awareness and open his eyes.

'Are you all right?' his rescuer enquired.

'Yes, I think so, thank you,' he answered. 'Do I know you?' he then asked after a momentary pause.

He seemed to stare into Jess's eyes almost as if he could see, when surely he could not.

'Yes, I think you do,' Jess confirmed.

'You have deep blue eyes, thick, black hair and a long beard. You travel from place to place, helping people as you go. Yes, I remember now. I never forget a face,' the vagrant said.

'But you can't see,' Mary protested.

'I can now,' the vagrant replied, leaving his stick and wandering off into the distance. 'He has saved me many times before this.'

CLOSE CALL

Mitchell was absurdly jealous. Here he was stuck at home with his wife Brenda, old before her time, whilst his neighbour, Steve Weller, went out to enjoy himself every night. It just wasn't fair. He wanted to get out and have a bit of fun himself before it was too late, but Brenda wouldn't even entertain the 100 or so yard stroll to the nearest pub at least to round off each monotonous evening with a drink. So mostly Mitchell stayed in to do the washing-up, put another shelf up or do some other mundane household chore Brenda had found him. Life in the bedroom too wasn't what it might have been. Sex to Brenda was something other people did, and certainly not her. Mitchell remained uncertain of the reasons behind her loss of interest. Perhaps she no longer found him attractive. Perhaps she'd just lost what little sex drive she'd once had. Whatever it was, they didn't talk about it, or anything else for that matter. There was no point. It would only end up in another argument, and he seldom emerged the winner.

Mitchell was jealous because his neighbour seemed to have everything he didn't. Steve Weller was in his early forties, a financial whizz and troubleshooter, with nice clothes, a fancy car and always an attractive woman at his side. It made Mitchell sick. He watched the women come and go from the house with envy. They were always younger than Weller, with slim figures, long, slender legs and flowing hair. Sometimes Mitchell would even sit by his bedroom window, with the curtains left slightly open, so he could see Weller's *Porsche* pull up and his latest bombshell get out. Mitchell would watch as they'd laugh their way up the garden path and go inside. Sometimes the lady would be tipsy and nearly falling out of her elegant dress, as Weller opened his front door and it was shut behind.

Later, after a few more glasses of wine, the lights would go out, and Mitchell would be left to imagine the soaring heights of passion taking place that were so absent from his own life. Sometimes Brenda would catch him as he was staring out of the window and ask what he was doing. *Nothing, darling*, he'd quickly reply, turning away, and she seemed to believe him. She remained remarkably unaware of the goings-on opposite, but then she was remarkably unaware of most things, or pretended to be, Mitchell reflected with a degree of sadness.

It was a dull, humdrum existence most of the time. It had been like it for years but had got worse since their only daughter had left for college. Mitchell continued to work in the same office, but when he came home at night, it seemed there was something missing. His daughter's absence seemed to highlight and epitomise how far apart he and Brenda had grown. They'd once been close of course, in the early days of marriage, but somehow the romance and excitement they'd once shared had fallen out of their lives. It wasn't as if they felt any hostility towards each other. They just felt nothing. They even found it hard to keep up a proper conversation. They did very little together, apart from sit at home in near silence. Brenda mainly occupied herself with the housework or sat in front of the television. Mitchell buried himself in work or a newspaper. It wasn't as if Brenda was an unattractive woman. She just chose to make little of herself, which made her seem plainer than she really was. She'd lost interest in appearance. She just couldn't be bothered any longer. She had no one to impress as far as she was concerned. Perhaps the problem was that Mitchell couldn't help but compare her with the glamorous women who visited opposite.

Weller had it all worked out. He hadn't got married for a start, and he had no children or responsibilities that Mitchell knew about. He was smart, suave and sophisticated. He ate out most of the time in expensive restaurants. He could afford to. He went to rugby and football matches whenever he wanted. Mitchell couldn't do that. He had the lawn to mow or the car to wash. Weller paid a cleaner to do his cleaning, and a gardener to tend his garden. He wore tailor-made suits and drank exotic cocktails. He'd even had his own bar installed and found time for a spot of squash or golf of course.

Occasionally he'd invite Mitchell and his wife round for drinks with some of Weller's posh work colleagues. Mitchell felt loathed to go, as it only accentuated the gulf between them and the failings of his own drab life and existence. Brenda would normally persuade him they ought to do the decent and polite thing and go along, much to Mitchell's reluctance. She didn't seem to care about all the trappings of Weller's wealth and the visible evidence of how much he was earning and how badly it reflected on their own frugal spending regime. They simply didn't have the money to throw around. They'd stretched themselves to the limit just to buy the house, and they had the added expense of a daughter at college. Mitchell wanted at least something to show for all the years he'd spent in the same suffocating office. Of course, buying the house had meant they'd had to make do with the same ageing, battered hatchback they'd had for a dozen years at least. It stood rusting in the drive, as a pertinent symbol of Mitchell's own stagnation and impotence. There was no *Porsche* for him.

It couldn't go on. He was firmly decided on that, but he wasn't quite sure what he was going to do about it. *Is anything wrong?* his wife had enquired rather dully and without any real conviction in her voice as he went to work one morning. Yes, there was, but he couldn't tell her about it. For him it had been a particularly sour night. Mitchell had seen the girl of his dreams, someone he'd admired from afar, turn up at Weller's house to be used like all the rest. The girl, who combined long legs and pouting lips with blonde hair and a short skirt, was someone Mitchell had bumped into on occasion through his own work. He'd never had the courage to talk to her of course, even though he'd very much wanted to. He'd tried to conjure up some excuse to strike up a conversation, but at the crucial moment had found himself unable to go through with

97

it. Now she was just another string on Weller's bow, or notch on his bedpost. It was the final straw for Mitchell and the final insult he was willing to endure.

On his way home from work that night, he stopped at a shop to pick up a bottle of scotch and some cigarettes. It was a very impulsive and uncharacteristic act for someone's of Mitchell's somewhat timid and conventional disposition, but he was determined to be impetuous for once. He was intent on taking control of his life and grabbing it by the scruff of the neck. He knew Brenda wouldn't let him smoke in the house even when they were young, so he'd light up just to spite her. It would provoke an argument of course. Then in the heat of it and with a note of triumph, he'd inform her he was leaving her and moving out and would be going to live on his own in a flat by himself. He foolishly imagined that once he'd made this daring move and broke the shackles of marriage, he'd be free to live like Weller did. He'd be able to go to the pub and eat out, to play golf and attend football matches. Best of all he'd be free to invite sexy women back. In short, he'd be able to do whatever he wanted.

His plan got off to the start he hoped and seemed to be working. Brenda couldn't believe it at first, as she peered through the clouds of cigarette smoke. Mitchell thought he detected a tear in her eye. There were none in his. This was exactly what he'd wanted. He was desperate to create a reaction and be noticed for a change and not merely invisible to everyone around him. He'd show that Steve Weller and the rest there was life in the old dog yet. Anything Weller could do, he could match, Mitchell decided with relish. It would be a form of rebirth. This was to be his great chance in life. He had to seize it.

Mitchell packed just one small suitcase. That was all he needed. Everything else could remain behind. It was all too closely associated in his mind with what was now his former self. He wanted a complete break from that sorry existence and to begin afresh. Brenda didn't get up as he made his way to the door. Once closed there was no going back, but he didn't stop or falter in his steps. He was determined to go through with it. He hadn't come this far to have doubts or second thoughts. Brenda said nothing. She just watched with a slight shaking of the head and in a state of mild disbelief and also some regret, as she witnessed her husband of more than twenty years pick up his things and leave.

Mitchell stepped outside with a renewed sense of freedom but was surprised by what he encountered. It wasn't at all what he expected. There was evidently some kind of commotion going on opposite. Mitchell stood there with his suitcase in his hand, glued to the spot and watching unfolding events with amazement in his eyes. Weller, in just a pair of soiled boxer shorts, was being carried out of his house on a stretcher. Despite a quantity of blood, Mitchell could make out the shape of a knife protruding from the top of Weller's thigh. Only the handle was visible. The blade was presumably embedded deep in Weller's flesh. The blonde Mitchell was besotted with, apparently in a state of shock and only half dressed, with just a blanket wrapped round her, was being comforted by a police officer. Another woman, a brunette in a smart, business suit, was being escorted into the back of a police car. Weller looked up and noticed Mitchell standing opposite. He motioned to the ambulanceman to stop for a moment as he beckoned Mitchell over. Mitchell bent down to hear what Weller had to say to him.

'I've had a spot of bother,' he said, with a ridiculous sense of understatement. 'I just could never understand women. That's my problem,' he continued. 'Mitchell, you're a lucky man,' he whispered. 'What I wouldn't give to have your settled marriage. To be faithful to one woman is all I ever wanted, but alas I can't be. It's not in my nature. This is just who I am.'

He paused for a moment to catch his breath and try to block out the pain.

'I think she was aiming for my penis. Perhaps it would have been better if she'd got it. It would save me having to go through all this again when I get out of hospital,' he said with a tone laced with sad irony.

With that Weller was lifted into the ambulance. Mitchell nodded quietly to himself and wandered back towards his house. He wondered whether Brenda would have kept something for him to eat. He decided they'd go out for a drink that night, wherever Brenda wanted. It had been a close call. Now it was time to celebrate.

A STING IN THE TAIL

It was a hot, sticky, summer afternoon. George Robinson would have preferred to have been sitting in the garden, lapping up some glorious sunshine, but there was something he was keen to watch on the television. It was a film he'd never seen but had always wanted to. Robinson opened a window to keep the air circulating and then sat down. He'd made himself coffee and to go with it he lit a huge cigar he'd been saving especially to enjoy that afternoon. He took a long, satisfying puff on it, before exhaling a great cloud of smoke that gradually filtered up towards the ceiling.

Robinson tried to relax, but it was just so hot. He felt little beads of sweat forming on the back of his neck. They were making his shirt wet. Why did it have to be quite so stifling on this of all days? he thought to himself. He'd been so looking forward to the chance of sitting inside and doing nothing except engrossing himself in a film. His wife had gone out, so couldn't bother him. It was just this dreadful, suffocating heat that was getting him down. He tried to block it out of his head. Perhaps he should have put on his shorts, and not the thick, flannel trousers he was wearing. He took a sip of his coffee. At least that was now only lukewarm. He tried not to move about too much in his seat. At last, the film's opening titles started to roll. He tried to concentrate his attention on that and not the torrid heat.

Robinson was a somewhat nondescript individual in his early fifties. Mostly he went about his business in an anonymous fashion, and it suited him to be that way. He was the kind of man who largely went unnoticed, unless there was some reason to speak and engage him in conversation. Robinson was of average height, but undeniably slightly overweight. A rather unsightly lump of flesh hung over his belt that however hard he tried to hide, by holding his breath and sucking his stomach in, refused to be concealed. He was fighting a losing battle in every sense, against the growing bulge of his waistline and his advancing age.

His light brown hair was also thinning visibly on top, which he disliked. He tried to comb those remaining hairs that steadfastly refused to leave his scalp, like seaweed desperately clinging to rocks, in such a fashion as to appear that he had more hair than he had. Needless to say, it didn't really work. His expert manipulation of the comb had little more effect than his feeble attempts to hold his stomach in. But what did it really matter? he asked himself. It wasn't as if he was a young man, so why did he vainly try to hold onto the few remaining crumbs of youth he kidded himself he still had left? It was pointless. They weren't enough to make anything of substance with.

Besides, he hadn't taken a day off to pick fault with his appearance, he remembered. He'd taken a day off to relax, to forget the pressures of work and to enjoy himself. It wasn't much to ask, to be able to sit down and watch a film in comfort and silence once in a while, and to have nothing hanging over him that had to be done. It was a luxury that only occasionally came along, so he needed to make the most of it. There was no point using it as an excuse to remind himself that he wasn't Robert Redford or Clint Eastwood in their 1960s and 1970s heyday. He knew that already, but there was no reason he couldn't enjoy them and their like on the television when their classic movies came on.

This time Robinson sat back determined not to allow his mind to wander onto other things. He was going to concentrate on the film and that alone. Nothing else would enter his mind or distract him from his viewing. He liked Steve McQueen, and this was one of his lesser-known works that he'd never seen, *Junior Bonner*. Robinson tried to imagine himself as the hero of the rodeo, however unlikely it might have been. Only by closing his eyes could he do so. Any sight of his own too ample figure would shatter the illusion that he was in any way equipped to take a bull by the horns and go six rounds with it. Still, it was a good film, he had to admit.

It was just this damned heat that was irritating him. Why did it have to be so hot? It hadn't been earlier in the week. Indeed, it had been cloudy and quite cool, with a stiff, northerly breeze for early summer. The weather had now taken a decided turn, most would have said for the better. Perhaps if he'd been planning to go to the beach, that might have been the case, but it was less than ideal for a quiet afternoon inside, watching a film on the television, that as a fan and a bit of a movie buff he'd always wanted to see, but had never got round to doing so until now, Robinson reflected with a strong sense of irony. He'd have been better off outside, trying to get a suntan. The gods were evidently against him and trying to ruin his best-laid plans for his day off.

Half an hour had now passed since the film had started. Robinson had finished his coffee and had replaced it with a cold drink he'd taken from the fridge and was sipping it slowly. He was trying not to fidget unnecessarily, but it was difficult. He could feel his trousers sticking to the backs of his legs. The sweat was continuing to drip from his forehead. He was trying to concentrate his full attention on the film but gradually became aware of a noise over the dialogue and soundtrack. It was a kind of buzzing, like the flapping of the wings of a large insect.

He looked around the lounge, at the curtains and the ceiling, but he couldn't see anything. Still the buzzing went on. Perhaps something had flown in through the open window. That was the obvious explanation, but then where was it? He could still hear it buzzing away, even louder now, but the source of the irritating sound remained a mystery. He wondered for a moment if it was in fact coming from the television. Perhaps it was an electrical fault in the set or a bad connection somewhere. Then he saw it.

It was the largest bee he'd ever seen. It was a good two and half inches long, and almost as wide. It floated nonchalantly around the room without an apparent care in the world, before landing on a book. It appeared to be watching him. It was almost as if it was goading him into making some kind of move. Robinson stared in disbelief for a moment. He just couldn't get over its extraordinary size. Being a somewhat cautious man, he wondered if a bee like that might be dangerous. Perhaps it was in fact a hornet, but it didn't look like one. Perhaps it was the queen, looking for a place to start a new colony. That was a plausible explanation. He'd read they could get very large. He certainly didn't want to provoke it, but it seemed to be challenging him into some form of action. He sensed it was almost demanding confrontation, as if the room wasn't big enough for the both of them.

It was the way it was boldly just sitting there that got to Robinson, but perhaps he was wrong. Perhaps it wasn't actually watching him. Perhaps it was watching the film instead. Perhaps like him it was a Steve McQueen fan. It was hard to tell what it was actually doing or thinking, probably nothing. Robinson was ceasing to find the bee a source of fear and more a plain irritant. It remained near enough to make its presence felt but was too far away to swat in one movement. Robinson tried to block it out of his mind and focus on the film. He reasoned that if he ignored it and left it alone, it might just return from wherever it had come. He had observed that whilst he was staring at it, the buzzing and peculiar flapping of wings had stopped. Robinson turned back to Steve McQueen. Within seconds the buzzing had started again. He cast his eyes around to see where it was coming from. He couldn't see the bee at first, but then he saw it. It was getting more daring. It was as if it was trying to get his attention. It had landed on a table situated between the bookcase and television, halving the distance between himself and it in one movement.

Robinson leapt out of his seat. He took a step forward to examine this monstrous thing that had dared to interrupt his enjoyment of the film. The bee appeared to be watching him also, and with a mild sense of amusement, as if to the bee it was all just a game. Perhaps it was, but it wasn't to Robinson. He didn't find anything about the absurd situation in which he found himself one little bit funny. He was feeling ever hotter and sweatier, and his temper was noticeably fraying. There was only one thing for it. He would have to eradicate the source of his annoyance. It was the only way he'd get any peace and quiet.

Robinson looked around on the floor for something with which to kill his malicious tormentor and picked up a discarded newspaper. He rolled it tightly in his greasy palm, before gradually and quietly inching towards the bee. Once within range, he took a swipe, swinging the paper through the air and bringing it crashing down on the table. He looked down to examine the dead or dying body of his quarry, but it had vanished. It had gone. There was nothing there. It simply wasn't possible, Robinson thought. He felt certain he'd scored a direct hit. He wondered if the bee had rolled off the table in its dying agony, or if its crushed remains had stuck to the newsprint. Robinson scrutinised the floor, but it wasn't there. Neither was it on the newspaper. He stood back with a puzzled expression creeping over his face.

Just when he thought he must have killed the bee, even if he couldn't locate its broken body, it shot almost vertically out from behind the sofa and made a triumphant circle through the air. It flew so closely to Robinson's head that he could even feel its wings touch the remaining wisps of his thinning hair. That was it. That was too much to bear. It had the audacity to mock him in his efforts to silence it for good. It would pay for its nerve, Robinson was decided.

The bee landed on a wall at the far end of the room. In a growing state of anger, Robinson made a wild lunge at it. At the very last moment, just as the newspaper thudded down on its intended victim, the bee moved. It was as if it was just toying with him and continuing to play some maddening game of cat and mouse. Surely it could have moved sooner if it had wanted to. Surely it had seen the paper come crashing down. Robinson tried again. It was just the same, and the next time, and the one after that, as the bee's deceptive movements drew pretty and intricate patterns on the wall.

Robinson could feel his face turning red with rage and sweat pouring down both sides and dripping onto his shirt. His pulse was elevated, and he was breathing heavily. He wasn't as fit as he'd once been, and it was showing. He could feel himself tiring already in this battle of wills. He wanted to collapse in a heap on the chair, but he couldn't, not whilst the bee was still there to torment him. It continued to study him, not even bothering to move unless he took a futile lunge or swipe through the air. There was only one answer. Robinson would have to try a new approach and think outside the box to eradicate the problem.

Robinson went into the kitchen. There was one thing there he could be sure would attract the bee's attention. He opened a cupboard and picked out a jar of strawberry jam. He then went back into the lounge. He unloosened the lid and placed it on the coffee table, with a generous dollop of the sticky substance on top. The bee didn't respond or do anything at first. It just sat and watched with indifference. Robinson remained poised with newspaper in hand, waiting for its first movement. Surely it would go for the jam, he thought, and dutifully enough, eventually it did. The bee floated gracefully down onto the jam jar lid and started feeding. So big was the bee that it covered the entire lid surface. Robinson couldn't believe it. The sheer size of the bee this close was incredible. It was monstrous. It was a freak of nature. Robinson imagined a whole swarm of them and the mayhem they could cause. Still, this wasn't the time or place to get emotional about the insect's obviously impressive proportions and physique. It was time to kill it.

Robinson lifted the newspaper high above his head and brought it crashing down. Again, he moved the paper away to survey his kill, but just as before, the bee was gone. But this time unlike the last, he could be sure he'd hit it. He could see the evidence for himself. An ugly trail of blood smeared the length of the table. Robinson looked on the floor to see if the body had fallen there, but it hadn't. For several minutes he continued his search. He wanted to find the bee to show to his wife, to prove its size and that he hadn't made the whole thing up. But however hard he tried, he could find no sign of the struggle that had taken place, except for the smear of bee blood and several marks on the wall. Eventually, he gave up looking. There was nothing else for it. After searching the floor on his hands and knees once more, he decided that was enough. He wouldn't waste further time and energy on the matter. However odd it seemed, the bee's body had disappeared. He could now relax and watch the end of the film in peace. It was the very least he deserved.

Robinson sat down and tried to get comfortable again. He still felt a little hot and bothered, so he reached down to take a sip of his drink, to help him cool down. He lifted the glass of refreshing, chilled liquid to his lips. What he didn't notice swimming in the bottom of the glass was the dying body of the bee. Robinson drained the glass, swallowing it down, juice, bee and all. He realised all too late there was something furry stuck in his mouth. The force with which he'd struck the bee must have carried it across the table and several feet further into his glass. Now he'd swallowed it.

He struggled to his feet and tried to spit it out, but it was too late. The sting got him in the back of the throat. He felt it like a giant needle prick. It stopped him in his tracks, as he realised the dreadful truth. Still he tried to get the bee out of his mouth, but the sting had already begun to do its damage. Its poison was starting to go round his blood system and Robinson felt like he was choking. His face began to change colour, first to an ugly purple, then blue. He had his hands around his own neck now, in a desperate attempt to aid his breathing and ease his suffocating, but it was no good. Suddenly he stopped struggling and fell back. As he hit the sofa with a tremendous crash, he was already dead.

INTERSTELLAR EXPRESS

One day a gringlegrunt walked into a bar, strolled casually up to the bartender and ordered a scotch and soda. He leaned back and let the warm, golden, malt nectar slide down his throat. He let out a sigh of pleasure and lit a cigarette. He told the bartender to pour him another and to get one himself whilst he was at it. It had been a good day. The grunt's stocks were up about fifty points. He could afford to relax. He could afford to live a little. No more jerking around, trying to make ends meet. No more scratching together a living. This was the big one. He was on a roll. The only way for him was up. A smile flickered on the gringlegrunt's lips. He knew the worst of his troubles were behind him. He knew he'd made enough today to keep him going and living comfortably for at least six months. The pressure was off. He could let the good times begin.

The gringlegrunt surveyed the bar. He noticed the resident hooker sitting on a stool in the far corner. He invited her over and asked her what she was drinking. She said she'd have a beer. He decided to join her. The bartender lined up two long, cool lagers for the odd pair. The gringlegrunt took a deep gulp of his. The soft, white, fluffy head of the liquid coated the fur around his mouth. He wiped it off with a satisfying sweep of his paw and offered the hooker a cigarette from a packet in front of him. She took one automatically without hesitation. She knew the routine all too well. The gringlegrunt guessed she was the wrong side of forty and carrying a few extra pounds she didn't need. He wasn't too concerned. She wasn't unattractive in her way, and he didn't care too much about the fine detail. He just wanted a bit of fun and to be entertained for the evening or perhaps the moment.

'Say, where are you from, mister?' she asked at last. 'I've not seen you round here before.'

'From out of town, baby. I'm just passing through,' the gringlegrunt replied, doing his best Clint Eastwood impersonation and imagining himself to be acting out a scene from a classic western.

He actually lived in a pleasant suburban home in a secluded avenue just a short drive away, but it sounded more exciting and romantic the way he said it. He hoped to impress her with tales of his thrilling, nomadic life in the fast lane.

'I'm just putting the final touches to an important business deal and making sure it all comes off with no hiccups or hitches,' he explained.

'That sounds impressive, man. What's the deal then?' the hooker enquired.

'I can't say too much, but we're talking megabucks here,' the gringlegrunt boasted.

If only his wife could hear him now. He'd be eating nothing but hay and leaves all week. He'd be put on a crash diet. She'd cut out all the cucumber, tomatoes and radishes, which were his favourites.

'Say why don't you and me go out back where it's a bit more comfortable and where we can get to know each other a bit better,' the hooker suggested. 'You're gonna find out I'm one mean mama in the bedroom.'

'Sure, lay one on me sister,' the gringlegrunt said confidently, but he was still putting on an act and playing some kind of part.

It wasn't really him talking. He'd never been like this before. He was beginning to feel hot under his fur, and his paws were twitching with both excitement and a degree of trepidation. The sweat on his down-coated palms made it hard for him to hold his glass. It was beginning to slip from his grasp. He wasn't sure what he was saying or doing. It was as if he was in some kind of trance, but he just couldn't help himself.

He and the hooker got up together and made their way out back. It was just a small room with a couch and a few chairs spread around. The hooker flopped onto the couch, which he presumed doubled as a bed or at least seat of passion and crossed her legs in a seductive fashion. She leaned back and took another cigarette from the packet in the gringlegrunt's outstretched paw. He lit it for her. He then slid one out for himself and pressed it between his oversized lips. He held it there by crunching his four large, rodent teeth together.

'Say, why are you all covered in fur then, man?' the hooker wondered.

'It's atomic mutation,' the gringlegrunt answered.

He didn't want to be too specific. He just thought of himself as regular, normal guy. He definitely didn't want any special treatment or sympathy.

'Do you want me to take off my clothes?' the hooker asked. 'I'd love to press my naked body against your soft, brown fur.'

'I'm not sure, baby,' the gringlegrunt replied.

He was beginning to have doubts and second thoughts.

'I've got a wife and kids to think about. They wouldn't like it very much if they knew I was here,' he explained.

'Forget about them,' the hooker said in her most alluring and tempting voice. 'I've never had sex with whatever you are. It would be a new experience. I'd like us to do it.'

'I'm sorry, but I can't,' the gringlegrunt apologised, starting to get up.

Perhaps he wasn't such a big shot after all. He'd let making a few bucks go to his head. In truth he didn't even find the woman that attractive. He longed to get back in his cage, to feel the gentle scratch of hay against his nose and to press his paws through the steel bars. He longed for his wife's touch along his furry back. He loved the way she fed him carrots and the way she made him get up on his hind legs and beg. He loved to give his children rides. He liked it when he was allowed to graze in the long grass, but only in the back garden of course. They didn't want the neighbours thinking there was anything odd about the way they lived. They even invited them round for drinks and snacks from time to time, although he'd noticed the strange way they looked at him when he sucked the heart out of a lettuce. Didn't they do that too? Perhaps not.

'Look, I've gotta go,' the gringlegrunt said at last. 'I'm sorry it didn't work out. Maybe another time, baby. I'm just not very good at this. I'm a novice really.'

'You don't have to go,' the hooker told him. 'You know I'm very good at what I do. I get compliments all the time.'

'I'm sure you do, but I've gotta be on the next interstellar express out of here,' the gringlegrunt said.

With that, he got up and left and didn't look back. It had been a narrow escape and one he wouldn't forget in a hurry.

ALL IN A DAY'S WORK

Why had she let it come to this, Sally thought, as she struggled back from the shops. Why had she given up her job to stay at home and look after the kids for a start? Why had she let him talk her out of going back to work, when it was the thing in her life she most wanted? Why had she given in so easily? Why did she always let him have his own way in everything? He spent half the day on the golf course but still managed to call it work. What kind of work was that? Of course, he always had the car, whilst she was forced to take the bus. He still managed to convince her it was all for the best. After all, it was the money he brought in that paid the bills and put the food on the table and the clothes on their backs, he frequently reminded her. It wasn't as easy as she seemed to think it was. At least that was what he insisted.

Sometimes he was forced to work late. These were the sacrifices he had to make. He was even forced to keep his pretty secretary, Angie, on after hours just to clear the backlog of work. Sometimes Sally had wondered if there was something going on there, but surely not. She dismissed the idea as unthinkable. He wouldn't do that, not with her. He wouldn't sink to such depths. She was so common and transparent, her appeal too glaringly obvious for a man of taste. Sally convinced herself that he couldn't possibly find that woman attractive.

With the late hours, the golf, the business lunches and evening dinners to secure deals, her husband had more or less missed the kids growing up. Sometimes Sally wondered if they even knew who he was. She was no longer certain she did. Where had he been when it was time to change a nappy or put the kids to bed? He'd been in the pub meeting potential clients or had some other excuse up his sleeve. He certainly hadn't been in the house with his family. He had a way of making everything sound so important and so vital to their long-term interests, even when it wasn't and when really he was acting out of pure selfishness and for his own personal pleasure and enjoyment.

Of course, she'd put up with it and just got on with life, as despite her complaints theirs was a comfortable existence. She'd been a good wife to him, despite getting little in return. Now for her pains, here she was struggling back from the shops with half a dozen bags in her hands at least. It was early afternoon, and the bus was predictably late again. Finally, it came, and she could think about getting home. She'd put the groceries away when she got in, she thought, and then would have about an hour to herself before she had to put his evening meal on.

The bus dropped her at the end of the road, and she walked the remaining short distance to their home. She started to walk up the garden path and then stopped in her tracks. Something was different and not quite right, but she wasn't quite sure what it was. She paused and then shook her head. It must just be her imagination, she thought to herself, although it was strange there was a huge motorbike parked opposite. Perhaps that was it. Perhaps that was what was different. It wasn't the kind of mode of transport normally seen in this particular middle-class neighbourhood. She wondered who it belonged it, and then thought nothing much more of it, as she continued to make her way up the path. She pushed her key into the lock and opened the front door. She carried her shopping into the kitchen and then put it down on the floor with a huge sigh of relief. She was just about to sit down herself when she heard a noise from upstairs, which was odd to say the least. She wondered what it was. Perhaps a lamp or ornament had fallen over. She decided to investigate further.

Sally wandered back out into the hallway and proceeded with caution up the stairs. The door to her bedroom was open. She wandered in and then let out a gasp of shock. An intruder was busy rummaging through her jewellery box. He was dressed from head to foot completely in leather. Presumably he was the motorbike rider. He only noticed Sally because of the little gasp she'd made at his unexpected presence. The man barely looked up but continued to cram various selected precious items into his jacket pocket. He was clearly very confident of himself and untroubled by Sally's arrival home.

'Don't worry, I'm not going to hurt you,' he told her. 'I just want a few things. That's all, and then I'll be on my way.'

He was a big man with an impressive physique. He had wild, blonde hair and a flowing, untamed beard. He had sharp, penetrating, blue eyes and Sally felt his stare boring into her. He seemed to exert some strange power over her. Clearly, she was unable to overpower him physically, so she just casually accepted the situation, and sat down on the edge of the bed to let him get on with it. She was strangely fascinated by his boldness and audacity and not a bit scared. She simply watched the man as he effortlessly went about his business and made no attempt to stop him. She found it impossible to guess his age or what he might look like in different clothes.

'Take anything you want. I don't need it, and we're insured,' Sally suddenly blurted out, and then wondered why she had.

What an odd thing to say in the circumstances, she thought.

'That's very kind of you. I will,' the mystery intruder in motorcycle gear replied. 'It's good of you to be taking this so well. Not everyone does. I'm impressed,' he said.

Sally continued to watch mildly in awe, as the man finished with her jewellery box and proceeded to her chest of drawers. He found some of her black nickers and put them back. She wasn't a bit embarrassed. Indeed, she'd begun to relax. She slipped her shoes off. For some bizarre reason she couldn't quite comprehend, she found herself loosening her dress. Sally had looked after herself. She might have been the wrong side of forty, although not by much, but she still had a nice, tight figure and attractive, brunette hair. Finally, the man looked up and said he was finished.

'I'd best be off,' he announced. 'Thanks for not make a fuss.'

'There's no need to hurry,' Sally suddenly blurted out, as something seemed to snap inside and take over her normal sensible self and good sense.

It had all been so exciting, different and out of the ordinary from her normal humdrum life. She was enjoying herself and didn't want it to end. In an act of spontaneity that surprised even herself, she undid her dress a little more, so her bra was now showing beneath. The man continued towards the door, so Sally let her dress fall completely off her shoulder.

'You've taken everything else, so why not take me before you go,' she said, quite shocked at her own audacity.

She wasn't going to leave anything to chance this time, so she unclipped her bra and let it slide off to her to reveal her strong, prominent breasts.

'Are you sure you want this?' the man asked in a mildly astonished voice.

'I'm quite sure,' Sally assured him, lying back.

The man slipped off his leather jacket and joined her on the bed. His large, powerful hands started to caress Sally's naked upper body. He did everything slowly, but with a degree of sensuality that made Sally's skin literally prickle with excitement. In the moments that followed, the rest of their clothes seemed just to fall away. Before Sally could begin to feel any guilt or regret, they were making love with a degree of passion she'd not known since before she was married. In truth, she'd probably never known anything like it. It was fantastic. The bed rocked and her body responded in a way she didn't know it could. Certainly, it had never been like this with her husband, but that was no great surprise, she realised with a touch of irritation. He'd always had too many other things on his mind and too many irons in the fire, to be bothered much about her sexual gratification. Now she was getting her own back and enjoying every moment of it.

Finally, they finished and collapsed in a sweaty heap. Sally let out a roar of sheer and pure delight. They lay back in each other's arms, warm and contented. The man, whose name she realised she didn't even know, reached inside his jacket and took out a cigarette, which he lit. He offered one to Sally. She didn't generally smoke but took one all the same. At that moment it just seemed the right thing to do. She inhaled deeply and it felt good. It had all been a wonderful experience. She'd never forget everything that had happened. It was about as far removed from the drudgery of her usual everyday life as it was possible to get. Finally, the man got up.

'I'd really best be off,' he said at last, with a twinge of regret. 'Thanks for everything. I've never known a job like it. I've really enjoyed myself, but I've got more work to do before I can call it a day just yet, despite this being a pretty decent haul.'

'That's all right. I'll come with you,' Sally announced.

The man didn't seem in the least bit surprised by this sudden revelation and took it all in his stride as he had everything else. He just paused for one moment, weighing up the pros and cons, and then said a brief OK, as if he got offers of a similar nature every day.

'You'll be needing this though,' he said, as he threw Sally his jacket. She didn't bother putting on a T-shirt but just pulled the jacket over her naked skin and did the zip up. There was something erotic and exciting about the feel of the rough leather on her breasts. It was sensuous and made her feel like she was someone else. She let out another yelp of delight, as they fled down the stairs, arm in arm, with plans to escape into the vast undiscovered distance that awaited them. They could go anywhere they wanted. They literally ran out of the house in their excitement to get out and start their new life together. The world was their oyster.

The couple jumped onto the back of the waiting *Harley-Davidson* bike, with their heads full of the magic and wonder they'd experience when they hit the road. He passed her the spare crash helmet, but she didn't put it on straight away. She wanted to feel the wind running through her hair for a moment first. Sally took another cigarette, which her lover lit for her. She laughed with joy as they roared off. She knew she wouldn't ever be going back.

FROM TOP TO BOTTOM

It had been a long, bad night. Brown couldn't remember exactly how much he'd drunk, but it must have been a lot. He had a sore head and nauseous stomach. The empty wine bottles and crushed beer cans littered across the dining room floor were rich evidence of what must have passed. He hoped he hadn't made a complete fool of himself yet again. The morning after the night before was never something he enjoyed. He dreaded the waiting office and the prospect of a day of boredom and humiliation, punctuated by intermittent bouts of sickness, ahead. Why he drank to such excess, he wasn't even sure himself. There was no obvious answer. It seemed a good idea at the time, he supposed. He just didn't know when to stop and go to bed. That was his problem. He just hoped he hadn't pinched anyone's bottom or done anything ese equally foolish. If he had, he was certain to find out about it soon enough. In the meantime, it was just a case of getting himself to work. He'd had enough trouble simply dragging himself out of bed. That had been the hardest part.

Now Brown went to the wardrobe to get himself a clean shirt. He put it on, backwards. He took it off, checked which was the front and which was the back, and tried again. Strangely, it still didn't look right, but he couldn't find a label to confirm which was the proper way round. He took it off a second, third and fourth time, but it seemed to make no difference. Eventually he threw it down in disgust and decided to opt to wear something else instead. He found another shirt, which also looked completely wrong when he put it on, but he couldn't be bothered to try a fifth time. He went into the kitchen with it still on backwards. He'd start a new fashion, he thought wryly to himself.

Brown's mouth was dry, and he needed a drink of water to quench his thirst. He got a glass from the cupboard and placed it under the tap. The water ran freely, but the glass wouldn't fill up. He left it there for several minutes, but all it gathered was a dribble in the bottom and barely enough to wet his tongue. He tried again, with the same frustrating result. In a fit of anger, he threw the glass on the floor, but it didn't break. It remained in one piece in an act of insolent defiance. In desperation, he bent over the basin, but his mouth couldn't quite reach the tap. The water just dribbled down the side of his face. Just then he remembered he had a carton of fresh orange juice in the fridge. He would drink that instead. He got it out, but it just burst in his hands, sending jets of wet, slippery juice spraying in all directions over the shiny, ceramic floor surface.

Well at least Brown could have something to eat. He went to the breadbin, but it wouldn't open. It was stuck firm. Nothing would budge it. In the face of such overwhelming odds, he decided to forget breakfast. It was best to quit whilst he was still ahead, if in fact he was, he thought. For once in his life, he'd give it a miss. It was better just to get to work safely in one piece. He'd clear up the mess later. It obviously wasn't his day, so there was no point prolonging the agony. What was wrong with him anyway? He must have drunk more than he realised, he reflected, with a somewhat disturbed expression on his face. He was a bundle of nerves, and his hands were visibly shaking. He suspected he was seeing things. He'd just finish getting ready and get outside. Perhaps the fresh air would do him good and revive him back to normality. It was probably just what he needed. He'd eat later. He'd get a coffee and sandwich at the office.

Brown went upstairs to continue getting dressed. He put on his trousers. They felt uncomfortable, almost as if the zip was at the back, but that was impossible. He put on his shoes, but they were at least a size too small. He found some sandals instead. Both were for left feet, but by squeezing his toes together, he managed to get into them, although they still felt too tight. He decided not to waste valuable minutes with a shower or shave. They'd have to wait until later or a day he felt rather better. He was all out of time and luck anyway. Instead, he just picked up his jacket and briefcase and hurried outside. He didn't notice that he'd left the entire contents of his case scattered behind, including vital documents he needed for work. It would be too late to go back once he realised his mistake.

Brown was relieved just to get out of the house and be on his way to work after such a bad night. He unlocked the car door and climbed inside. He sat in the driver's seat and eased the key into the ignition. The engine started at once. He pressed the clutch down and pushed the gear lever into first. He gave the car some throttle, let the handbrake off, and attempted to set off, but the car stubbornly wouldn't move. It was stuck. He tried second gear, but the same thing happened. The car wouldn't go forwards, despite his best efforts. Third, fourth and fifth were all similarly useless. He opted for reverse and was mildly surprised when he was greeted with relative success. The car lurched backwards. Luckily, he'd parked outside in the road and not in the drive, he thought to himself, or he'd have had to push the car out. Using the mirror and sometimes looking back over his shoulder, he reversed to work. He was aware of more than a few strange looks, but he did his best to ignore them and put them out of his head. He needed to concentrate solely on the road. With care, he eventually arrived at his destination and reversed into the car park.

Brown got out, carrying his empty briefcase, and with as much dignity as someone wearing a back-to-front outfit could muster, attempted to stroll casually in the direction of the main entrance. It was a tall building with its own official doorman. It gave the impression of somewhere where important decisions were made and to a large extent that was the case. Normally the doorman greeted everyone who came in with a smart salute and a sharp click of the heels. Earlier in his career he'd been a military man. This time the doorman didn't observe the usual formalities. Either he didn't recognise or just plain didn't notice the man he regularly saluted every morning. Perhaps it was the strange back-to-front clothing Brown wore. Perhaps it was the cheap sandals on his feet that somehow disguised him. Either way it was no way to treat a head of department. He might be hungover, but he deserved a little respect, Brown thought to himself. Yet, he said nothing. He just sighed and carried on inside. He didn't have the time or inclination to reprimand the old boy. It would serve no purpose, and it would only make him later getting started.

Brown had his own office, on the fourth floor. The lift was out of order. Oh well, the day might just as well continue in the same vein as it had begun. He'd have to take the stairs. At least it would help him sweat off one or two of the previous night's beers. On his way up he passed one or two faces he knew, but they just looked straight through him. He wondered if he'd done something foolish or embarrassing at the party after all. What mortifying and mindless act could have deserved this kind of cold shoulder treatment? Perhaps he'd usher one of his closer friends to one side during the course of the day and ask if anything untoward had happened. Perhaps he'd made a clumsy pass at someone else's wife or been intolerably rude and boorish. Perhaps his somewhat explosive nature had got the better of him. If it had, he had absolutely no memory of it whatsoever. If he had to make an educated guess, he suspected somewhere at the bottom of the situation would be a woman. There usually was. That was his one great weakness that he tended to lose control of when he'd been drinking. On the other hand perhaps he was just the victim of some cruel practical joke. None of it quite made sense to him, but he'd find out the truth of the matter in his own good time. Of that he was certain.

Reaching the top of the stairs, Brown came to the outside of his own personal office, at least where it had always been, but to his astonishment the nameplate on the door had been changed. It no longer bore his. It bore a name he didn't recognise, and which meant nothing to him. What the hell was going on? he thought to himself. He tried to fit his key into the lock, but for some strange reason it didn't fit. He banged on the outside and tried to force the door open, but it wouldn't move. Then he heard someone inside announce the words *Come in*, and the door miraculously opened of its own accord, as if on command of the voice alone. Sitting at what he believed to be his desk, sporting an expensive grey suit and smoking a fat cigar, was a young lad of no more than eighteen. He recognised the face but couldn't quite place it. Then he realised it was one of the cleaners sitting before him. The lad's smart appearance had momentarily disguised his identity, but it couldn't be denied. He was employed by the cleaning company all right.

'Ah Smith, please sit down,' the lad said, in a smug and self-satisfied manner. 'What can I do for you then?'

'Smith? Smith? I'm not Smith. You're Smith,' Brown, the man in the back to front outfit, protested in an indignant voice, as he was reminded of what he believed was the lad's surname.

'My dear fellow, have you been drinking? Come now, be a good chap and run along back to your work. There are walls to wipe, floors to scrub and toilets to clean. They won't do themselves you know,' the young lad declared.

'But, but…' Brown stuttered, struggling to get his words out. 'I'm the boss. I always have been,' he insisted. 'I worked my way up from the bottom of the heap. It used to be my name on the door. Only yesterday it was.'

'Well, you might get there one day if you keep trying and keep your nose clean, but not with an attitude like this,' the lad said. 'Now take your mop and bucket and get on with it. And by the way, do you realise your shirt is on back to front?'

'Oh, sorry,' Brown apologised meekly.

'Appearance is very important. I'm prepared to forget about it just this once, but don't let it happen again. Take note, if I catch you bursting into my office again, sprouting nonsense that I'm Smith the cleaner not you, you'll be looking for a new job. Do I make myself clear? I trust I don't need to say any more on the subject,' the lad said, taking a long puff on his cigar and with an authority of manner that suggested he was way older than his tender years.

'No, of course not, sir. I don't know what I was thinking. I'll change my shirt right away. I don't know what came over me. I must have been dreaming or something. I thought I was the boss for some reason. Of course I'm not. I can't be. It was just a joke. Yes, I was the only joking. I thought…' a very confused and still hungover Brown started to say.

'Look, I don't want to hear it. I'm not really interested. It will have to wait. I haven't got time for this now. I've got work to do. Tell me about it another time if you have to. Meanwhile, I must get on. Shut the door on your way out,' he was told in no uncertain fashion.

With that Brown, or was it Smith after all, picked up his mop and bucket and left. His head was filled with thoughts of endless walls to wipe, floors to scrub and toilets to clean, stretching into eternity. Yet, he was still racked with doubt and the suspicion that something wasn't quite right, and he'd been duped in some way. Then he resigned himself to his work. Better get on with it, he thought, and stay off the booze for a bit. There would be no more parties for him for a while, he realised with a tinge of regret but also a degree of muted acceptance and an air of resigned inevitability about his new name and new position in life.

WILLIAM JONSON'S SCHOOL DIARIES

Johnson was a worried man. End of year examinations were all set to begin on the first Monday after half term. A lot was expected of both him and the students he'd been teaching these past two years. The Headteacher had even had a quiet word with him to say he'd be paying special attention to the results of Johnson's form. The exams would be the first any of his classes had faced from an outside examining body since he'd joined the profession. Johnson had been a brilliant student himself, and it would be a good test of what knowledge he could pass on. He'd left the sixth form of this very school just seven years earlier with the best grades across the board ever achieved by a pupil in the school's long and illustrious history.

It was a lot to live up to and in truth he had little faith in his ability to do so. The central problem was the two years had just sped by too fast. He hadn't prepared his teaching notes well enough in the first place, and he was always trying in vain to catch up. When it came down to it, the sad reality was he just hadn't worked hard enough and put in the necessary time and effort required. He'd rested on his laurels and had allowed himself to be distracted. He hadn't really put himself out, at least not as far as actual lesson preparation went. He hadn't put in the hours needed in the areas that he should have, and the regrettable fact of the matter was he hadn't really perfected the art of how to teach.

Perhaps it had all just come too easily to him when he'd been a student. He hadn't been fully able to adjust to working with those less naturally able than himself in a strictly scholastic sense, though he had in other more vocational ways. He didn't know how best now to rise to the challenge. He'd singularly failed to recognise the root causes of the difficulties he faced until it was too late. It wasn't that he didn't get on with his class. He knew that much. In fact, they got on very well in many respects. Perhaps he had become too close to the project to see the wood from the trees and impart them with the educational tools that were essential for actual academic success. Instead, he'd dwelled more on life skills than educational learning.

Johnson had allowed them to sidetrack him from the core curriculum and what he should have been teaching. They'd talked about other things, like life, love, religion, politics, fears and anxieties, puberty, adolescent development, even sex. They'd drawn him out on these issues at length and extracted his opinions where they could. They'd enjoyed great debates that had taken over normal studies and had replaced the lessons that should have been taking place. Johnson was of an age, not so very much older than his students, that he could still relate to their ideas, beliefs and general concerns. Some of the keenest had even come round to his house in the evenings to carry on these momentous arguments and expound their views.

Johnson was a single man, and it seemed he had all the time in the world to listen to their hopes and dreams. He was fascinated by their boundless energy and their complete faith in the ultimate goodness of mankind and a world that would only let them down in the years to come, even though they were blissfully unaware of that then. The strength of their youthful convictions absorbed him. He wondered where they derived the power source to fuel their unshakeable moral standpoints, and it saddened him to think how during their lives ahead, their beliefs and plans would gradually be diluted and forgotten. They would be sacrificed to the reality of mundane, everyday living, and the daily disappointment it would inevitably bring. All the more reason then why for the time being he should celebrate with them in the joyful glory of their boundless optimism.

They had views on everything, from eating meat to banning the bomb. One thing was a recurrent theme whatever they were discussing. They always took the moral high ground. They always opted for the obvious, easy option, as if everything was black and white and had a simplistic solution. It probably did to them. In the safe confines of Johnson's home, they solved all the world's problems. Famine, fear, war and death, were just minor issues that could just be waved away by the touch of a hand or the sweep of a magic wand. They had answers to everything and for a while Johnson himself had been taken in and carried along. Perhaps everything was in fact so simple that all the politicians and world leaders had just missed the point and the answers that were before their very eyes, because they were searching for remedies that were unnecessary complex.

Johnson wanted to believe that, but when it came down to it, he knew he couldn't. In his heart of hearts, he knew that these meetings of

118

the mind would never progress to anything concrete. They'd never bear real fruit or create an end product of lasting worth and meaning in the long run. Yet, it was fun while it lasted. He was enjoying himself and he realised in his own clever way he was influencing these young, hopeful and naïve personalities and leaving his mark on them. That gave him a feeling of authority and power. He was aware that they looked up to him as some kind of guru and mentor, as he gently pointed them in one direction and then another. As a result, the real work that formed the basis of the course had just never been done. Sure, Johnson had given them a brief outline of the themes and study areas he was meant to have covered, but he knew it was far too thin and incomplete to achieve the kind of results that were expected of him. Now the day of reckoning had finally come.

Johnson had given it all little thought, until in a flash it had caught up with him. He'd pushed it to the back of his mind and for the most part it had remained forgotten. Suddenly he was struck by the realisation that not only his future lay in the balance, if he didn't live up to the high expectations of him, but the future of a class of promising, young students also lay in his hands. Truthfully, he'd let them down. He'd been more than happy to let them distract him from the work that should have been going on, when he knew better and shouldn't have allowed it to happen. He'd welcomed every opportunity to take a break from the teaching of the mundane and boring. Now he was going to pay the price for his folly.

In fairness the syllabus he'd been stuck with wasn't one of his own choice. In fact, it was far from it, but that was no excuse. He'd singularly failed to bring his personal knowledge up to scratch and up to the standard that was required on the aspects where he was a bit rusty and not fully confident. Now these failures were coming home to roost. He was in trouble and what's more he knew it. In the last few frantic days before the exams started, these worrying thoughts had started to spin wildly in his head. He wore a slightly anxious expression on his face and had developed something of a nervous tick. It was simply too late to imbue his students with all the knowledge they needed, he realised. Besides, if he was to do that, he'd have to give himself a crash refresher course first to ensure he got everything right.

Perhaps it had been a mistake to opt for teaching maths and science. At the time he'd been so brilliant at everything that it seemed to make no difference. He thought he couldn't possibly go wrong whatever his choice, and he'd convinced himself that was where the money was. He might have been right, but now despite what he taught, he felt himself being pulled inexorably towards the arts. In class, even as he spoke, he found his thoughts drifting somewhere else. Perhaps he just wanted to escape the pressures of work. He didn't know the true cause. Perhaps he'd just been pushed too hard all his life, by his family, his tutors and even himself, that he was now beginning to resist and push back. He wanted to relax, put his feet up and take a break, but he couldn't.

As the discussions about the nature of the cosmos had drifted ever further from the set syllabus and into debates about the meaning of life itself, so Johnson had distanced himself ever further from the curriculum as it had been plainly outlined to him. When they were discussing the very essence of self, that was the only time he could really be himself. He was in his element. Perhaps he'd found a sense of freedom of expression in their lines of philosophical questioning that he couldn't find in a normal lesson. Proper teaching, in the traditional chalk and blackboard sense, had no longer seemed important or relevant until this moment. Now, alarmingly for Johnson, it did. His overconfidence, general casualness and disregard for formal learning to explore broader themes had unwittingly been his undoing.

He came out of his last lesson before the half-term break, vaguely scratching his head and deep in thought. He guessed that his students had suspected something wasn't right and he wasn't quite himself. He'd tried to offer them words of encouragement for the weeks ahead, but he didn't even believe them himself. He thought about going to the Headteacher's office to confess his neglect of the recognised course. He even started walking in that direction before thinking better of it. He realised that only he could dig himself out of this mess, but where should he start?

Johnson lit a cigarette in the car on the way home that night, an act that was out of character for him, and tried to ponder the few options he had left. The customary broad-ranging discussions in class that day had been noticeably flat and lacking their usual zest, devoid as they were of his accustomed interest and effortlessly natural leadership. He knew he had failed but was less certain what he was going to do about it. His last chance to take decisive action would come when his band of most favoured students visited him at his house one last time before their exams began. He would need a definitive answer before then. If only he could implant all the formulas and equations they needed in their willing heads at this late stage, but he knew he couldn't. It was just pipedreams on his part and pointless pretending otherwise. He needed another solution and perhaps a more drastic one. This was the time for clear, unsentimental thinking and meaningful decision, however painful and hard it might be to make. It was now or never, and Johnson knew it.

As he sat down that evening and drank from an open bottle of wine, he braced himself for the course of action he was going to take. He drew up a devious plan inside his head. It would all start when Ben, Michael, Stewart, Tom and Mark, his most gifted students, and perhaps a handful of others, arrived at his house for their last-minute pep talk and words of advice. He'd give them that, but also something they wouldn't expect from their trusted mentor. When they found out and discovered the truth, it would be too late to act and reverse the effect. It hurt slightly to think about, but he knew he had no choice. This wasn't the time for regret or sentiment. That would come later, if it came ever. Besides, why should he worry unduly? None of it was going to come back on him, he reflected rather foolishly.

The arrangement was they'd come round on the Friday during half-term, before the exams started the following Monday morning. In theory that would give them the rest of the weekend to complete their final revision. Johnson had the few days from now until then to put his plan into operation. It was easy for him. The school was empty as everyone had gone home. He was easily able to get in with his key and work away in his private laboratory alone. If anyone saw him, he'd simply explain he was taking advantage of the students being away to get on with some of his own research and study. As it was, he was lucky. He remained undisturbed and was able to do what he needed to in peace and quiet. Strangely, as he worked he felt no sense of worry, remorse or regret. It was as if some great weight was being lifted from him, and it felt uplifting. It was their young skins or his, he told himself callously, as he bevered away with a peculiar sense of relief and satisfaction.

Then the day came. It was upon him all too soon. He waited patiently for the bell to ring, at it did around 7pm. He answered it, and there they were, standing before him in total unsuspecting innocence. It was everyone he'd expected, but also some others from his class. He wondered if any of them had any inkling something was up. He wondered if any of them realised for a single moment that their brilliant tutor hadn't covered the work he should have and that they were doomed to failure. Johnson guessed not. At least he hoped that was the case.

They fired questions at him, and he answered them as best he could. He continued to maintain the pretence, almost forgetting what was to come next. He tried to forget how much he liked them, Ben and Tom in particular. It was difficult, but he had his career to think of. The discussions continued until late, and then it was time for them to leave.

He called them back. It was then he handed them the case he'd prepared. He explained it was wine, a bottle each, to wish them luck. He said it wouldn't hurt them to have a celebratory glass or two together that night to relax and unwind, before getting stuck into exam fortnight. They tried to persuade him to join them, but he said he never touched the stuff. He knew they'd never notice how he'd tampered with the bottle tops, adjusted the contents and expertly resealed them.

Johnson congratulated himself on his cleverness. He knew the exact chemical compounds to mix that would have no taste but would nonetheless kill them outright. Death, however, wouldn't be instantaneous. It would take a few minutes, just long enough for them all to drink a sufficient quantity to be lethal, before its effect became apparent. He reasoned when they were found, it would be attributed to pre-exam nerves and the pressures built up by the high expectations of parents and peers alike. He would of course express his profound regret. He'd speak of their brilliance, and how it had been plucked all too soon before having a proper chance truly to develop and reach its full potential. He'd convey his sadness they'd never know adulthood or maturity or live to see the prime of their lives. He justified his actions by telling himself he was saving them from the future disappointments they'd surely face. The failures of the rest of his class, Jonson would attribute to shock, caused by the *suicides* of their friends, in some misguided, fateful suicide pact. It all made logical sense, and he was confident his plan would work. Just in case he kept one bottle for himself, lest they should ever suspect or find out. He'd enjoy drinking it. It had been a particularly good year for Burgundy, he reflected as he went to bed.

IF LOOKS COULD KILL

She was beautiful, but very unhappy. Everyone who met her was left to ponder the reasons behind her inexplicable melancholy. To the casual observer, she seemed to have everything. She had the looks, a good job, a nice car and a pleasant home to go back to at the end of every day. She oozed success, but to her it obviously just wasn't enough. She wanted something more in her life, but no one could tell exactly what it was.

Men competed to buy her drinks, but she'd taken just to brushing them away and making her excuses of late. It seemed she'd lost all interest in the opposite sex. Their pathetic attempts to seduce her just didn't do her justice. They were beneath her and an insult to her intelligence. Lately, she was often to be found sitting on her own in the local pub, or propped up against the bar, or sat on a stool in the corner, smoking a cigarette and sipping a glass of wine or a short, normally a double, with a look of sadness on her face. She simply didn't want to rush home after work. She had nothing much to rush home for. She just chose to drown her sorrows instead, whatever they were.

I knew all this because I'd been observing her from a distance. I'd formed the conclusion she was a bit like me really in some ways if not others. I didn't rush home either, but that was another story. On this occasion, it wasn't about me. I wanted to buy her a drink, or offer at least, but I didn't have the nerve. I didn't want to appear like all the other guys who'd tried and failed. Even the one or two who got to first base just seemed to disappear out of the equation after that. They didn't come back for more. Perhaps they just grew frustrated at the painfully slow progress they were making in breaking down her shields and barriers, or got their fingers burned in some other way. It was hard to say. Who knew the truth of the matter? Perhaps she was just too demanding to form a proper, lasting relationship with. Perhaps none of them quite measured up or came up to scratch. One thing I was certain of, I wouldn't either, not with my luck. I just didn't have what it took to make a positive impression on attractive women. I went up to get another drink. I was surprised and a little taken back when she turned and returned my glance. I thought I saw the flicker of a smile for once.

'You've got a kind face,' she said. 'I've seen you around. Do you want to talk?'

'Sure,' I replied rather hesitantly and uncertain of my myself, fully aware I was betraying my lack of confidence when conversing with such as her. 'Can I get you something too?' I asked, as I paid for my own drink.

'No, I'm all right for a moment,' she said, as I sat down beside her. 'Do you want one of these?' she asked, offering me a cigarette. 'I only started recently. It's a filthy habit and I should give up.'

'If it makes you feel better, I'll join you,' I said, extracting a cigarette from the packet she held and allowing her to light it.

I didn't usually smoke, but I thought it might calm my nerves, and it seemed the right thing to do in the circumstances.

'Yes, you've got a kindly face,' she repeated, studying my features in some detail and making me feel slightly uncomfortable at her scrutiny. 'You look like someone I could trust. That's nice. It's what I need right now.'

'Kindly perhaps, but a little ugly I'm afraid,' I suggested, with a philosophical shrug of the shoulders. 'I'm not blessed with good looks, not like you. You're very lucky,' I told her.

'Am I?' she asked, taking a puff on her cigarette. 'Is that what you think? Is that how it seems? Then why am I alone? Why don't I have someone?'

'I've seen you drink in here many times,' I said. 'Numerous men have tried to win your affection. You reject them.'

'It may appear that way, but let me tell you, it isn't so,' she explained, flicking her long, auburn hair out of her eyes, so I could see more of her soft, pale, flawless flesh.

She was probably in her late thirties, but her skin was unblemished and perfect.

'So, you're not married then?' I enquired.

'No, never, and you?' she replied.

'Me? I'm not important,' I said, failing to give a direct answer to her question.

She didn't persist with her line of questioning. Her attention was suddenly caught by a newsflash on the television placed over the bar. The volume was on low, and I could only just hear.

'Two more middle-aged men have been found dead in the Fulham area,' the newsreader announced. 'It's not known if the incidents are connected, and there were no marks on either of the bodies. Police don't know how the men died, and their deaths are being treated as unexplained. One was found…'

Then the voice trailed off.

'Always bad news,' she commented.

'That's the way it generally is,' I agreed. 'People don't want hear about joy and happiness.'

'But then it's not so easy to find it,' she suggested.

'Perhaps,' I nodded.

She was right of course. There was far more misery in the world than contentment and delight. What was more, that would probably always be the case. I knew it, and so did she. There was nothing we could do to change that fact. It was just how it was and always would be. We talked for a little longer. Without invitation a guy I knew as another regular and considered a sort of casual drinking friend came over and joined us. I was mildly annoyed. He was a handsome fellow and unsurprisingly she seemed more interested in him than me. I gradually started to drift out of the conversation. He said something about taking her off to dinner. To my disappointment, she agreed, and they left together. I finished my drink alone and was left to contemplate the tedium of the morning to come.

I didn't see either of them again for a day or two. On one occasion the worried wife of my fellow regular and drinking buddy came by and asked me and the barman if we'd seen him. We said we hadn't since that last evening he'd been in. She said he hadn't come back that night, but I pretended to know nothing about it. What choice did I have? I certainly didn't say he'd left with another woman. I was aware their marriage was on the rocks and in a bad way. I didn't want to do anything to worsen the situation and put the final nail in the coffin. It was odd though. Perhaps he and my auburn beauty had run off to start a new life together. Three days later, when she turned up alone, I knew they hadn't. I asked what had happened. It just hadn't worked out, she replied. She looked a little sad, so I left it at that.

The following day I learned my drinking friend was dead. Apparently, he'd died of a heart attack. It was hard to believe. He'd always seemed so fit and energetic. I was beginning to get suspicious. Could my auburn-haired love have had something to do with it? And what had happened to all the other men I'd seen leave with her and never come back? I decided to confront her and find out the truth. At first she was evasive and pretended she didn't know what I was talking about, but slowly she started to open up.

'I just have bad luck,' she said. 'I want to get married and live a normal life, but I can't. It's just fate.'

I thought I saw a tear well in the corner of her eye, before she choked it back.

'But you're beautiful. Men fall at your feet. You can have anyone you want,' I protested.

'Looks aren't everything. They may seem to be to people who haven't got them, but believe me, beauty really isn't that important. It's only skin deep. It can't bring happiness in itself. Hell, I should know. I've spent twenty years finding out,' she said, taking a sip of her drink and lighting a cigarette.

'Why do you say that?' I asked. 'Was it someone in particular who hurt you so much?'

'No, I'm just cursed,' she answered.

I needed to understand more of what she meant before I could act or offer meaningful advice, so I persisted with the direction the conversation was taking.

'Don't be silly. No one's cursed. It's all in your head. You just haven't found the right person yet,' I said.

'No, listen, I mean I'm really cursed,' she insisted. 'I don't know how to tell you this, but every man I kiss dies. It's as simple as that. I'm a lethal weapon. The moment I kiss them they die in my arms.'

I could barely believe what she was saying. I could easily have concluded she was mad, but I knew inherently she wasn't. I needed to know the rest and understand the missing pieces of her story.

'Don't be ridiculous,' I said, anxious to probe further for the truth of the situation. 'People don't die just because you kiss them.'

'With me, they do. I don't know why. All I know is that it happens just as surely as I'm sitting here. Perhaps I carry some kind of venom in my mouth like a snake. Perhaps I'm a genetic mutation or a throwback,' she speculated, shaking her head with sadness and taking another drag on her cigarette.

'Is that what happened to Frank?' I asked.

She silently nodded.

'And the others?' I enquired.

'Yes,' she said simply.

It was hard to believe, but it was the answer I'd come to anticipate.

'Do you really kiss that well?' I asked.

'I suppose so,' she said.

'Is it aways fatal?' I continued.

'I kiss them, and their eyes just roll over in happiness and they slump into my arms,' she explained.

'Stone dead?'

'Yes,' she confirmed.

'And if you kissed me now?' I wondered.

'I expect so. It's always been the case. I doubt it would be any different with you,' she said.

'Then go ahead and kiss me,' I told her.

'I can't. It wouldn't be right,' she said. 'I've killed enough. Each time I thought it would be different, but each time it was always the same. It was always the identical outcome.'

'Listen, I'm alone. I've got nothing to live for,' I said. 'Just do it. Let me die a happy man. Let me be like Frank. I've got nothing. Give me this one thing. It's all I ask,' I begged.

'You've got a kind face,' she said, just as she had when we'd first spoke.

She then leant forwards to embrace me as I'd asked. Our lips met and my tongue pushed open her waiting mouth. Without warning I sunk my fangs into the fleshiest part before she could even move or react. I released all the venom I could harness from my glands in one long spurt. She looked up and smiled before she died. She now understood.

I kissed her lightly on the forehead and carried her outside. That was one less to worry about. Perhaps I was the only one left now and the only one who hadn't been put out of his misery. I departed quietly to continue my search. I had a job to get on with. I couldn't relinquish my duty, at least not just yet, until I was certain there was no one else. Then finally I'd be able to finish my ongoing quest and finish myself afterwards. That would be my last dying act.

THE WORD

Why won't they believe me? I keep telling them. Why don't they take it in? Don't they understand? He came to my in my sleep and told me to spread the word. He told me of the end of the world. It's nigh, he said.

It's upon us. It's coming soon. He even told me when. He told me to warn them. He told me to say the apocalypse was approaching. That was to be my purpose in life. I was to be the messenger. His was the message. I'm doing what he said, but they won't accept the message. They prefer to ignore the truth and deny the obvious, but it's coming all right. It's coming for certain. I can see it as clearly as day follows night.

I've been blessed. I've been told first, so I might be spared. Those who listen may be spared too. I'm giving them that chance, so they can be prepared for what lies in store, but they're just dismissive. They just think I'm mad, but they can't escape their destiny. They ignore me at best. At worst they're abusive. They laugh at me in the street as I try to spread the word. Some throw eggs and rotten fruit, but I'm not to be deterred. I've been told the reality of the situation we face. I know I'm right. I know what to expect when I venture forth. It no longer hurts. I've learnt to shut it out. I just carry my board. Its message is clear enough. *The end of the world is upon us.* I've even been given the date, so there can be no doubt. It's September 1st. That's when God will strike and vengeance will be his. That's when it will all finally end, and our greed and malice will be punished. That's when everything will go up in a puff of smoke. I'm almost looking forward to it. After all the mockery, it will be gratifying to be proved right. It will bring a degree of satisfaction when they see I wasn't joking and was right all along.

I've tried everything to sound my warning. I've placed adverts in magazines and newspapers, so that people would know what was inexorably heading their way. I've written to radio and television stations, to councils, committees and departments, to MPs and ministers of state. I've done everything I can think of to spread the word and inform the masses of the truth, but it hasn't worked. Daily I've preached in public. I've gone door to door, but no one's listened. It's fallen on deaf ears. They just laughed in my face. So now I just carry my board and my message. It's my full-time job. God gave it to me himself. He gave it to me and not to anyone else. I'm his anointed one. I jacked in the real job I had, but I don't care about that. It was nothing special, and I have no need of it anymore. I have my board, which I carry from town to town and then back to where I started from.

I've lost my friends, those few I had. They went in an instant. They didn't hang around when I started preaching of course. They said I'd lost my mind. I suppose that's no surprise. What can you expect? My meagre social life also vanished. It dried up quickly, what there was of it, once I embarked on my new purpose in life. I don't have a girlfriend or partner. I never really have to speak of, so nothing much was lost there. I have God instead. He's my true friend and the only one I need. I don't need anything else, only him and his message. That's enough. That should be enough for anyone.

Nine months he gave me; the time it takes to produce a baby. He came to me in January and said by September it would all be over. I carried his message through the end of winter and into spring, and then through summer. Now that's nearly over and soon it will be September. It's hard for me, seeing how people continue to ignore me and look through me like I wasn't there. They fail to prepare for what is to come. They don't even seem to care. Their souls mean nothing to them. They appear unconcerned where they end up. Heaven or hell, it's all the same to them. I shall watch them burn one by one. I shall see them go up in flames, until nothing remains of the world they've known.

I'm prepared myself. I know what I'm going to do when the day finally comes. I'll take to the hills. I'll give them one more chance to hear the truth first of course. After all it was the job that he chose me for and gave to me personally. I can't let him down. I must continue whilst there's a heartbeat and breath in my body. I'll go on television if I can. I'm confident of getting a spot on some local station if nothing else. I should be able to stir up that much interest. They love a crackpot.

I'll warn them. I'll explain this is their last chance to save themselves. Then it's up to them. I've done my best. I can't make them listen if they don't want to. If only I could. Heaven knows I've tried. What more can a person do? I'm just a simple man, but one who's been approached by God to carry his word. I've carried it to the utmost of my ability. It's not my fault it's fallen on deaf ears. Why do they choose not to hear? Why do they act like they don't care? Doing the shopping, going to the pub, getting home in time for *Eastenders* or *Coronation Street* are all more important. And they say I'm the one who's mad. I'm the one who's lost his mind. Nothing could be further from the truth. I'm the enlightened one. I know what's going on. They know nothing. They'll only find out when it's too late and when Armageddon actually hits them.

On August 31st they gave me my television spot. The local paper picked up on it first, and that got the TV people interested. Naturally I agreed to go on and do my bit. It was my opportunity to repeat my warning, the one I'd been giving time after time for nine long months, and now for the last time. They introduced me like this:

129

'A local man who's been predicting the end of the world for the last nine months says the world will finally end tomorrow morning. Why September 1st? How do you know this, Dave Clarke?'

'God came to me in my sleep,' I replied. 'He told me what was to come. Don't anyone doubt it. It's going to happen, as surely as I'm talking to you now. He told me to warn everyone. He told me to tell them to save themselves while they still could. He told me to spread his word.'

'Did he tell you how it's going to happen?' the female interviewer enquired.

'He didn't tell me that. He only told me when,' I answered simply but truthfully.

The interview carried on in a similar vein for a bit and then seemed to be winding up. I started to get a bit exasperated.

'Listen, you fools, save yourselves before it's too late. Embrace God. Let him into your lives. This is your last chance. Take your families. Get out of town. Don't die not believing. Believe in him. This isn't a joke. It's really going to happen,' I declared.

'Dave Clarke, who claims the world's going to end tomorrow morning. Watch this space,' the interviewer concluded.

After that I went to pack my few belongings. I knew where I wanted to be when he finally came. I wanted to be up on the common that overlooked the town. I wanted to be there to watch it happen. I left the sparse flat I've barely seen since my quest began for the final time. I took some food and a tent to keep me warm. I ditched my board. It had served its purpose. It had given its warning. I had no further need of it.

As I left, I looked back on those I was leaving behind. They imagined themselves so safe in their little homes. They had their jobs, their cars, their credit cards and their mortgages. If only they knew, if only they realised what little use they'd be to them now. They were so secure in the knowledge they couldn't be touched and that they were above the rules of natural law. How wrong they were. How sad were their lives that were about to end. I pitied them, for they hadn't listened to a single word I'd said. None of them had joined me, and in the morning they'd be no more. That would be it.

With an air of slight nervousness and trepidation, I tried to settle down for the night and wait for the sun to come up. I wondered whether it would. I wondered whether perhaps it would just stay dark instead. There would be no more light, and without light everything, all plant and animal life, would eventually just shrivel and die off to nothingness. Or would the sun come up and then just explode in some almighty cataclysm of the skies and heavens? I didn't know which. Perhaps a deadly virus would be released, and every living thing would be struck dead in an instant. I didn't know the method. I only knew the outcome. I only understood that the world and all its history and all its myriads of people and cultures would be erased in a second. Everything on it and all we'd ever known would shortly be brought to its brief conclusion.

Dawn came. It did so slowly with the sky gradually lighting up, just as it did on any other day. Was it slightly late? Was it slightly early? I think it was probably just about on time. What time would it end? I hadn't been told that bit. Why hadn't he told me? All this waiting was making me edgy. I was getting impatient. I wondered for a moment if I'd been deceived and whether I'd been tricked in some way, but surely not. His message had been so certain and so definite. Surely there was no mistake. Surely an error hadn't been made.

Six became seven then eight and still nothing. Nine o'clock became half nine. Had he got it wrong? Had he let me down after all? Then it happened suddenly and without warning. There was a huge explosion, and the sky turned from clear blue to a fiery red. A bright light of flame shot across the horizon, followed by the grey and black of thick smoke. This was it. I'd been right all along. Why hadn't they listened? Why hadn't they done what I'd said? Why hadn't they followed me to safety? Now it was too late. The town was going up in flames and they'd all be dead. Other towns and cities were no doubt also burning. Only I was left.

God had passed judgement. They'd been punished. They'd paid the price for their sins and for refusing to listen and for not hearing the truth as it was told to them. Nine months they'd had. Nine months to heed the warning and change their lives. They'd had nine months to mend their ways. They hadn't done it and now they'd suffered the inevitable consequences of their complacency and failures.

Soon he'd be coming for me. Soon he'd be coming to take me up to heaven. He'd probably send an angel as his emissary. Now I'd finally get my reward, after nine months of derision and mockery. Now I'd get my just desert. It was only right. I'd done wat he'd said. I'd dutifully carried his word. Now I'd be by his side. Meanwhile, at a roadside café serving breakfast just three or four miles away, a radio played. Music was on the airwaves, although it was suddenly interrupted by a news flash.

'We've just had reports of a major gas explosion which has severely damaged a town in Wiltshire, leaving a large number dead and many more injured. Multiple emergency services are in attendance. It's not known yet whether the explosion was caused by a terrorist act or by accident, but it's already been described as the worst of its kind ever to take place in this country…'

VOICE OF A GENERATION

You had to admire the man. He was the greatest singer of his generation and perhaps all time. He really was. You certainly couldn't convince his many fans and admirers otherwise. Put bluntly he knew his chops. He was the coolest in the business. His name was Ray Phillips, and his music just seemed to say something no one else's did. He was in touch with real life. His lyrics carried a distinct message. He was the voice of his peers and people of all ages. There had been nothing like it since The Beatles. He understood the scene and how best to manipulate the industry to his advantage. He was the big thing that was happening, and he was getting bigger and bigger all the time, if such a thing was possible. Together with his band, The Centaurs, he was being catapulted from a cult independent act into ultimate big-time fame and fortune. His number one fan was Sam.

Sam had followed Ray since the beginning. Sam had been into The Centaurs when they were nothing, when they were still playing pubs and clubs and had yet to sign a record contract. Sam had followed them from one success to the next, as they'd made it up the music ladder to become true pop stars. Ray had been Sam's hero, even in the early days. Even then Sam had recognised this man, this human god, had something no on else did. He was special. He had a magnetic presence and personality. He had star quality stamped over every inch of his body. Sam had even taken to dressing like his hero. He'd gone to great trouble to copy Ray's distinctive look, his clothes and his haircut, down to the smallest detail. Most of all Sam wanted to be Ray, but he knew he never could be. There was only ever one Ray Phillips.

Success had come for The Centaurs, but nothing had changed for Sam. He'd bought the first record, and he continued to buy every new one after that. He bought every badge, every poster, every T-shirt he could get his hands on. his bedroom was full of the stuff. It was like a shrine to the band, with the lead singer at the centre of it. Sam went to every gig. It was the most important thing in his life. In fact, it was the only thing in his life. Nothing else mattered to him. Everything else was irrelevant and just trivia. Sam lived his life through Ray's words. In them he could find everything he was looking for.

Ray had been touched by the mark of genius. He was blessed with supreme talent. He had a rare insight into how young people thought and felt, and he knew how to express it in words. The Centaurs were good. Hell, they were great, but next to Ray they were mere mortals. His was a gift no one else could match. They didn't even come close to it. He was just something else, a one-off in a league of his own. Even the music papers were starting to realise it. They were calling him the most important songwriter in popular music since Bob Dylan, but Sam knew he was even better than that. History would show he was the best and the greatest. Sam had absolutely no doubt. Ray would be immortalised. For years and decades to come, his impact would remain undiminished.

Sam made a convincing lookalike. He'd now had a year or two of practice getting the look just right. He'd dyed his hair a slightly darker shade to make it more like Ray's. He'd backcombed it slightly to give it that same bounce Ray's had on top. He had all the clothes that he knew made up Ray's regular wardrobe, at least what Ray wore on stage and in public. Some had been hard to get, but Sam had managed it, even if he'd had to have some handmade. Ray was a sharp dresser. His style was nothing too fancy, fussy or jazzy, but just classic and cool.

Ray favoured straight black jeans and hip Chelsea boots, although he would have looked good in anything. He had the tall, slim figure of a model. He could have pulled off any look and made it work. He tended to favour fitted T-shirts and body-hugging polo necks, to best show off his impressive physique. He only wore the most expensive brands and labels. Sam had all of these too, even though he'd sometimes had to go without food to get them. Having what Ray had was all that mattered. Even when it meant forking out over £1,000 to have the same leather jacket, Sam had somehow done it and felt it worth it. Furthermore, he'd done it without a thought.

Sam spent hours in front of the mirror each night trying to look more and more like Ray did. He was obsessed with his endeavours. It occupied almost every waking thought. Sam would sit examining himself and playing with his fringe, combing it forward and then combing it back, to see what looked best and what was the most faithful reproduction of Ray's distinctive hairstyle. He leafed through books, magazines and newspapers, featuring Ray, to perfect the look and get it exact, but remained frustrated. He could get the haircut and clothes to almost an exact match, but he was never quite satisfied. Despite his best efforts, Sam still had a larger, wider nose than Ray had, and his ears stuck out more than Ray's did, but Sam could do nothing about that. That was just Mother Nature's cruel trick.

Why did he have to have stupid, obtrusive ears and a big, fat nose? Sam thought. If only he could get rid of them or disguise them in some way, he'd look exactly like Ray. They were of a fairly similar build, even if Sam wasn't quit as toned. People would barely be able to tell the difference. They'd think he was Ray. He'd certainly be able to deceive most but the highly trained eye. When he went out, people in clubs would already occasionally stop Sam and remark how much he looked like the singer. Imagine what they'd say if he got his ears and nose cosmetically altered. They'd be convinced they had a pop star in their midst. They'd think Sam was the frontman of The Centaurs. Imagine the looks and comments he'd get. It would be brilliant, and he'd play up to it of course. He'd play it for all it was worth, even signing autographs if asked. He'd have everything he ever wanted.

Then it struck Sam like a thunderbolt, why not? He could get his face permanently changed. With plastic surgery, they could turn him into anyone he desired. It would cost a lot, but surely it was worth it. Afterwards, his greatest ambition would be realised. He'd be Ray Phillips. The more Sam thought about it, the more he convinced himself it was the way forward. He resolved that he was going to do it. He was going ahead with his plans. He couldn't really think of any valid arguments or reasons against, so there was no point delaying it. It was only a nose and ears job after all. It was no big deal. People had them all the time. It was just the money he was worried about, but even that could be managed. If necessary, he'd just have to borrow it. He could get a loan to fund the procedure if he had to. It shouldn't be that hard, particularly these days. Banks were desperate to lend you money, just so they could claim the interest. It was comparatively normal to have multiple credit cards all maxed out to the limit. Sam would just have to get into debt like everybody else, but he was unconcerned. He had no doubts or second thoughts about the plan of action he'd decided on. To him it would provide the perfect outcome.

Sam spoke to a couple of surgeons in his local district and after several consultations eventually chose the cheapest. It had been harder to get the cash together than he'd expected, but with a bit of effort it had been achieved. Enough had been scraped together to secure the services of the one surgeon he could just about afford without having to go abroad. Even that had been done by arranging a massive personal loan and greatly increasing his overdraft, which he'd eventually have to pay back. Still, Sam was comparatively relaxed. It was only money, he reasoned. What was that compared to his happiness? Money shouldn't stand in the way of his intended progress. Of course it shouldn't. Looking exactly like Ray was the only thing that mattered.

Sam took a few days off work to book himself into the clinic. The operation hurt more than he'd anticipated, but he could live with the discomfort if it worked. He had to spend the first few days after surgery with his head covered in bandages, whilst his nose and ears healed, but eventually it was time for the moment of truth when they could take the bandages off. He barely dared to look. He was afraid in case it hadn't worked. He'd shown the surgeon a picture of Ray's face, and he'd been confident he could make Sam's match, without delving too much into the ethics of the request. Of course, such procedures were easy in theory. Would it work as well in practice? Had the surgeon been true to his word? Sometimes these things went wrong. Other times they were fine. Slowly Sam's bandages were peeled back and pulled off. To Sam's relief, the surgeon had done his job. Sam was Ray Phillips. Even to a trained eye, it would now be hard to tell them apart.

Sam's life changed almost completely after that. No longer did people notice Sam bore a passing resemblance to Ray, they stopped him in the street and asked for his autograph. Sam was only too happy to oblige. It was brilliant and a massive boost to his ego. If people thought he was Ray, who was he to say otherwise? Sam quit his job and decided to move. He wanted to be nearer his idol. He wanted to live in the same city as Ray and hang out pretending to be Ray all the time. He was becoming addicted to perfecting the impersonation and the adoration he was enjoying. It made him feel good inside. It made him feel he was really someone, someone special, someone important and significant and not just a nobody, the nobody he'd been for most of his life before Ray and The Centaurs had come along like a breath of fresh air.

Sam even found there was a healthy living to be made from being the exact double of a famous pop star. Local nightclub owners wanted him to appear at their venues, pretending to be Ray Phillips. Just an appearance was all they needed. Sam didn't even have to sing or perform. His mere presence was an endorsement in itself and enough to boost numbers through the doors. The owners didn't care if he was the real Phillips or not. He and Sam were almost indistinguishable anyway. No one could tell them apart or discern any obvious difference between them, now Sam had taken to working out in the gym too.

Even when Sam told the truth that he wasn't Ray, some weren't convinced and didn't believe it to be the case. They suspected it was just an elaborate hoax, and he was merely pretending to be someone else, a double at that, to deflect excessive and unwanted attention from himself. Often it was easier just to go along with it. If they thought he was Ray Phillips, he'd simply give them what they wanted. He'd tried telling those who mattered the truth, and if they chose not to believe it, it was hardly his fault. He'd done his best at first. Now more and more he went along with the deceit. He started calling himself Ray not Sam and living his life as the man he so admired.

The reaction he got every time he waked into a local club had to be seen to be believed. It was something else, the like of which he'd never experienced. Sam was virtually mobbed. It was just fantastic. People kept buying him drinks and the club owners would give big wads of cash if he promised to come back the following week. He started really to believe he was Ray. He was getting confused between fiction and reality. He could no longer tell the difference himself. He was even consenting to singing a few of Ray's songs now and again and from time to time, when the pressure to became immense and claiming them as his own. Sam had spent years listening to Ray's music and could now do a more than passable version of Ray's distinctive voice, certainly enough to fool a crowd of drunken nightclubbers and keep them sweet. Every time he agreed to sing, they went absolutely mad.

Sam had written fan letters to Ray going way back to when he first started out, but once Ray had hit the big time they'd largely gone unanswered. Ray would even have found time to have a quick word with Sam in the early days, when The Centaurs were still playing the pub circuit and knew most of their fans by face if not by first name. They were just a small, hardcore band of loyal followers then, but they'd grown and grown out of all recognition and proportion. It was no longer like it had been sadly.

136

Since they'd made it big, The Centaurs no longer had time for individuals like Sam and the others who'd helped put them where they were now. Everything had changed as Ray had got bigger. It just wasn't like it had been anymore. They were too big for all that personal fan interaction and contact. In some ways they'd got too big for their breaches, Sam thought. In some ways he'd started to resent the real Ray Philips. Sam himself was the one doing all the small cubs on Ray's behalf. That was where Phillips should be playing, not the massive stadiums and arenas. The man had forgotten his grass roots and spiritual home. He'd forgotten the humble beginnings from which he'd come, and the people like Sam who'd made him what he'd become, the biggest pop star on the planet.

Sam had taken to following Ray's movements. He wanted to get an even closer insight into the man and his habits, so he could make his impersonation even more complete. Sam wasn't happy with everything he found out. These days Ray spent far too much time being driven around in fancy limousines for Sam's liking. He spent too much time drunk or out of his head on drugs, and not enough time writing songs. He was letting the side down. He was letting himself go. It was true The Centaurs had always liked to indulge a bit, as Sam did himself, but not when it started interfering with his real purpose, blunting his talent and stopping him doing what he was good at and what he'd been put on this earth for the sole purpose of. That was when it had to stop, Sam thought. It was no good Ray spending his time with high-class hookers, snorting coke and smoking crack, if it meant he was neglecting his music. Sam was beginning to wonder if in fact Ray was the imposter and not himself. Sam had started to believe perhaps he was the real Ray Phillips.

Then news came that Ray was going to give the true fans what they wanted. He'd been on the road too long, he said. He'd travelled the whole world and was now going to play his hometown again for the first time in two years. He hadn't been on the road at all, not in recent months, Sam thought. It was crap. He'd been living it up. He'd been enjoying the good life. He didn't even have the excuse that he'd been in the studio or anything like that. He was full of bullshit. Even so, Sam would still go to the gig, if only for old time's sake.

Ray himself had heard rumours there was a guy who was the spitting image of himself, and he was intrigued. He was anxious to meet Sam to see if the rumours were true and they looked as similar as people said.

He'd even arranged a backstage pass for Sam, just so they'd have a chance to meet face to face. Who was this person going round the local clubs saying he was Ray Philips? Was he dangerous? Was it just a harmless prank to make a few quid?

Sam gratefully received his backstage pass and thought to himself maybe old Ray wasn't quite so bad. Maybe he hadn't gone soft. Maybe he hadn't forgotten his real fans after all. Maybe he was still OK. Then Sam heard him play. He was horrified. Ray was shit, a pale caricature of the performer he had been. Something was just missing. The bite and the edge had gone. Where was the rawness? The guitars, bass and drums were all too quiet, as if they were now merely incidental to Ray's voice. They'd been replaced by keyboards, and even a strings and horn section. Ray himself was just some sorry, ageing crooner, like Jim Morrison or Elvis when they'd gone to seed and were out of shape. It was sad, even pathetic. It was a joke. To a man they'd sold out good and proper. People shouldn't have to pay money for this, Sam thought.

With excruciating difficulty, he endured the rest of the limp set, shaking his head at how far downhill they'd travelled since he'd first seen the band. Sam waited until Ray left the stage, before returning for his first encore, not that he deserved one. That was Sam's cue to act. Sam rushed backstage and held up his pass. He was let in without question. The security men probably thought he was Ray's brother or something.

Sam caught sight of Ray wandering off towards the toilets and followed him. Sam surprised even himself with how quickly he could move when he had to. Before he knew it, he was alone with Ray in the toilets. Ray was using the urinals and had his back towards Sam. He didn't even wait for Ray to turn round but put one hand over Ray's mouth to stop him screaming and the other hand round Ray's neck.

Slowly and purposefully, Sam squeezed the life out of Ray's body. He didn't put up much of a fight. Sam had expected him to be stronger than that, but the years of drink and drugs had taken their toll. Ray departed this mortal coil with barely a whimper. It was as feeble as his set. Maybe he realised he'd lost it, and it was no less than he deserved for failing his true followers. Sam stripped Ray of his clothes and put them on himself. He put his own on Ray in return. He then dumped Ray's body in a cleaner's cupboard. He reasoned when Ray was found, it would be assumed it was his now infamous impersonator, or the brother the backstage security staff had admitted. No one would think it was Ray.

Sam then went out to face his audience. He'd done the real fans a service, he thought.

'Ready for the encore?' someone asked.

'Sure,' Sam nodded with confidence.

He was ready all right. He'd been ready all his life. He was now going to be Ray Phillips in a way not even Ray could.

A STEP BACK

It was hard coming back. Perhaps I shouldn't have done it, but I guess I had no choice in the matter. There were mother's things to sort out for a start, her clothes, possessions and the house, and there was no one else to do it. As her only offspring, I was her closest living relative. It was my burden to face. So I'd decided just to get on with it. I'd grin and bear it and do the decent thing by the old woman, not that we were very close or anything. In truth we hadn't spoken much in years. We'd been close once, but that was all in the past. A lot had happened since, and we'd failed pretty miserably to patch things up. It was a shame, but that was life.

It was odd coming back to the town where I'd grown up. It hadn't changed all that much. It was still as dreary as it always was. Still, I'd decided for better or worse to hang around for a bit and see what might turn up. I even considered getting a little job, just for a while, until I was ready to go back to London. I just needed a break from that place. It was great of course, but sometimes it could get a bit too hectic and on top of the unsuspecting and careless individual like me. Sometimes it was necessary just to take a step back and take stock of your life. I'd reached that point in mine. Mother's death had been a perfect opportunity to do just that.

The funeral had been a very quiet affair. There hadn't been all that many people to invite in truth. There were just the few friends she'd had, and one or two more distant relatives. Not even all of them had turned up. Not that I was too sorry about that. I wanted it kept quiet. I wanted the minimum of fuss. I wasn't exactly the most popular person in town it had to be said. Hence perhaps the general surprise I was staying around for a bit. Most people had expected me to scuttle off straight back to London as quicky as I could, but not this time. This time was different. Besides, what could they have against me now?

I'd done my duty by the old lady. Anyone could see that was the case. I'd given her the kind of send-off I thought she would have wanted. It was quiet yet dignified. Hadn't I done my bit and atoned for the sins of the past? Didn't I now deserve a little forgiveness? Well, I'd find out in due course. They say in time all memories fade, but I was a living reminder of the hurt that couldn't be forgotten. My mere presence would bring it all flooding back, but there was nothing I could do about it if it did. I'd just have to face whatever they had to give out.

It hadn't always been like this. I'd been popular once or well liked at least. I'd had friends in the town then, back in the years before I left for London. What great harm had I done them? Didn't they know I was still the same person, the one they'd liked at the time. But you couldn't persuade any of them of that. They were so insular, so narrow-minded, so one-dimensional, so virtuous and moralistic, so set in their ways, so certain of what was right from wrong. Perhaps I shouldn't go on too much. It wasn't good for my own mental health. If they wanted to be like that, let them get on with it. There was nothing I could do to change their minds, so it wasn't even worth trying. It still hurt of course, to feel shunned, let down and frowned upon, but I was stronger than that. I could rise above it, and I knew I would. I could tough it out, if that was required. I was used to doing just that.

There were still the looks of course, even now after so much time had passed, every time I walked down the street. There were those who remembered and who'd lived in the town when I had. There were those who'd just been warned by others to watch out and keep their distance. Perhaps they should have just put the whole town on alert. It would probably have been easier and saved the gossipmongers a lot of time and trouble. Still, they had to have their fun and their pound of flesh. It was just the fear and loathing they stirred up that I resented, and the implication I was going to do them some great harm. Why should I do that? I'd done nothing wrong. Even so, young mothers pulled their children out of my path and grown men and women turned their heads away in hatred. Old people scuttled inside merely at my presence. It was amazing to see, that little, old me could have such a powerful and dramatic effect on them. It was amazing, but also faintly ridiculous.

I was greeted with coldness every time I went into a shop, just to buy a paper, a loaf of bread, a pint of milk or some cigarettes. Even that was too much. They had to demonstrate their disdain. Frostiness was the best I received in truth. Most of the time they were just plain rude, but

I didn't respond. It was what I expected. I just noticed it more now, after a period away. I didn't receive this treatment in London. I'd half forgotten what the people here could be like. I'd half hoped they'd be different. It had been a while. Water under the bridge, forgive and forget and all that, but not in this case.

I'd hoped in vain. They were still out to get me. They didn't want me back here. They were making that very clear. They'd driven me out once and probably thought they could do it again. They were no doubt surprised to see me hanging around. They probably thought it wouldn't be long before I was off with my tail between my legs, if they kept the animosity up. Little did they know, but the longer I stayed the more the pressure would increase and the more they'd make it their business to get me out.

I couldn't get served in the local pub. I'd been a regular once, but when I went in now it went very quiet. There was a deathly hush as I went up to the bar to order a drink. People waited with bated breath to see what would happen next. Would the barman serve me? Would he not? Would he turn me away? I was told in no uncertain terms my custom wasn't wanted. I was told I'd upset the other customers. Basically, I was told to get lost. It was hard, but I tried not to let it get to me. It was the same when I tried to find a job.

I'd had a job here before, several in fact. I'd been pretty good at them, people had said. I'd been respected in my roles. All that counted for little or nothing now. Perhaps I'd been over optimistic even to hope that I'd find work. I just thought things might have changed a bit. I vainly imagined attitudes might have relaxed, but not at all. In fact, it was quite the opposite. I tried a number of places, looking to be taken on in some basic position, but in each one the answer was the same. I tried offices, banks, shops, cafés, all sorts. None of them had anything at present. At present, they said. That was a laugh. That was a joke. They'd never have anything for me. That was obvious.

Some even came right out with it and said as much. They told me I wasn't wanted and just to clear off. It pained me, but I'd become used to it. I just had to accept and disregard their contempt. Mostly I didn't dignify it with a response, but it made me think. What was my great crime? Most of these people didn't even know me. Their only information was through rumour, hearsay and assumption. How could they presume to know so much about me? They knew nothing really. It was easy for them. Their lives were simple and straightforward, and they could make black and white judgements. Mine wasn't. That was something I'd learnt to live with. Why couldn't they? No, they had to be so high and mighty.

Perhaps I shouldn't have come back. Perhaps it was a mistake. Perhaps I should have just got the funeral over with and made my exit. Perhaps I should have put the house on the market straight away and not decided to stay living in it for a bit. What on earth did I think this place held for me? What was its appeal? If I wanted a holiday and a break from the big city, surely I could have chosen somewhere else. Anywhere would have been better, just not here.

It had just been so convenient I supposed. The opportunity had come up and I'd taken it. I'd been looking for an excuse to get out of London, just for a short period, and this had seemed perfect. Well, perhaps not perfect, but I was intrigued to see if memories had faded and hatred softened. They hadn't. I'd found that out to my heavy cost. It was every bit as bad as it ever had been. They were just as prejudiced and bigoted and just as determined to make me remain an outcast in my own hometown.

It was strange. They'd had all this time to come to terms with whatever they thought they had to come to terms with. To think some of these people had once been my friends. That was what made it so hard to accept. They wouldn't give me a chance. I was still the same person underneath, the one they'd formally liked and hung out with. I hadn't changed so very much, but what did I really expect? I was never going to be greeted with open arms. You can't fight discrimination of that kind. It was too embedded and too fundamental to their narrow-minded way of thinking and living. No one could change that, not in a lifetime. I'd done something so apparently unnatural and disgusting, it could never be forgotten or forgiven. It couldn't just be brushed over and skirted around. Sure, they'd liked me once. Of that there was no denying. But I'd been a man then. Now I was a woman.

PANIC ATTACK

Brian didn't know what was happening. He'd never felt like this before. He told himself in no uncertain terms to pull himself together and get a grip. He was a grown man for god's sake and not a kid. What the hell did he think he was playing at? This was a public place. People would

142

stare, but the urge was so great. He wanted to scream. He wanted to shout out. He felt like he was about to have a fit, but he couldn't allow himself to lose control like that. What would Angela think? And the rest of the audience for that matter? They'd think he'd gone mad. Perhaps he had. Perhaps that was the explanation. He was losing his mind. Yesterday he was all right. Suddenly he wasn't. He'd somehow blown a fuse and flipped his lid.

He couldn't think straight. His forehead and palms were covered in sweat. He could feel it dribbling down his neck and sticking his shirt to his back. He prayed Angela wouldn't ask him to get up and buy an ice cream or popcorn or anything like that. It would push him over the edge. He wouldn't be answerable for his actions. He wouldn't be able to hold himself back and in check. He'd be all over the place. He'd be kicking and screaming in the aisles. They'd have to get him a straitjacket to take him away. There would be nothing else for it. As it was, he was rooted to the spot, unable to move or breathe.

What was he playing at? What rubbish was he telling himself? He'd never actually do it. He'd never actually leave his seat like that. He just needed to relax, sit back and watch the film. That was all he had to do. He just had to forget about everything else and concentrate on the movie. He was just being silly. He was having a nice evening out with his girlfriend. What could possibly happen? What could go wrong? He was there to enjoy himself. He was there to have fun. Why did he feel compelled to spoil it by letting all these strange demons into his head? There was no need and no point in his irrational behaviour. He just had to restrain himself and everything would be all right. In another hour he'd be outside in the fresh air. He'd be able to calm down and think straight. Yet, there remained this nagging doubt in his head.

Brian looked around at the other members of the audience. He looked at their faces and was struck by how totally absorbed in the film they were. They didn't have his problems and insecurities. They didn't have his issues and nightmares. Weren't they the lucky ones? Why did he have to be so different? Why couldn't he be more like them? Why did he have to be the mad one? Look at them, he thought. They were so content and so at ease with themselves. Their carefree demeanour was the polar opposite on his own. Compared to him, they were models of sanity and serenity. What was wrong with him? Why couldn't he be the same? Yesterday, he had been. He'd been one of them or considered himself to be. Now he was someone else, someone he didn't recognise.

Something or someone had taken him over. They'd taken control of his body and taken control of his mind.

What was he on about? It was all total crap, the whole lot of it. There was nothing wrong with him. He'd just had a bad day at work. That was all it was. There was nothing untoward happening. He was just a bit tired. His brain was playing tricks on his overwrought imagination. He just needed to sit still and ride it out. The moment would pass soon enough, and it would all be all right. He could work through it, he was certain. Everything would be fine in due course. Just wait and see, he told himself. He'd be back to his normal, assured self before he knew it.

For a few minutes he managed to turn his attention back to the film. It was a good film. He couldn't say it wasn't. Normally he would have been able to get right into it, and it would have absorbed him totally. It clearly had Angela's full focus and concentration. Her eyes were glued to the big screen, and she seemed completely oblivious to his torment and suffering. Why would he want to shout out anyway? What possible reason, motive or justification could he have? It was during the quiet moments of the film he felt the urge most acutely. He wanted to break the silence. It was too much to bear. He wanted to break it in two. He wanted to scream out loud and shatter it for good. What would Angela think if he did? She'd probably never speak to him again. She was so correct, proper, formal and proud in everything she did. She wouldn't be able to stand the embarrassment. She'd be so humiliated. She'd dump him there and then on the spot. It didn't bear thinking about.

Subconsciously Brian found himself raising his hand to his mouth and covering it, lest he should let out a squeak or the tiniest noise. He was scared to move in his seat in case it set him off. He'd never felt so unsettled and anxious in his life. He was sure he was going to do it. The urge was so great. His face was turning red as his blood pressure rose and his pulse raced to almost unbearable rates. He felt he was a pool of sweat. Surely people could sense his discomfort. His head was beginning to spin. He could no longer focus his eyes. His vision was blurred. He could barely see the film. Everything was misty. It was like a dark curtain coming down. He wondered if he was having a heart attack, but somehow he knew he wasn't. It was just blind panic.

He had to get out. He knew he just had to get up and leave the auditorium. He couldn't stay another moment. That was it. Enough was enough, but he couldn't just leave. Angela would be extremely cross if he caused her to miss the end of the film. But what other choice did he have? It was either get out or risk having a fit there and then. What would they think at work if they ever found out and if news got back? He'd be the laughing stock. He'd never live it down. They'd never be able to look at him in the same light again. He could forget all about a pay rise or promotion. That would be it. His chances would be dashed forever. He might just as well start looking for a new job. In fact, come to think about it, there were probably people from work in the cinema at that very moment. It would be just his luck. Imagine what they'd say afterwards. Just consider the gossip. He'd gone in a normal, healthy man and been taken out a gibbering, broken wreck. It didn't bear thinking about.

In some ways it made his plight even worse. He was even more sure he was going to do it. He was even more certain he was going to break. One second he had himself under control and in check, the next he could feel a rising sense of panic that threatened to overwhelm him and knock him for six. That was what he feared most. That was what he couldn't get to grips with. He disliked the sensation that he wasn't in control of himself and that someone else or some other mysterious force was driving him onwards that he was powerless to resist. Logic had no part. He was the puppet of some greater power and greater spirit, much stronger than his own. It was beyond the bounds of normal reason. He couldn't fight it, however much he tried. That was what he hated. By nature, he was something of a control freak, it had to be said. He liked to have his life neatly planned and set out. He approved of structure and order. He resented the fact some greater will had imposed itself on him. It had just come along and blown his ordered world and existence out of the water.

Then he thought what would happen if he did break? What would happen if he did shout out? Would it be so very bad? People might just assume he was shouting at the film, or that he had Tourette syndrome perhaps, and so what if they didn't. So what if they thought he was mad. Did it really matter so very much? Would it really matter if Angela was humiliated? Would it really matter if she left him? She was a bit snooty anyway. She deserved a bit of a comedown, that one. She had it coming. She was too high and mighty by half. He wasn't really sure what he'd seen in her in the first place. It was someone else in the office he'd been after in truth, not her. She wasn't really all that interested in him either, if he was being strictly honest. She'd just seen him as an easy path to get on. Maybe it was worth having a fit just to see the priceless look on her face, and that of the rest of the tossers at work.

Brian didn't like his job so very much. Maybe it was time to get out. But why should he do it for them and for their entertainment, just to see their reaction? He had too much self-esteem for that. Bugger them! He wasn't a performing monkey. He wasn't going to perform for them. He wasn't about to lower himself to their level. They could make their own fun and entertainment, not at his expense, he decided. It just wasn't going to happen, not now or ever. He was just going to sit back and enjoy the film.

Just then Brian heard a horrible, strangled scream from somewhere behind him. The shock and suddenness of it almost threw him out of his seat. Even Angela looked around startled. It sounded like someone was dying, but they weren't. A man in his late twenties, not dissimilar to Brian, was shaking uncontrollably and bellowing at the top of his voice. His arms and legs were flaying in all directions and tears were rolling down his cheeks. He was rocking back and forth, beating his own chest and banging his head with his hands. People in the seats next to him were moving away as fast as they could, to give him space as he slid onto the floor. No one knew what he was going to do next, but he just lay there sobbing and crying.

'I wonder if he's an epileptic,' someone speculated.

'A drug addict more like,' another responded.

Emergency lights went on. Ushers came to assist. A manager appeared on the scene. As they went to take the young man out, he suddenly leapt up and started to run about wildly, tearing at his clothes, trying to rip them off. It took four members of staff to catch and subdue him, and even more to remove him from the auditorium.

'Well, can you believe that?' an astonished and mildly indignant Angela commented. 'I've never seen anything like it. I'm so glad I don't go out with someone like that. I'm so glad I've got you, Brian, someone so sensible and straightforward. You'd never have a fit or do anything like that in public.'

'Of course not, my dear,' Brian replied calmly, trying to forget how close he'd come to a similar breakdown. 'How silly even to have such a thought. As if I ever would,' he added, with a forced chuckle on his part.

At that moment the cinema manager reappeared. He was still a little befuddled and trying hard to regain his composure.

'On behalf of the cinema may I apologise for the interruption,' he said. 'The film will resume again very shortly.'

'I wonder how it will end,' Brian commented, reclining back in his seat and feeling at ease for once.

ISLAND FORTRESS

I've lost track of time. I was a boy then, when it started. Now I'm a man. Middle age has come and now largely gone. I'm growing old. I can feel it. My body is gradually slowing down. Forty years at least it must have been, maybe more. I can hardly believe it could be less, but still the war goes on. Originally there were four of us. Four of us were washed up. Now I'm the only one left. The last of my companions went about ten years back, as near as I can estimate. Since then I've been by myself, but I haven't surrendered. I've continied to fight and do what I can, and will continue to fight to the end.

Everyone else died when the ship that was carrying us went down, after being hit by a torpedo from a submarine. It happened so quickly that most never even made it into the water. Some of us did only to be taken by sharks. Just four of us made it onto dry land that we know of. One went within a year from fever. Another took his own life three or four years later. He thought it was the only thing to do to preserve his honour and dignity. He couldn't stand being so far removed from the real war that everyone else was still fighting.

That left just two of us. We carried on as best we could. We built huts from bamboo sticks tied together by reeds. We survived on a diet of fruit and nuts, fish from the sea and the odd animal we hunted. We kept the only rifle we managed to save from the sinking clean using leaves and vegetable oil. It wasn't in the army manual, but it seemed to work. It could still fire a bullet, although we only had a few cartridges, and that was all that mattered. We could still make a fight of it, if anyone came to take this island from us. We could still make a stand.

Over time we made other weapons to add to our armoury. Using the natural resources at our disposal, we fashioned bows and arrows, spears, catapults and all sorts. No one would catch us unprepared. We'd be ready for any eventuality. We littered the island with booby traps. We dug and then covered holes full of ugly spikes that could impale a man in an instant. We perfected the art of jungle warfare. We had it all worked out in fine detail. We made plans and strategies to defend ourselves. We intended to defend our island down to the last man, even as our numbers dwindled over time. Our collective spirit and commitment to carry on wasn't broken. There could be no surrender and no question of it. We knew that. Surrender was worse than death itself. We wouldn't give up until every last drop of blood had been shed. We'd defend our island in the name of our glorious Emperor. That was the cause we were fighting for. We fought for our leader, for our homeland of Japan and our women and children.

Then we sat and waited for them to come. We didn't know who'd come first, whether it would be our forces or theirs. Would it be a rescue team? Would it be our fellow comrades in arms, or would it be the dreaded Yanks with their pale, white skin? We expected them to come soon. We knew it wouldn't be long. The island was after all in the heart of the Pacific war zone and in the centre of the main fighting, even though it was small and uninhabited. Someone would come. Of that there was no doubt. It was inevitable that they would. Every island was precious. Every one was being fought over to the last.

We climbed to the highest point and erected a flag. We proclaimed the island Japanese and part of the Empire, although now with each passing day and hour, the Empire was getting smaller. Soon it would be gone altogether, but not if we had our way. We'd fight to keep this island forever. It was ours and that's how it would stay. We erected the flag so it could be seen from land, sea and air. That way anyone who came would be forewarned whether we were enemy or friend. With their sophisticated military binoculars, they'd know instantly whether they were a rescue party for the island's band of ragged inhabitants or whether they'd come to do battle. We may not have looked like much, but what we lacked in weaponry we made up for in bravery and guts. It made me feel proud to see our flag fluttering in the breeze. It made me feel proud to be what I was, an officer and a gentleman in the Imperial Japanese Army. I was those things above anything, and they helped to sustain me through all I've had to face both before and since. I've never given up. I've never abandoned hope or my role in life.

We sat and waited. A day passed, then a week and a month. We waited with bated breath. We fully expected that any moment we'd see a boat, a ship or a plane overhead perhaps. We were sure of it. Any second we'd be called into action and have to fight. It was what we'd been trained for. It was what we were here for. It was why we wore the uniforms we did. It was our allotted purpose and the reason for our existence. Others had been born to till the soil, to be teachers or to go into business. Not us; we were soldiers first and foremost. It was the fate of our generation to die in combat. Maybe future generations would be able to return to peace. We never would. We could never be at peace with the dreaded United States, or Britain or Australia. We'd been through too much turmoil and suffering even to contemplate it. Our personal pride and honour were at stake. Our dignity was too great merely to lay down our arms now. There could be no compromise, no ceasefires, no treaties or armistices of any sort whatsoever. There could be no reconciliation for us. We'd battle until we fell exhausted. We'd fight until death.

We sat and waited. At first it was hard to sleep, lest they came in the dead of night. At any moment a flare could illuminate the sky and herald the start. It didn't. It was eerily quiet. It was odd. It was peculiar indeed. It made no sense. Surely this island was every bit as strategically important as every other tiny island in the Pacific. Apparently not, as nothing happened. No one arrived to take it from us. No one came from either side in fact. It was as if we were being bypassed and forgotten. One month became six and still nothing. Six months rolled into a year. We went through four seasons – spring, summer, autumn and winter, but still we didn't fire a single shot, not in anger.

It was a strangely unsettling state of affairs to find ourselves in. What was taking them so long? How could we simply have been forgotten? Surely that was impossible. I couldn't understand or comprehend it at all. Four loyal men, then three, then two, then just one, me, all soldiers of the Imperial Japanese Army were making their stand, against the odds and against the might of the Allies and everything they could throw at us. My compatriots and comrades were itching for a fight, but no one landed. No one attacked. Was the enemy scared? What was it? Had there been a reversal of fortunes? Were they now in retreat and beaten, rather than our own forces on the back foot? Had someone one or lost?

Sometimes I wondered if it had somehow finished without our knowledge. One side was the victor, and the other was the vanquished. Only which was which? Sometimes I wondered if it truly was all over, and the war had ended. A truce had been declared. Surely there was no chance of that. I knew the Japanese people would never surrender. Maybe a peace with honour had been agreed. Surely if it had, someone would have come to tell us. Someone would have relayed the information that we could lay down our weapons and go home. We could never go home. There could never be peace for us. Only death could bring peace.

In the second year the relationship between the remaining three of us began to deteriorate to some extent. One was starting to get noticeably slack in his attitude, for my liking at least. He was letting his guard down. He was becoming too casual and too relaxed, as if the war for him was already over. I tried to warn him they could be here anytime, but he didn't listen. He started to sunbathe and swim and neglect his duties. It made me sick. I found it painful to watch. They could arrive any minute, and that waster would be sunning himself off. I reminded him why we were here. I put him straight on a few things, but he just laughed. He laughed in my face. I should have just shot him there and then on the spot, but I didn't want to waste the ammunition. Things were hard enough as it was. We needed every man we had, however useless.

'No one's coming, not now, not ever,' he scoffed. 'Don't you get it? We're here for life, my friend.'

Maybe he was right. That was the saddest part, but I refused to believe it. Even if they had forgotten us, I hadn't forgotten them. I'd fight on, until my final breath expired. Some years after that we finally saw our first aircraft. I couldn't tell if it was one of ours or one of theirs. It was like no plane I'd ever seen before. It was longer, sleeker and flew faster, much faster, leaving a long trail of vapour behind it. It sounded different too in engine tone. It was nothing like the *Zero* I was accustomed to, or the American *Corsair*. We wondered what it was at first, and whether it was a plane or just some trick of the atmosphere or weather. We thought it was perhaps the sound of approaching thunder. We heard it long before it came into view. Even then it was flying at very high altitude. It was like a bolt of lightning across the sky. There was no hope of signalling to it. There was no hope of being seen by the pilot. Then no sooner had it come into sight than it was gone, over the horizon and beyond in a flash of speed and light. I hoped a plane as sophisticated as that was one of ours. I prayed it was, off to smash the United States.

There's been no contact since. There's been nothing, and now I'm the only one left. I still have my rifle. Remarkably I still have some health, for a man of my age, who's been forced to live in these trying circumstances and surroundings for so long. There's been no more contact, not in all the years, during which I've buried three comrades.

150

There's been no more contact, that was until this morning. Now they choose to come, to invade my island, when I'm all alone. Only then, and not when we had a fighting chance.

I saw the boat cutting through the waves and I could hardly believe my eyes. I thought it was a mirage, but as it continued to sail steadfastly towards the beach, I realised it wasn't. They were coming to invade and take my island as its sole remaining inhabitant from me. For a moment I wondered if I still had the strength to defend myself. Then I realised I did. I was still prepared. I hadn't forgotten my training and planning. I'd been through it all a million times. I'd pick them off as they tried to land. I'd pick them off one by one, in one last glorious strike for my homeland of Japan.

I got into position. The boat had now dropped anchor. It was gleaming white, with a bright blue stripe along the side. It was hardly the design and colour of a proper Japanese fighting vessel. Something that garish had to be Yank. It was the enemy all right. Of that there could be no doubt. Of that I was absolutely certain. They'd finally come after all this time. The defence of the island rested in my hands and on my shoulders.

A smaller rowing boat, apparently their landing craft, had now been launched and was pulling away from the larger mother ship and was heading towards shore. It contained maybe six or seven, perhaps even eight, men. It was hard to tell with the overhead sun beating down, and my eyesight slowly failing. I was unconcerned about their numbers. I'd get all of them. I had enough bullets. I'd wait until they got in the water. That was when they'd be at their most vulnerable. That was when I'd shoot. They'd be like sitting ducks. I'd cut them down as they struggled to shore. I'd show them no mercy. They made me sick anyway. I could see them better now, with their casual clothes and white skins. They weren't even in proper uniforms. They obviously didn't realise the island was defended. They were going to pay heavily for their arrogance.

I waited until they entered the water. That was when I squeezed the trigger of my rifle. The first shot hit one on the arm and he fell back. Another I caught in the head. I was sure of it. My third shot missed. My fourth didn't. It was too easy by half. They were so unprepared. They weren't even fighting back. I decided to leave the safety of my cover and get a little closer. Those who were left were frantically trying to get back in their boat as I picked another off. There were just a couple remaining I hadn't hit. I'd soon see them off. I was only thirty yards away now. I could properly survey my handiwork. I could really admire the carnage I'd caused.

'You never take my island,' I screamed in my best pidgin English, learnt from a spell in Singapore, as I fired a couple more shots from closer range.

Three were drifting wounded and helpless. Four more lay already dead in the water. I'd put those still alive out of their misery. I'd finish them off and send them back to their maker too. I'd do it quickly. It was the decent and honourable way to conduct oneself, even in battle. I had no desire to prolong their agony.

'For god's sake, don't kill us,' one shouted. 'What are you doing, you crazy Japanese maniac? Don't you know the war finished forty years ago.'

'What?' I roared. 'Is this some cheap American trick?'

'No, really, it's all over. It's finished,' the wounded man insisted.

That couldn't be right. There had to be some mistake. There could be no end, not ever. There could be no surrender, not from the Japanese people. Everyone knew that.

'Who won then?' I asked, more out of curiosity than any real interest in his reply.

'The Allies did. Japan surrendered,' the bleeding man coughed.

That was it. Now I knew he was lying, and I shot him in the head where he floated.

'We're not Americans, we're Australians. Please believe us,' his two companions begged, before I finished them off too.

No one would take my island, not through lies and deceit. No one would take it while I lived. I would defend it with all my will and strength until the day I died. There could be no compromise. This was my island fortress. Only when I'd departed could it pass into another's hands.

SCHOOL TRIP

Ben couldn't bear to look at them. Everyone was going, everyone that was except him. It was just so humiliating. It was always the same. It didn't matter what it was. Everyone else's parents could afford it, but not his. That was how it seemed, ever since his dad got laid off. There was just no money coming in, they kept telling him time and time again. If he wanted a new pair of trainers, or a new football shirt, or if he

152

wanted to go to a party or on a school trip, it was just hard luck. At best, if he was lucky, they might buy him some cheap substitute, but it was never what he actually wanted. His classmates wore *Nike* or *Adidas* on their feet. He was stuck with some lesser brand. It was almost worse than having none at all. Better that than being laughed at every time he went to school.

It was so bad that sometimes he'd even feign illness just to get out of games, because he didn't want anyone seeing the embarrassing kit he had. They all wore proper England or Manchester United replicas made by *Umbro*. He had some fake, unofficial shirt his dad had picked up at the local market. Even that had been a birthday gift. He should have been grateful, he supposed. He knew they weren't well off. His dad had done the best he could. It wasn't his fault he didn't have a job. It was just so hard. They just didn't understand the pressure he was under to wear the right things and have the right gear. They just didn't understand what it was like. For kids who didn't have the right stuff, it was as if their face didn't fit. They almost became some kind of outcast. Ben was sick of that and being the butt of every joke. He was just too embarrassed to wear his England shirt. It was better not to play at all. It was better just to give it a miss.

Ben's performance at school was beginning to suffer, just because his parents were poor. His class work, his relationships with other pupils and his sporting prowess were all going to pot. It hadn't always been like this. He'd had friends once. That was before they'd started getting so competitive about the things they had, and he'd no longer been able to keep up and had become labelled the poor kid. He was fed up hearing how they lived in posh houses, how their parents drove expensive cars, how they went away at weekends and travelled abroad, how they had ponies and boats and other things he'd never have. He was fed up, because he couldn't do any of it, however much he wanted to. It would always be nothing more than a pipe dream to him. He was stuck with the rest of his family in the cramped, poky flat they'd had ever since they'd lost the house. He was stuck having to walk to and from school, and everywhere else in fact, ever since they'd sold the car just to pay for food. He was stuck, and now this on top of everything else.

Ever since he'd been told his class were going on a week's residential trip to an outdoor adventure centre in Northern France, he'd desperately wanted to go. He wanted to so much, but he knew it was more or less out of the question. It was just about impossible that his parents could ever find the money, not in a month of Sundays, let alone by the day it had to be in by. It was just about impossible, yet he couldn't stop himself from hoping. Some small part of him refused to let go of the dream, but the more he hoped, the further away it seemed to get from him. It was the most important thing in his life at that moment in time. He was desperate to go with the rest of his class, and for once be truly one of them, if only for a week, but it was such a forlorn hope for him to cling to. He knew there was little or no chance of him actually going. Even so his cautiously approached his parents on the subject, keeping his fingers crossed and hoping for the best.

'You know we haven't had a holiday since dad lost his job. Well, there's this school trip coming up,' Ben explained.

'Oh yes,' his dad replied, without taking any real interest and not looking up from the paper he was reading.

'Yes, they're going to France,' Ben continued.

'And who do you think is going to pay for that?' his mum interrupted.

'I just thought…' Ben started to say.

'Forget it. I'm sorry, Ben, but you know our position. We can't even pay the bills or buy new clothes, let alone pay for holidays,' he'd been told in no uncertain terms.

Ben left the room in tears. It just seemed so unfair. Everyone else was going, every single one of them, but not him. He wasn't going. He was staying at home. He'd be staying at home, whilst they swam, went pony trekking, paintballing, canoeing, completed assault courses and all kinds of other exciting stuff. Until then he'd have to endure their withering, pitying looks and snide, little jokes that his parents were too poor for him to go. He'd have to endure their derision and suffer it in silence. He'd have to put on a brave face, however much it hurt inside.

'Why aren't you going on the school trip, Fowler?' one boy asked. 'Can't your parents afford it?'

'Being cheapskates as always,' another commented. 'You know you want to get them to get you a decent pair of trainers. People are laughing at you in those,' he added.

'Yeah, I wouldn't let my dog wear a pair like that,' someone joked.

'This pair aren't my best,' Ben protested, but no one listened to him. 'I'm not going on the trip, because I'm going with my parents later in the year,' Ben lied again.

'What, to Margate?' someone laughed.

'Or to Bogna,' someone suggested. 'I don't suppose you've ever been abroad, have you Fowler?'

'I don't care. I like it here,' Ben insisted, but he didn't.

Nothing could have been further from the truth. He didn't like it one little bit. He just wanted to get away from it all. He just wanted to be accepted. He wished he was rich. He wished his parents had money, and he wouldn't have to tolerate their abuse. He wished it was happening to someone else.

As the date of the school trip drew nearer and nearer, Ben got more and more depressed. He wished he was dead. All they talked about was the trip and the preparations being made for it. It wasn't much better in class, as whole lessons were being given over to the planning and itinerary, and some of the educational aspects of the visit.

'Perhaps you'd like to do something else, Ben,' one teacher suggested, as the others put together worksheets, maps and all sorts.

It was bad enough being the one missing out, without some misguided person highlighting that fact, Ben thought.

'They'll have forgotten all about the trip by the start of next term,' Ben's dad tried to reassure him.

Ben wanted so very much to believe him, but he knew his classmates too well. No doubt they were eagerly looking forward to rubbing it in about the amazing time they'd had. They'd grab any excuse to make him feel small and run with it. They wouldn't forget. He knew all too well what they were like. They'd remember this humiliation for the rest of his time at school. He'd always be remembered as the only pupil who didn't go on the French trip. He'd forever be labelled as the one big loser who'd stayed at home. It would be a label that would stick for the rest of his time there. He'd never be able to lose it. It would be with him for life.

Ben started playing truant. He started wandering out of school at lunchtimes and then just not going back. He started taking whole days off. It was just too much for him to be with them. He wanted to be alone. He didn't want to be with anyone. He was getting run down. He looked sick and tired. His teachers discussed sending him to a child psychologist. His parents were worried. He was withdrawn and moody. He was finding it difficult to eat. He was losing weight, and all because of the impending trip.

'You know if we could afford to let you go, we would,' his mother said. 'If there was any way at all, but we're in enough debt as it is.'

155

Finally, the day came when his classmates were due to set off. They were going by coach to the ferry and then coach again on the other side. Ben was being assigned to another class for the week. Even that was humiliating in itself. He saw some of his classmates taking their cases and rucksacks out but couldn't bear to watch. They looked so happy, chatting and laughing away, and he was the complete opposite, about as sad as anyone could get.

When they were all on and the coach pulled out, his heart sank. That was it. His last chance had just evaporated. It had disappeared down the hill with them. He'd maintained some futile hope to the last that there might be some last-minute reprieve or some divine intervention of fate. Perhaps the Headteacher would tell him to forget the money and he could go with them, or that they'd all chipped in to pay his fare. It wasn't the case. It wasn't to be. He wasn't going. There was no way, and now they'd gone without him. Ben couldn't concentrate in class. He felt sad and deflated. He disappeared early again, not for the only time that week.

'They'll probably be there by now,' he said to his dad, as he tried to eat his tea that night.

'Try not to think about it, Ben. I bet it's not all it's cracked up to be anyway. A lot of those foreign hostels aren't that great when you get there. Why don't you watch some TV? That might cheer you up,' he advised.

Ben did as his dad suggested and switched on the television, although he wasn't really interested in watching anything. It was just better than sitting about moping, he supposed. The screen flickered into life. It was the news. He could immediately gather that much by the presenter's stern face and the informative and authoritative tone of his voice, although Ben wasn't really paying any attention at first. He was just vaguely aware of scenes of twisted metal wreckage. It must be a car crash, he thought to himself, before taking another bite of his food.

'The coach was travelling south,' the newsreader informed his audience.

Coach, Ben pondered, the word suddenly striking a chord inside him.

'When it sped out of control and left the road,' the newsreader continued.

Coach? His classmates had been travelling on a coach, but he was just being silly. It was too much of a coincidence. It couldn't be. There

156

were no doubt hundreds if not thousands of coaches travelling south every day. Surely it couldn't be them. Surely it was some other coach and not theirs.

'It was containing a party of school children about to start a week's residential visit at an adventure centre in France,' the newsreader explained in a solemn manner.

France? Residential visit? Every word struck another chord in Ben's brain.

'Unconfirmed reports say that at least fifteen are dead, and many more injured. Parents of the children, all pupils of the Ashley Community College, have been informed and are rushing to be with their children's at this very difficult time.'

Ben had heard enough.

'Turn it off,' he screamed in horror.

He knew the truth. They were all dead or dying on that French road. Then it struck him. He should have been with them. He would have been there too if his parents had had the money he'd always craved and if they'd been affluent like the parents of the others in his class. Maybe being poor wasn't such a bad thing. He'd never complain about it again, he thought. On this occasion and for once in his life, it had actually done him a favour and probably saved him in fact. If he'd gone, like he'd begged to be allowed to, in all likelihood he'd be dead or injured too and not sitting safely in front of the television as he was. It was a very scary realisation for Ben. Perhaps someone was looking out for him and his wellbeing after all, when he'd always assumed no one was. It was with a mixture of sadness and yet some relief that he finished eating his meal in silence.

AN ANSWER FOR EVERYTHING

Barbara had begun to suspect something was wrong. She couldn't quite put her finger on it, but she was aware of it all the same. At first she'd barely noticed it was happening. It was mainly just little things really, but they'd slowly started to mount up into something bigger. She'd started putting two and two together, and they seemed to add up to something that wasn't quite right. She just didn't know what that something was. She just had this nagging doubt in the back of her head. She began to suspect another woman, but she didn't want to do that, not after 25 years of reasonably contented marriage, that had produced two kids who were now more or less grown up.

It was just little things she noticed. She wanted to put them down to overwork or stress perhaps. Her husband, Bob, was staying later and later each night at the office. He no longer wanted to spend time with the mutual friends they had. He'd largely lost interest in sex, with her at least. He started to lose weight and had become more concerned with his appearance.

'Do you think I'm looking older?' he asked her. 'Is my hair thinning on top?' he enquired, as he was getting ready for work one day.

'Of course not,' Barbara tried to reassure him, but she wasn't sure her assurances were enough.

She wondered if he was going through some kind of midlife crisis, particularly when he started to update his wardrobe and wear different clothes.

'What does it matter anyway?' she responded. 'None of us are as young as we used to be, are we?'

Then she discovered a note. It had seemingly fallen out of Bob's wallet. He tried to deny it at first, but he couldn't really. It was obviously his. It contained the name and mobile phone number of a woman, Fiona, and a request to meet for lunch at a local hotel.

'She's just a client,' Bob explained. 'I didn't mention it, because I didn't want you to get the wrong idea.'

Just what wrong idea might that be? Barbara wondered to herself, but instead she just nodded. Outwardly she accepted her husband's somewhat unconvincing explanations, but inside they just confirmed what she already suspected. He was seeing another woman, the cheating, lowlife bastard that he was. How could he do it? How did he have the nerve?

Whilst inwardly she quietly seethed with bitterness and resentment, outwardly she tried just to carry on as normal and busy herself with her usual everyday household activities. But now everything he did that was a little unusual or odd, she added to the mounting weight of evidence against him. In her eyes he was already convicted. It was just the final proof she needed. She just wanted to know who this other woman was. She started listening in on phone calls and examining his mail, but she found nothing conclusive. He was a clever one all right, or maybe she'd just got it all wrong. Maybe he was telling the truth about the note. Maybe it was nothing.

Barbara thought about hiring a private detective to follow her husband, but decided it was too expensive. Instead, she'd just follow him herself. A day or two passed and she was ready to put her plan into operation. She decided to start by seeing exactly what it was he got up to after work. She put on her hat and coat one afternoon and drove down to his office to wait outside for him to come out. She got there in good time, so she couldn't possibly miss him. She then planned to follow him home to see what he did, if indeed he did anything at all. She waited and waited, but he never came out. Eventually every light in the building was turned off. Surely he couldn't still be in there, she thought, not unless he was doing something she'd rather not think about. Finally, she decided to give up. There was no point hanging round any longer, she thought.

Barbara drove back ever more confused and with her suspicions even more aroused than they had been in the first place. What was odd was that when she got back, Bob still wasn't home. He was still out somewhere, but he definitely wasn't at his office. She was pretty certain of that, so where was he? When he eventually returned home, she asked him where he'd been.

'Just working late at the office again,' he said. 'We've got so much extra work on at the moment, I have to stay late to finish it.'

Well, he was certainly looking tired. That much was the truth, but she wasn't sure about anything else he said. He hadn't been at the office, unless he'd been working in complete darkness, perhaps with a pretty secretary on his lap. Again, Barbara decided to let it drop for the time being. She'd keep her suspicions to herself temporarily at least but would try and follow him again the next night. She intended to get there even earlier, to see what time he really left.

Barbara waited outside from four o'clock until gone eight. She waited more than four hours, but there was no sign of her husband. The last person left about seven. No one emerged after that, not Bob or any of his colleagues. It was very odd. On the way home she stopped at a corner shop and bought a packet of ten cigarettes. She hadn't smoked for nearly fifteen years, but Bob's erratic and unexplained behaviour was proving a great strain. It was making her very stressed, but she was determined to get to the bottom of it. She also bought some strong mints, so Bob wouldn't be able to smell the smoke on her breath. He didn't approve of women smoking cigarettes. He considered it unladylike. That was why she'd given up in the first place. Now he'd unwittingly driven her back to it.

She sat in the car and smoked for the first time in fifteen years. She wasn't used to it anymore and it made her feel lightheaded, but that was almost good and a relief. She sat and pondered. Nothing made any sense. None of it did. What the hell was Bob up to? Where was he going when he claimed to be at work? What time did he actually leave his office? Where did he go after that? Where did he spend his lunchtimes? Where did he spend his evenings?

Then Barbara remembered the note she'd seen. It had mentioned something about meeting a woman in a hotel. Which one? She tried to recall the name. She should have paid more attention. It was all so frustrating. It was all exceedingly annoying. It was driving her to distraction. She had so many pent-up emotions inside. She wanted to get them out. She wanted to know the truth about what was going on. The problem was she didn't feel there was anyone she could really talk to about her inner turmoil and the suspicions she was having. There was no one she really trusted or felt she could confide in, and she wasn't ready to confront Bob, not quite yet. Barbara decided to follow him one more time. She'd give it one last shot to get to the bottom of the situation. This time she'd make it a lunchtime, to see if that would shed any more light on what he was doing and what exactly was going on.

'What time do you usually take your lunch breaks these days?' Barabara casually remarked that night while they were talking, after Bob had finally got home around ten, looking drained and exhausted.

'Oh, about one,' he replied. 'Why do you ask?'

'No reason,' she said, and left it at that. 'Just checking you're eating enough.'

The following day Barbara was waiting outside the office from about half past twelve. Bob never came out, not at one, not at two, not even at three. Eventually she gave up. She'd had enough.

'What time did you have lunch today?' she asked him later that night.

'Usual time I expect,' Bob answered, not even looking up from the paper he was reading.

'Really? Are you sure? About one, was it? Only I was driving past your office about then. I didn't see you leave. I actually looked out for you, as I just thought by chance I might have done, but you weren't there when I passed,' Barbara explained.

'Actually, I gave it a miss today, now I come to think of it. I didn't have time. We were too busy,' Bob suddenly remembered.

He was a wily one. He always had an answer for everything. There was only one thing for it. She'd have to trap him. She'd have to come up with some clever plan of her own, to find out what he was really doing with his time. Then she remembered the note again. She'd write a note of her own, asking him to meet up, and pop it in the post. Then perhaps she'd finally get to the bottom of it. Then she'd find out what was really going on.

Barbara knew Bob would recognise her handwriting, so she went to her local library to type her note on a computer. She constructed her letter with care. She wanted it to be just right. It had to be, if he was going to take the bait, if he was going to swallow it hook, line and sinker. She asked to meet up. She said it was a matter of urgency that couldn't be discussed on the phone. They had to meet in person. Then she signed it, Fiona. She finished it with a little flourish. She was pleased with her efforts. She put a stamp on the envelope and took it to the post.

Then she waited for her letter to arrive. She wanted to watch Bob open it. She wanted to observe the expression on his face and see how he reacted. Barbara posted it first class, and it arrived promptly the next morning just as she hoped it would. Bob went to pick it up. He'd been doing that more often of late, she realised, now she came to think of it, and his volume of post had increased. There was a time when he would have left it to her to collect the post. Now he was quick to jump up and fetch it himself.

Barabara watched as Bob opened her letter. She knew it was hers as she recognised the label she'd put on the front. She watched as carefully as she could without making it too obvious. She could feel her pulse begin to race, as he took the note out and started to read. He evidently got the gist of it, as he quickly put it back in the envelope.

'What was that?' Barbara asked, trying to stay as calm as she could in the circumstances, and appear as if she was just making idle conversation and had no particular interest in the letter's contents.

'Oh, nothing important, dear,' Bob replied, doing his best to be equally nonchalant and unconcerned, so as not to arouse undue suspicion. 'Just something to do with work. Nothing for you to worry about. I'll sort it out at the office,' he added.

Bob had evidently taken the letter to be genuine and at face value. He clearly didn't realise it was from his own wife. Barbara had asked to meet on the Monday of the following week in a hotel restaurant of her choice. Well, she might as well make it one she liked, she thought. It was silly not to make the most of it and at least get a decent lunch out of her torment.

The next few days went extremely slowly. She was so on edge, both nervous and excited. She could hardly wait for Monday to arrive. She wanted to put an end to this once and for all. She wanted to find out the truth. She wanted to find out whether Bob was having an affair or not, and if he was, who was the lady he having an affair with? She needed some answers, and she was determined to get them, one way or another. She'd had enough of the uncertainty and the cloak and dagger stuff. She was at the end of her tether. This was it, make or break. She wanted to know where the hell was he, if he wasn't at his office. She was fully intending to confront him face to face and find out exactly what he was playing at.

'Got anything special planned today?' Barbara enquired when Monday finally arrived.

'No, just a normal kind of day really,' Bob answered.

It was his final test, and he'd failed. It was his last chance to come clean, and he hadn't. He hadn't taken the opportunity to say he was meeting someone, a woman, for lunch. Barbara put on her very best formal clothes for their date. She wanted to appear smart and businesslike, but also wanted to look attractive, to remind Bob what he was missing. So she did her hair nicely and put on some bright, red lipstick. She wanted Bob to know what a fine wife he was getting rid of, if indeed that was to be the case and the way it was going to finish. She also slipped a packet of cigarettes into her purse. She wanted him to know he wasn't the only one who could spring surprises.

Their date was to be at one, the time Bob claimed he generally stopped for lunch. Barbara had already decided that she'd arrive at twelve and enjoy her lunch by herself before they even met. It was for the best, she realised. If things turned ugly and awkward, she knew she wouldn't want to hang about and eat with the man who'd betrayed her.

Barbara had her lunch by herself just as she planned. It was a rather nice fish dish done in a white wine sauce. She'd chosen something quite light, and it had gone down a treat considering how nervous she felt. She then sat and waited for Bob to arrive. She ordered a gin and tonic and lit a cigarette. It felt good to smoke and she felt emotionally stronger for it. She felt somehow empowered, as she knew how strongly Bob

162

disapproved of smoking. She was just blowing out a coil of smoke when he arrived.

Barbara held her head high and proudly, to preserve her dignity as best she could, and gave Bob a gentle wave. He stopped dead in his tracks, with an absolute look of shock and horror on his face. He started to turn and head towards the exit, before realising it was too late. She'd already seen him. He couldn't just escape. He'd have to stay. He'd have to go back and speak to his wife. He couldn't just ignore her. He couldn't just run out. He wandered over to where she sat, with an appearance of extreme discomfort. Barbara almost let out a laugh. Bob was wearing some kind of peculiar designer suit that she'd never seen before and was far too tight-fitting for a man of his age. He'd also done something odd to his hair. He'd put dye on it or something of the sort, that he hadn't had when he'd left that morning. It was all an ill-advised attempt to look younger than he was, she presumed. He looked quite strange to her eye, but that wasn't the most pressing of matters really, and it wasn't what she'd come here to say.

'Surprised to see me?' she asked.

'Barbara, what are you doing here?' Bob replied, still with a glazed look of bewilderment on his face.

'I've come to see you. I've come to find out what you're up to,' Barbara explained.

'I don't know what you mean. I've come for lunch. I've come to meet a client,' Bob stammered.

'The note was from me, Bob. I sent it, I'm afraid. You've come to meet me, your own wife,' Barbara said to stunned silence. 'Look, I know you haven't been staying late working at your office as you claimed, and I know you've been getting notes from women asking to meet you. I just want to know what's up. I want to know the truth. Are you having an affair? And by way, you look ridiculous,' she added, taking another cigarette from her packet and lighting it.

'Of course I'm not having an affair,' Bob insisted.

'Then why are you dressed like that? Is it for her? is that what she likes? Is she a younger woman? Is that what it is?' Barbara enquired.

'It's none of that. Look, you've got it all wrong,' Bob said. 'All right, you want to know the truth. That's fair enough. I lost my job. OK, that's what it is. That's the truth of the matter. This is what I do instead.'

'What do you mean, you lost your job?' Barbara repeated.

'I was made redundant some six months back. It's as simple as that,' Bob explained.

'Why didn't you tell me?' Barbara pressed him.

'I didn't want to worry you, what with the mortgage and all our other outgoings, and the redundancy money wasn't as much as I hoped. Besides, I was embarrassed. I have my pride,' Bob said.

'So what have you been doing since, whilst pretending to go to your office?' Barbara stuttered, a feeling of apprehension and dread suddenly stirring inside, as she began to suspect the truth but was uncertain she was quite ready to hear it.

'I'm an escort, Barbara. I'm a gigolo, a rent boy, a male prostitute, whatever you want to call it,' Bob announced.

'I don't believe it,' Barbara sighed, the colour draining from her face. 'You can't be surely. You mean you have sex with other women for money?'

'Yes,' Bob confirmed. 'Don't you see? I had no choice. I did it for us,' he pleaded, looking forlornly at his wife. 'I hoped you'd never find out.'

'Why didn't you just get a normal job?' Barbara wondered.

'Believe me, Barbara, I tried,' Bob said.

Barbara just shook her head. She didn't know what to think. She was just too confused. She didn't know which was worse, him having an affair, or this. She didn't know whether she should stand by him or whether she should walk out. He just looked so pathetic. She didn't know whether she'd still be with him in the morning or whether this was it. She only knew it would take one hell of a lot of sorting out.

ACCIDENT OF BIRTH

He was just about the ugliest man alive, Lewis thought to himself. How unlucky he was to be born with a face like his. Not everyone could be a model of course, but this was ridiculous. He might have made something of himself, if it hadn't been for his excessive ugliness. It was always holding him back and destroying his confidence. He'd been a bright kid, but it was such a burden to have to carry through life. It had been bad enough at school, but it was no better now he was an adult. Maybe it was even worse, as he started to realise all the things he was missing out on, just because he had a face like the back end of a bus. It was too wide and too flat, and even a little crooked on one side. He couldn't bear to look at himself in a mirror or catch sight of his reflection as he was walking. It was a constant reminder of how ugly he was. He felt afflicted. He felt like he came from another planet, certainly not the same one everyone else was from. He was just so different in appearance to others around him. He stood out like a sore thumb. It was like chalk and cheese. He was the chalk. Everyone else was the cheese and got to eat as much as they liked. They got what they wanted from their pampered existences. Lewis felt like he never would.

There was the not insignificant matter of girls for a start. How would he ever get a girlfriend with a face like he had? He had no chance. To date he'd never had a woman in his life. He hadn't got close. He couldn't even get to first base. On the odd occasion he agreed to go out with some of the guys at work, he was always the one who'd end up by himself, whether they went to a pub, club or restaurant, whatever they did. The others pulled, at least more often than not, but not he, Lewis. He was probably only invited out of sympathy anyway, he realised. He was a romantic failure of the highest order.

He didn't even like to be looked at. If his eye caught someone else's, he had a tendency just to look away. It was a kind of automatic, internal response mechanism that he'd developed over many years and was now incapable of changing. No one should have to look at ugliness like his, he thought. It shouldn't be inflicted on anyone else. He should keep it to himself where at all possible and as far as he could. As a result, he preferred to stare at his feet when he spoke, or to look slightly to one side, but not straight ahead. That was too much.

Sometimes he was aware people would wince as they caught sight of his face. That made Lewis feel terrible inside. He'd even been asked if he'd been in some kind of accident. It was just an accident of birth, he replied. He tried growing a beard to disguise his unusual features, but it hadn't worked. The hair had only grown in patches, and he'd ended up looking even more of a freak. He was now even starting to recede somewhat on top, which was making his massive forehead look even bigger and more horrific than it was.

It was a cruel joke nature had played on him. It was a cruel joke indeed. His parents weren't especially ugly, which he found hard to understand. They looked perfectly normal. Some might even say they appeared moderately attractive. He had a brother and sister, who'd turned out all right, so why had he been so afflicted? Why had he been cursed? Why had he been beaten with the ugly brush within an inch of his life? He'd even been taken to the doctor as a kid, to ascertain if there was anything fundamentally wrong with his bodily construction, and to see if anything could be done to improve his appearance. No abnormality or deformity had been found. His parents had been told there was nothing wrong with him. He was a perfectly normal child, just a little on the ugly side. He wasn't actually deformed as it appeared. He just wasn't very nice to look at.

Since then he'd had to learn to live with that fact and put up with it every day of his life. At school someone had even taken a picture of him and photocopied it with the caption *Animal, vegetable or mineral?* Others had just dubbed him *The Elephant Man* or *The ugliest boy living*. It was cruel, but it was hardly their fault. Lewis had an ugliness that was rare indeed, that shone out and begged to be poked fun at. He was every bit the freak. He even thought of himself as such, so why wouldn't everyone else? He was an easy target.

He'd found it difficult getting a job. He was intelligent and worked hard, but who wanted someone who looked like him hanging round their office, shop or business? Eventually he'd got a job in a warehouse, where he could be kept away from the glaring eyes of the public. It was a pity because he knew he was better than that. He knew deep inside that he had the ability to do something really worthwhile with himself, if he was only given the chance, but who was going to give him a chance with a face like that?

He'd thought about plastic surgery, but it was just so expensive. He'd never be able to afford it, so he was stuck. He was stuck with people either turning their heads away in shock or staring at him almost in a trance with some kind of morbid fascination. What was even worse were the people who tried not to show the obvious horror they felt. They always gave themselves away in the end by the tiniest glance, the slightest crease of the forehead, the furrowed brow, or the merest twitch at the corner of the mouth. They were desperate not to hurt his feelings, but in some ways they hurt him the most, because he respected them, whereas he couldn't care less for the others.

Any girl who was willing to talk to Lewis at all always touched his heart, but only ended up breaking it, because he knew it could never go any further than that. He was just too disgusting for love. Perhaps if he met a blind girl, he might have a chance, he thought. But why should someone have to put up with him just because they were blind? They had enough on their plate as it was, without him on top to add to their woes. He just had this nagging feeling inside him that he had something to offer, if only he could meet someone who would accept him as he was.

It got so he didn't like going out. He'd given it a go at first with the boys from the warehouse, to see if his luck had changed since school, but it hadn't. It was just the same. Time and again he was the one left on his own. He just ended up getting drunk and depressed. There was no pleasure in that. It just made him more aware of what he was. It just brought home the truth and made him realise it would always be like this. He'd always be the one left by himself, and there was nothing he could do about it. What was worse his birthday was coming up. He'd be twenty-four in a week, and he'd never even kissed someone of the opposite sex, let alone made love. He'd probably die a virgin, he thought. It would be just his luck.

'You've got to go out for your birthday,' they told him at work.

'I don't know,' Lewis replied. 'I don't really feel like it. I may just have a quiet night in instead.'

'You can't do that. You've got to go out. You've been staying in too much,' they insisted.

Eventually he agreed to go out for a curry with a few of the boys. He didn't seem to have much choice. At least they seemed to accept him for what he was. That was something, he supposed. They were all up for going to a club after, but Lewis said he would see how he felt on the night. He wasn't really into clubbing. He'd had enough of being stared at and rejected and left to feel humiliated.

When the night came Lewis tried his best to make an effort, but it was hard. He tried to put a smile on his ugly face. He tried to look like he was enjoying himself. His workmates had even clubbed together to buy him a present, which he appreciated, but it was difficult to appear like he wanted to be there, when he didn't. He wanted to be somewhere else, at home or anywhere in fact. He guessed they could see through his pretence. Not that it was all bad. The food was quite good for a start. At least he could enjoy that. And the boys from the warehouse gave him some much-needed company and companionship, which was more than most people did. Most people just couldn't see past his ugliness.

The problem was they just helped to make it better on the surface. It was simply papering over the cracks. He needed something more than that to find fulfilment. He wanted a girlfriend, a better job and success of some sort. He wanted what he believed his intelligence and hard work merited, but he couldn't make the first step because of his damned ugliness. He wanted a clean break and a fresh start. Just some kind of lucky break would be good, but was he ever going to get it? It seemed unlikely in the extreme.

'Try and look like you're enjoying yourself, mate,' one of his friends, John, commented.

'Yes, perk up a bit,' another, Mike, added. 'It's your birthday and the night's still young yet.'

'Yes, sure, you're right,' Lewis agreed, trying desperately to look happier than he actually was. 'You've all been great. I really appreciate this,' he said.

Even if he wasn't enjoying himself all that much, he wanted them to know he appreciated their efforts.

'Anyway, it's time to eat up lads,' Mike announced. 'We should be moving onto a pub and then a club soon I reckon.'

'I don't know about that,' Lewis protested.

'Of course you do, mate,' Mike insisted. 'We're not taking no for an answer. You're coming with us, all right.'

It seemed it was all decided, and Lewis was stuck with it, whatever his feelings were and what he wanted to do on his birthday. It was easier just to give in to their plans and accept them, rather than fight the inevitable, he thought. They were just about to leave the restaurant, when suddenly a rather strange little man came rushing up to Lewis. He was about forty, with a shiny, bald head, and was wearing a rather garish sports jacket and crimson chords. Even next to Lewis he made rather an odd sight.

'Hold it right there,' he demanded, looking straight at Lewis and none of the others.

Oh no, not another one about to make some joke about his appearance and extreme ugliness, Lewis feared, almost recoiling back from the man's rapid advance.

'Turn around,' the man continued. 'Let's see you from the other side.

'Are you talking to me?' Lewis asked, getting a little annoyed at the unwanted attention.

'Of course, who else?' the man replied. 'Look at that face,' he said to a companion who had now joined him at his side. 'It's perfect. It's a godsend. It's just what we need,' he remarked.

He then turned back to Lewis before continuing.

'Do you want to be in the movies, kid? You can be in my next picture. I'm going to make you a star. I'll get your face on the cover of every magazine and newspaper in the country.'

'I don't know what you mean,' a confused Lewis started to stammer some kind of response.

'Of course you do. Forget Bela Lugosi. Forget Boris Karloff. You're the new face of horror and I'm going to make you rich,' Lewis was told.

Perhaps being a freak, looking different and standing out from the crowd wasn't such a bad thing after all, Lewis began to reflect. Who was he to argue? This could be just the break he was waiting for. It might not lead anywhere, but he was ready and willing to go with the flow for once in his life.

FEMALE INTUITION

For those who don't know me, I grew up in a small village in Gloucestershire. Things were much harder then. We didn't have much money to go around. We had to make do with what little we could find. We had to survive on what could be scraped together. Six of us there were, four girls and two boys. Six children meant six hungry mouths to feed and just a few pounds a week coming in for everything. It was hard all right then, but they were good times, happy times. Sometimes you're happier when you have nothing and have to settle for less. Sometimes you're happier when your life is simple and basic. It was certainly basic for us in the old farmhouse, the First World War not long finished and the Second something not yet on the horizon, still future and distant that we dared not even contemplate.

I left school at fifteen, or was it fourteen perhaps, to go to work in the local shoe factory. I had no exam qualifications or anything like that to speak of that come in such abundance these days. Far less emphasis was placed on them then. It was all about getting out into the real world and finding a job as fast as possible to help the family. It was all about contributing and starting to bring some money in to make it a little easier at home. So I went to work at the shoe factory.

That was where I met my love, Robert. He was an impressive sight for any young woman. I was quite bowled over by him. He was the most handsome man I'd ever seen. I couldn't even dream he'd ever be mine, but that was what he became. When he first spoke, I thought I was in heaven. I could barely breathe, let alone speak or summon up the words to return his conversation. My face went bright red with embarrassment. I remember it quite clearly almost like it was yesterday. It was so mortifying and yet so wonderful at the same time. Then when he asked me out on a date, I could hardly believe it. I could hardly believe it was happening, but it was, and it did.

We got married when I was seventeen. Mother made me wait that long. She wanted me to be sure I knew what I was doing. I knew all right. I knew all along from that very first time. There could be no one else, not for me, not ever. He was all I ever wanted, and it remained the same ever since. We had a lovely wedding and grand hotel reception, although I have no idea where the money came from. We certainly didn't have any. Everyone in the family must have just clubbed together. That's the only conceivable explanation. I drank wine, even though I was too young. It went straight to my head, but I wasn't really drunk. I was just drunk with pure elation, happy to be with the one I loved. Looking back, it was simply marvellous.

We spent the first few years of married life living in his mother's house, before we'd saved up enough to get a place for ourselves. Susan arrived not long after that, and then James. I wanted a third, but he said two was enough. We couldn't afford more than that he said, not to give them a decent life. I still think we should have had the third. I was right about that, what with James going off the rails like he did. It would have been tough at the time, but surely we could have managed it with a bit of scrimping and saving. We were a proper family then. We were never happier than we were in that first place we had, an old, rundown cottage.

Then war broke out again and took Robert away. Those were the worst times, not knowing if my love was coming back or if he was gone for good. I don't know how I got through it. I really don't. Maybe it was because I wasn't the only one suffering. It was the same for everyone else. We were all in it together. We all sat at home with bated breath for six long years, waiting for news and always fearing the worst. Yet still keeping alive that faint hope our loved ones would be kept safe.

I thought the war would change him more than it did. How could anyone be the same once they've seen so much death? But after a few months, he wasn't so very different, not to me at least. It was coming into money that changed us if anything did. It was when my premium bonds came up. I could hardly believe it at first. I only had a handful of the things and had more or less forgotten those. Yet overnight we went from having to watch the pennies, day to day, week to week, month by month and year to year, to being rich. We became well-off just like that, as if a magic wand had been waved. Even then I didn't know if it was a good thing or not. I still don't. I'd never had a lot of money, and I wasn't entirely comfortable when suddenly I did.

We moved into a bigger house. We got a nice car to sit outside on the drive. We ensured the rest of the family were all right. Robert even wanted a boat. I suppose it was a symbol of our newfound wealth, so we got it, although I don't remember ever going out to sea in it that much. It was the money that did for James I believe. He liked it more than he should have. It gave him a taste for the expensive things in life. Of course, it was our fault as much as his. We made it too easy for him. He got in with the wrong crowd, and then we lost touch over time, once he became a fully-grown adult. We heard stories of drugs, fallen women and prison. Robert probably remembers better than I do. I tried not to listen. I still think having too much at an early age made him like he was. He might have turned out all right if we'd stayed in the cottage and hadn't come into all that cash.

Months and then years passed without news, and we learnt to get on with our lives. We did our best to make the most of the affluence that good fortune had given us. We no longer had to work, and we had Susan to be proud of, but there was still that aching hole that James had left that no amount of fine things and lavish holidays could ever quite compensate for. Naturally we tried to contact him. We did our utmost to trace his whereabouts, but he'd have nothing to do with us. He made that clear enough, although we had no idea of the reasons for his ongoing and continued estrangement.

That's why I think we should have had the third, Robert. It's a terrible thing for a mother to lose her child, just as it is for a father. It's just about impossible to get over. It's so hard knowing they're out there somewhere, but you just don't know where. Maybe they need your help but are just too proud to ask for it. I always maintained some small amount of hope that James would come back, but eventually even I had to accept it wasn't going to happen. He was never going to get in touch. He'd separated himself from us for good.

Coming to terms with James was painfully difficult, but once we had as far as we could, I think we enjoyed nearly twenty years of comparative happiness, when we could do more or less whatever we wanted. We had no money concerns to think of, and we could devote ourselves to our leisure interests and the two grandchildren Susan provided. I had my clubs, societies and dinner parties. You took up golf. We went to shows, opera, ballet, the theatre and other such things I probably would never have dreamt of before we became wealthy and before we hit the jackpot. We ate out more often than not. Life was pretty good to us, until we discovered my illness.

Robert was very good throughout. I have to say that. He provided me with wonderful support. He did more than anyone could have reasonably expected. He did more than I would have done myself I think. I recall we were just about to go on another holiday when I first discovered the lump on my breast. Inevitably, I feared the worst, but I didn't want to think about it too much. I decided to wait until we got back before getting it checked out. Perhaps that was a mistake in retrospect. I didn't want to tell Robert at first. I wanted to keep it to myself. I wanted it to be my secret, but it became impossible to conceal the truth. I began to lose weight. Then there was the shocking diagnosis, and the treatment that followed. I don't think Robert could quite believe it. He struggled to accept it was happening to his wife. I'd always been so strong before that. We'd made it through the war for Christ's sake, but this was a battle of an altogether different type that I just wasn't destined to win. It became obvious as the cancer slowly spread, and slowly I became resigned to my fate.

Now by the time you hear these thoughts I shall be dead. I've instructed my executors to read this letter aloud on my deathbed, when my final breath has passed from my body and I've departed from this world, and I must presume my wishes are being carried out as requested. I want it read out before I go cold and stiff and while I still look more or less as I did in life. I want it read out to my assembled family of Robert, Susan and my beloved grandchildren. I want you all to know what I'm thinking and how I'm feeling. I expect you want to know what I'm doing with the money. I imagine you think that's the most important thing, although I have to say it was never the most important thing to me. Other things matter so much more than wealth, and one day I hope that all of you will find that out for yourselves.

Of the actual details, half of my worldly possessions will go to Susan, in time to be split equally between my grandchildren. I have also set up a small trust fund for James, which he can call on in the unlikely event he should ever return. The rest, just under half of everything I own, I'm donating to Cancer Research, in the hope that in the future they may be better able to treat those struck down with the illness I have endured. That's it. For my husband and lifelong love, Robert, I leave nothing I'm afraid, except perhaps the shirt on his back and anything else he can claim to own outright. That's correct. I've instructed my executors to sell everything, so the split I've outlined can take place as fairly and equally as it's possible to manage.

I realise of course that my actions will make Robert homeless, which is regrettable but also inevitable and a price that must be paid. You see I know, Robert. I've always known in fact. There are some things you can't hide. Call it female intuition. Call it whatever you like. All I ever needed was the proof, and it didn't take me long to have that. It was such a long time ago, I know, and forgive me for harbouring some small grudge in part ever since. Perhaps I shouldn't have. Perhaps I should just have let it go. Perhaps I should have learnt to forgive and forget but I couldn't, and this is my way of getting a modicum of revenge and some payback in kind.

I said some things are more important than money, and this is just one of those things in life. Robert, I'm leaving you to find that out, by leaving you nothing in fact. It's a harsh lesson, but one I feel you need to be taught. It's such a shame you did it, my love. All of this could have been yours, all of it, every penny, every pound, but it was never going to be, because I knew the truth all along, even before I fully realised it myself, and even though I managed to hide my knowledge and keep you in the dark for so many years. I still knew. I always knew inside.

I knew the moment you came back, not because you had changed or were in any way different, but quite the opposite. You were calm, content, confident and collected. Only a woman and her love could have done that, but it wasn't my love, was it, Robert? It was someone else's. I assumed she was French, and I was right, wasn't I? You see over time you gave yourself away. It was just little things that did it. An odd word, a phrase here and there out of place, but to a woman that was enough. You gave away what you most carefully tried to conceal. In the end you gave it all away.

An old friend who was with you in France confirmed what I already knew many years ago now, and all this time I didn't tell you. I waited. I bided my moment, and now revenge is sweet. I've hurt you back when you are at your most vulnerable, just as you once hurt me, and I hope you can excuse and forgive me for that. Knowing you as I do, somehow I think you probably will. You also know me well enough to know I'm not one to be crossed and that's why I've done this and couldn't just let it pass and take my knowledge with me to the grave.

I gather there was a child born from your adulterous relationship. Was it a boy or a girl? I never found out, but I gather your French mistress is still alive. I suggest you go and live with her. You've been once before, haven't you, Robert? You told me it was a trip organised by your old regiment, but it wasn't, was it? You see, I found out. You went to see her and your child grown up. I don't blame you. I would have wanted to myself. I would have done the same, but with every choice made there is a cost. I can rest easy now knowing the score between us has finally been settled and your outstanding account has been paid in full.

NINE LIVES

Carter looked at his watch. He was running out of time. He knew he should have left sooner, but something inside him had made him stay. He wanted to be the last one. He'd always been the same. Nothing had changed, even after all these years. He wanted to be the last reporter out of Saigon before it fell.

It was determination like this that had helped him make his reputation. It was his willingness to push himself to the outer extremities of his own physical and mental limits and beyond to get the story he wanted that had made him one of the most sought-after journalists of his generation. His readiness to put his life at risk time and time again was second to none. Like a cat, he had nine lives but had just about used up every one of them. Finally, his luck was running out.

Carter had always possessed some kind of inner sixth sense that had allowed him to walk the tightrope, to hover over the proverbial precipice and still escape, but this time he'd left it too late. He was in serious danger, and he knew it. He had been warned. He'd been told to be at the airport by one o'clock at the latest. Be at the airport then and they could still get him out. Leave it later than that and he'd have to take his chances. Naturally, he hadn't listened. It was now two o'clock and he was still stuck in a huge queue of traffic heading towards the airport.

Everyone was going that way it seemed. Everyone wanted to get out. He hadn't anticipated so much traffic. How stupid of him to be so negligent. He should have done of course. He was a bloody journalist for Christ's sake. He knew the situation better than anyone else. These people were running for their lives, just like he was. And there were only so many more runs the planes could make, before the airport was taken with everything else.

The Cong were already at the edge of the city. It wouldn't be long before they overran it. He had an hour or two at most. He had an hour or two to get to the airport, get on a plane and get out. Commercial flights had long since ceased. Only military aircraft were continuing to fly and still undertaking the hazardous evacuation. Carter had never wished to be safe and sound back at head office so dearly in his life. He'd had some narrow escapes in the past. He'd been to just about every trouble spot in the world. He'd been in Africa, the Middle East and South America at the heart of conflicts, when things were kicking off all around him, but he'd never felt quite like this. It was largely his own fault and a situation of his own making, he realised. There was no getting away from that. He was the chief architect of the perilous position he found himself in.

It didn't help that he'd allowed himself to become separated from his film crew. That was a contributing factor without doubt. Carter had instructed them to leave whilst they still had a chance of getting a flight out. It had seemed like the decent thing to do. They'd been very good to him in the past. He wanted to give them something back and to show they were appreciated. He wanted to repay a little of the faith they'd shown in him. They had wives and families waiting for them back home to think about. They'd stayed as long as they could. He'd felt mildly heroic letting them go. He didn't feel quite so stoic now. Without them he suddenly felt terribly alone. Despite the incessant, humid heat, a strange chill went through him. It was as if he somehow knew this time he wasn't coming back. This was it, his last assignment.

Carter feared what would become of him if he got left behind. He feared what would happen if he fell into the hands of the Cong. He guessed they'd love to get their hands on a foreign journalist and make an example of him. Rumours of their cruelty to prisoners was legendary. In fact, the atrocities carried out by both sides had been stomach-churning. Carter had witnessed it first-hand. He'd seen whole villages laid to waste, women raped, and children burned. No one wanted to fall into the hands of the Cong.

That was why what seemed like the population of the entire city was heading towards the airport with him, with a sense of desperation he'd

175

rarely experienced. No one dared be left behind. Carter was scared he'd be taken for an American. He knew what they thought of Americans and did to them, perhaps with some justification, but he was British. He just hoped they'd know the difference. That was if he didn't get back to the airport, if he didn't get on a plane and didn't get back to London. He still hoped he might just do it yet. He hadn't given up entirely. There was an outside chance they might have waited. It had only been an hour, but they wouldn't wait forever.

It was just this bloody traffic jam. He was still stuck in it, and the cars just weren't moving. Horns were beeping, people were shouting, screaming and gesticulating, but nothing was shifting. It was gridlock. It was blocked solid. That was when he decided to ditch the Land Rover he was driving. He'd just leave it where it was and try to get to the airport by foot.

The pavements were as busy as the roads, he found. Carter tried to push his way through the crowd. Whole families were trying to move with him, weighed down by their most precious possessions they couldn't bear to leave behind. For his part he still had a camera and a tape recorder. He'd dumped everything else, but he hadn't forgotten he was still a journalist. That was the reason he was there in the first place, and he'd continue to document what he could and the fear and despair on the faces he passed.

The sound of gunfire was getting nearer, although Carter was aware it had become more sporadic. Resistance to the advance of the Cong had more or less ceased. It was pointless and a lost cause. Like himself the Cong were now more inconvenienced by the volume of people on the streets than any serious military opposition they faced.

Carter decided to take to the backstreets. It seemed to be his best chance. Everything else had failed. After all this time he was still a good half mile from where he needed to be, and time was really running out now, if it hadn't already done so. He just didn't know. That was one of the most terrible things of all. Even if he got there, even if he reached the airport, there was only a small possibility there might still be a plane, a helicopter or something to take him out.

There were using the runway at the American Embassy. It was the only one left where pilots could still fly in and out from. Some of the city folk had been camped outside for days trying to get a flight. Luckily, Carter didn't need to do that. He was a priority case, as a foreign national and as a member of the international press corps, and as such had been assured of a seat. He just needed to get there.

He'd been told one o'clock, but that time had come and passed. He'd blown it, but he was still trying, now more in desperation than anything else. It was just his instinct to survive that was driving him on. He could have just given up and surrendered. He could have just waited to turn himself in to the first VC soldier he encountered, but something inside wouldn't let him. He had to keep going and keep trying, whilst there was still a smidgen of hope.

There were now men in uniform in the streets. Carter didn't know if they were government troops or the dreaded Cong. He wasn't going to take any chances, so he double backed to avoid them. He'd do anything to avoid being taken. He was running now. He was running for his dear life. He was panting and sweating. For the first time, he was really scared. As he ran, he feared a bullet in the back at any moment. He feared the pain of a bullet tearing through his flesh. He feared the sensation of blood seeping through his shirt. He feared death.

He was now at the perimeter gate. In the distance he could make out a small aircraft being boarded. Instinctively he knew it was his. He should have been on the flight, and he would have been if he hadn't been so bloody late. It was his own stupid fault, and now he was paying the price for his own carelessness. As the plane filled up with those fortunate enough to have places, stewards and military police battled to keep the rest back.

There was a surge towards the gate, and some spilled onto the runway. They were frightened, desperate people. Others were crushed against the huge metal fencing, in their forlorn efforts to reach the plane that would take them to freedom. Carter knew if he was to get on, he'd have to somehow get through them, but there seemed no chance of that. It was a scene of increasing mayhem. There were simply too many to battle his way through.

Carter should have been on that plane. He should have been going home, but instead he'd be forced to watch powerless as it took off, with him not on it, with him still here on the ground, and the Viet Cong breathing down his neck. He knew they were there. They were now on the airport approach way, coming into view, jeeps and tanks, barely 100 yards away, and there was the plane manoeuvring onto the runway, starting to pick up speed, but with him not on it.

Carter watched the aircraft and as he did so he felt his heart sink. This was really it. He'd lost his last chance to get out. He'd seen it evaporate before his very eyes, and there was nothing he could do about it. He was about to be captured by the conquering rebel forces, and heaven knew what fate lay in store for him then. He could be tortured, murdered or incarcerated for years. He didn't know which. And there was his plane, moving down the runway and about to take off.

Carter started to look away and prepare to surrender himself to his captors, when he caught sight of something out of the corner of his eye that made him look back. A small group of people had somehow got onto the runway and were running towards the plane, causing it to veer off course. In his attempts to avoid them, the pilot was getting dangerously close to some outside hangars that bordered the runway. It was hard to watch. Would the pilot be able to straighten the aircraft in time or would he not? It was desperately tight.

Suddenly a wing made contact with the hangar wall, causing the plane to tilt violently. The pilot battled to get it back on the right course, but it was hopeless. It careered sideways, before hurtling into the solid bricks of the hangar wall. There was a dull explosion and the plane burst into flames. It was engulfed in an instant. There was nothing anyone could do. Those on board never stood a chance. They were roasted to death, as he, a British journalist, watched in numbed, awful silence. No one could have escaped the inferno that engulfed them. It was gut-wrenchingly obvious. The crew and passengers were incinerated in their seats in seconds.

As the flames burned brighter, the stench of burning human flesh began to fill the air and made Carter want to vomit. Then he was struck by the thought he should have been with them. He should have been dead also and his flesh and blood melting down to their component parts. He had a strange feeling inside. Suddenly the prospect of taking his chances with the Cong didn't seem so bad. It was better than being in the twisted wreckage of an aircraft, burning to death.

Perhaps fate had intervened on his behalf, he reflected. Perhaps it had somehow contrived to save him, by making him miss his flight. Perhaps he still had one of his nine lives left and had just used it. He now turned to face his captors with more relief than he could ever imagined possible only a few seconds earlier, ready to embark on a new chapter in his life and whatever that held in store for him. He should have been dead anyway, so anything else now would be a bonus.

178

POETIC JUSTICE

'Spread the butter thinly and evenly,' mother always said.

He'd heard her say it a thousand times at least.

'Get into every corner of the bread.'

She was always right. She knew what was what.

'Butter makes the world go round,' she explained. 'It's the very structure and foundations on which this great country of ours is built.'

He'd heard her say it all many times, but he'd never seen it himself, not the outside world that is. This was all he knew – this little piece of earth. This was his place. He had nothing else.

Apply the butter thinly and evenly, with a knife. He didn't have a knife. He wasn't allowed one. It wasn't safe. He wasn't allowed clothes, let alone something sharp. He couldn't be trusted with anything he might hurt himself with. Apply the butter thinly and evenly, on his hands, and then put them between two slices of bread he'd found discarded in the old barn and presumably meant for the chickens that wandered about and occasionally produced eggs. The barn was his home most of the time. The chickens were his companions and he theirs.

Apply the butter and feel it on his skin. It felt all greasy and warm. Put his fingers between the bread and try to eat them. He knew nothing of cannibalism and self-harm. It meant nothing to him. He only knew what he'd learnt within the confines of this limited space. Nothing else mattered or had any relevance. He knew nothing of art, religion or politics. They were alien concepts from an alien world. They were something else beyond his comprehension that had no meaning, not to him, not here in the limited confines of his tiny domain. They simply didn't count. They were from a life and a world he had no part of and never would.

Sometimes he was allowed out, out of the barn at least. Sometimes he was allowed to stretch his legs. Sometimes he was allowed out for a brief walk, like a caged beast given momentary respite. Maybe that's what he was. That's what he felt like. Sometimes he could be seen in his swimming trunks in one of the fields beyond the farm. He could be seen lying in the long grass, his arms stretched out and pretending to swim. He wished he could just swim away. He longed to swim away to somewhere else, somewhere different.

Surely there was more than this, if he could only find it, if he could only escape, but he couldn't. He dared not even try it. He feared the big stick. He feared that most, the big stick she beat him with. If he strayed too far, it was sure to come out. It always had, since he was a kid. He was almost a man now, but he still feared it. It still held him captive. It still had some kind of power over him. It had broken almost every bone in his body that stick had. He had every reason to fear it. She knew how to wield it with precision. She was an expert. She knew how to inflict maximum pain and maximum impact.

If he was ever going to escape, he'd have to get it right. There could be no second chances. If she caught him, the stick would surely come out. He could be certain of that. She'd beat him within an inch of his life and maybe more. Maybe she'd actually go the whole way. Perhaps it would be a mercy if she did. Perhaps it would be a mercy and a blessing if she just put him out of his misery. How he hated that stick. He imagined breaking it into little bits, burning it or even turning it on her if he had the strength, but he couldn't. She was built like an ox. She was a farmer's wife, and she was a brute. He had no chance of overpowering her. There was no point even thinking about it. It wasn't an option. She was just too strong for him.

He liked to slither through the grass. It was one of his small pleasures in life. He'd seen grass snakes and slow worms. He liked to imitate them. He liked to imitate the animals around him. Sometimes he thought he was one of them and not a human. It was only seeing her and recognising some of her in himself that made him realise he wasn't. He had two legs and not four. He had some very vague recollections of a sister from the very distant past, but he couldn't quite remember, and his mother never mentioned her.

What had become of his sister? Did he really have one? Had he ever done? Was it just a dream? Had he just imagined it all? Something deep inside him locked away in his brain told him that once as a child there had been playing and laughter, even fun, but no more. It had all gone. What had happened? What had gone wrong? He still felt some minute connection with that past, and the sibling he wasn't even sure he had. Sometimes he liked to pretend he was a sheepdog. His mother appeared to like that. It seemed to give her some kind of perverse pleasure seeing him run around on all fours, barking out loud. She liked that, as much as she liked anything in life.

'I could use you in the fields,' she joked. 'You could round up the sheep as well as any dog.'

On other occasions she'd tell him to be a pig.

'I want to hear you oink,' she merrily demanded. 'I want to hear you squeal like a hog.

He'd oblige by doing his best impersonation of one. If it kept her happy briefly, he did it. If it kept her away from the stick and using it, it made good sense on his part. It was best to keep on the right side of her if he could. He'd learnt that. It was a mistake to rile her up. It was foolish to cross her. It was a mistake to get her upset. If he did, he knew the price to be paid. He knew what to expect for his impudence.

She kept him chained up at night, sometimes in the barn or sometimes in the yard, depending how cold it was. Then she'd go inside and come back with a bowl of food. It was all the scrag-ends and leftovers of course from something nice she'd had. He ate it just to fill himself up and keep himself alive. Afterwards he'd watch in the dark for an hour or two until eventually the light in the old cottage went out and she'd go to bed. He knew he was safe then until morning, left alone to himself, staring up at the star-filled night, with just his own thoughts for company. He often wondered if anything good would ever happen, or would it always be like this?

When dawn came, everything would be the same. It would still just be the two of them. Once he'd had a father. He must have done, but he'd gone longer ago than he could remember. What had she done to him? What had she done to everything? Was she a normal mother? Was everyone like her, keeping their son locked up? Were they any others? Was there anyone else on the outside? Perhaps he could contact them. Were they alone in the world? Would he ever find out? Would he ever get the chance to live a proper life?

Occasionally she talked of the outside, of shops, villages, towns and other people, but he'd never seen them. He'd never seen them for himself. He only had her word they existed. That was all he had. She could have been lying. She could have been making it all up. He wouldn't have known any different. That was until the night when they arrived. They finally came in a big white car with a flashing blue light on top. Two of them got out, police officers, but he didn't know that. He just watched in stunned silence as they went up to the door of the farmhouse. They knocked once, then twice. Eventually and somewhat

181

reluctantly she came out. He didn't know whether to be scared or delighted. He was a bit of both in truth.

'What do you want?' his mother scowled in a gruff voice.

'Do you mind if we have a look about?' one of the officers asked, who was wearing a tall, blue helmet.

'I do mind as a matter of fact,' his mother replied. 'Have you got a warrant?'

'You are Mrs Greenwood, are you not?' the officer continued.

'I am. What of it?' his mother said curtly.

'Well, we're investigating the alleged disappearance of your daughter, Katherine, and your husband, John. Where are your husband and daughter, Mrs Greenwood? Are they here?' the officer enquired.

'They've gone,' she announced.

'Where have they gone?' the officer pressed.

'I don't know. They just left. I never did anything to John,' she insisted.

'And where is your son, Mrs Greenwood?'

'He's here. There's nothing wrong with him,' she said.

'We've had a report you keep him chained up at night. Is that right?' the officer asked.

'What business is it of yours?' she answered, with no intention whatsoever of helping them in their investigations.

'My god, look over there,' the other policeman suddenly shouted out, alerting his colleague to a sight he barely dared believe.

He was pointing to the shape of a small, teenage boy lying stretched out in the corner of the yard like a dog. The boy had a collar around his neck, which was attached to a chain that was secured to a post. They hadn't noticed him at first, as he was half hidden by the shadow cast by the barn opposite.

'Is that your son?' the officer continued, in a voice full of disgust. 'What on earth have you done to him?'

His colleague rushed over to try to release the teenager, who was almost too unsightly and disgusting to touch, all covered in bruises and his own excrement.

'It wasn't my fault,' the boy's mother protested. 'I didn't mean to kill Katherine. I only hit her once or twice. I didn't hit her that hard.'

'What about your husband, Mrs Greenwood? Did you kill him too?' the officer asked.

'I never touched him. He killed himself. He couldn't live with the truth after Katherine's death. I had to keep Mark here in case anyone ever found out,' she said.

At that moment Mrs Greenwood rushed back inside the cottage. One of the policemen started to follow her, but she returned almost immediately, waving a shotgun menacingly around her head.

'Duck,' the policeman called out in warning to his fellow officer, as a single shot was fired in their general direction, but with no real sense of aim or accuracy or which officer she was trying to hit.

'Keep away. I'm warning you,' Mrs Greenwood threatened.

She then turned the shotgun on herself, pushing the barrel into her own mouth and squeezing the trigger. It was all over before either of the policemen could even move to stop her. They found the key to Mark's padlock in one of her pockets. It was smeared with her blood, but no one seemed to care very much. Sympathy for Mrs Greenwood was in very short supply. She'd evaded justice, but it was almost good it had ended like this, one of the officers commented. It would save the courts a lot of time and expense. She'd got no less than she deserved, both policemen agreed.

'Come on son, we'll get you cleaned up,' said one of the officers, helping Mark into the back of the police car.

'I just don't understand how she got away with it for so long,' his companion commented, with a puzzled look on his face.

'Well, it's very remote out here with barely a soul for miles. Maybe it was lucky we got her at all. It was only the odd remark here and there from the occasional chance visitor, the postman and his like. As you can imagine, she didn't have many of those, but that's what did it in the end. That's what made us suspicious. She might have got away with it forever, keeping him locked up like that,' the police officer declared.

'I suppose we'd better call an ambulance and get her remains cleared up,' his fellow officer suggested.

'No, leave it. We'll alert all the correct authorities when we get back. Let the animals feed on her for a bit. She's been eating them and treating her son like one of them. It will be a form of poetic justice,' the officer said, with an ironic tone in his voice.

All three watched with a peculiar mixture of horror and delight, as the farmyard animals, chickens, ducks, geese and pigs, slowly started to descend on Mrs Greenwood and tuck into the bloody mess that had been her face. It was an ugly sight, and yet at the same time it somehow wasn't. It was something strangely satisfying and almost uplifting to witness.

UNIVERSAL

This was strange, really strange, Wilson thought to himself. There was no accounting for taste, but this was ridiculous. It was a job interview he was attending, wasn't it, and not an audition for the circus? He'd just never seen people dressed like this for a job interview, at least not on this planet. He wondered whether he'd come to the right place. Had he taken a wrong turn somewhere? Had he gone into the wrong waiting room?

Here he was, one of six patiently waiting their turn to be interviewed for the position of clerical assistant, but he was the only dressed in a suit, or indeed even remotely smartly. He understood it was a job for which a suit was required sartorial wear, and not the peculiar assortment of outlandish outfits the other five had on. What on earth were they thinking of? What did they know that Wilson didn't? Who'd tipped them the wink? Who'd told them to dress up like they were going to some freak, alien, glam rock party? Wilson felt every bit the odd one out, with his conservative choice of traditional collared shirt, tie, suit jacket and trousers, and polished leather shoes.

His fellow interviewees sported pink, purple, lemon and lime dayglo clothes in textiles and fabrics Wilson had never seen before, at least not in the shops he frequented, and a wacky assortment of multicoloured wigs. Two even had horns coming out of the sides of their heads. Were the Vikings making a comeback and invading again? Wilson wondered. He very much wanted to ask someone if he was in the right place, but he felt a bit awkward. He didn't want to be the first to speak. He felt rather foolish, but none of the others looked like they felt in the slightest bit uncomfortable. They acted like they did this every day of the week. They seemed calm and confident. Wison felt anything but. He felt uncomfortable and uptight. He wished he'd worn something different. He'd clearly made the wrong choice in his selection of attire. He clearly should have dressed like a zany children's television presenter. Eventually he summoned up the courage to speak.

'I have come to the right place for the job interview?' he asked.

'Yes,' they all replied at once.

'For the clerical assistant position and not something else?' he added.

'Yes,' they all confirmed.

'Say, you've dressed down a bit,' one observed. 'That's very brave. Do you think you'll get away with it? I wish I had the nerve.'

'He's just trying to be a bit different. He thinks it will mark him out from the other candidates. Maybe he's right. Maybe it's not a bad ploy. Maybe they'll go for that,' one of Vikings commented. 'I tell you these horns are murder on my head,' he added.

'I'll bet,' Wilson agreed.

'That's why I left mine at home,' said another in a lime dayglo suit.

'Well, if he can get away with it,' said a young woman in a fluorescent pink suit and purple wig, who up to that point hadn't spoken.

The he in question was clearly Wilson. That's who she meant. It was weird being talked about like he was something outrageously different, Wilson thought, when he considered himself to be just about as straight and normal as it was possible to get. In fact, most of the time he was a bit too reserved and sensible for his own good. Now suddenly he was being treated like he was a freak. It was strange indeed. All he'd done was wear a standard shirt, tie and suit. He'd done nothing more than that. It wasn't as if he'd turned up naked, or wearing an empty baked beans tin on his head. In this particular company in which he found himself, he'd probably be considered more normal if he had.

What he had on was a suit he'd purchased from *Marks & Spencer*, if he remembered correctly. Their clothing was considered pretty middle of the road and inoffensive by most standards. It wasn't the most expensive or top end of the market by any means, but they were a company known for their classic, timeless styles and good quality. He'd never heard wearing their clothes being described as *dressing down*, well not before this. But then this was just something completely beyond his previous experience and comprehension. Now he just wanted to get it over with.

Eventually the first of those waiting was summoned, but not in a fashion Wilson might have anticipated in normal circumstances, but these were hardly those. A woman with dark brown hair, wearing a deep red, velvet catsuit, complete with pointy ears, a tail and whiskers, suddenly appeared at the door. She surveyed the room, carefully taking everyone in, and visibly turning her nose up when her glance fell on Wison. Her eyes then went back to the others, who seemed to please her more.

'I think we'll see you first,' she said, motioning to the candidate in the lime, dayglo suit. 'Let's see what you're made of.'

On any other day Wilson would have found the prospect of being interviewed by a woman in a velvet catsuit as a little odd, and he did to some extent, but after what had gone on already, he took it in his stride. There was no point doing otherwise. He was just somewhat perturbed by the way he'd been looked at, with a mixture of pity and disgust. He didn't like that. He didn't appreciate it one bit. It made him feel even more wretched than he already did. He also wondered what the reasoning was behind being given a time to attend, when they were just going to be picked out one after another in no particular order. It didn't make any sense, well not to him at least. But then none of this made any sense, not if you came from planet earth, as he thought he did.

It was no great surprise to Wilson to find he was made to wait until last. The others were obviously in on something he wasn't part of. Either it was all an elaborate practical joke, or they knew something he didn't. If only they'd told him in advance to wear the most outlandish costume he could find, he would have obliged. It would have been no problem. He could have done it. He'd just never been asked. He'd never got the memo or message. It was a shame. He could have gone to a fancy dress shop and hired something. It would have been worth it. He needed this job or at least thought he did. That was before all this had taken place.

Eventually, after everyone else had been seen and left the building, Wilson's turn came. He was led into the interview room by the woman in the red catsuit. They were four in total on the interviewing panel it appeared, of which she was seemingly the chairperson, if the way she was taking control of the situation and leading proceedings was anything to go by. The other three, all men, sat waiting patiently as she took her place in the middle of them, in what could only be described as a throne, decorated with ornate, gold carving. Wilson had never seen an office with one of these before. He would certainly have remembered and taken note if he had. It wasn't something he witnessed every day of the week. That was evident, but then everything was significantly out of the ordinary as far as Wilson was concerned. He was about as far out of his comfort zone as he could get. And worse was still to come. The actual interview hadn't even taken place yet.

Having already taken in her red catsuit, Wilson quickly glanced to see what the rest of them were wearing. Although their legs were partly hidden by a desk, he could still clearly see to his horror that they wore high heels, black stockings and short, plastic miniskirts, in blue, pink and white respectively. Were they taking the mickey? They were men, weren't they? Wilson suddenly thought with a jolt. Well, they appeared to be, it had to be said, although they looked like something out of a drag show and about to go on stage. Wilson should have been astonished, and he was to an extent, but after what had gone on before, it was no longer such a surprise. It was almost to be expected in the circumstances. He was beginning just to accept things as they were and not think about it or question it too much. There was no point. There was just this nagging doubt in the back of his head. There weren't hidden cameras somewhere, were there? They weren't filming his reactions for the amusement of the audience of some *Candid Camera* style reality TV show? All these things crossed Wilson's mind. Was he to be the star of some twisted porno flick? Were they going to ask him to take his clothes off? He dearly hoped not.

'Well, it's good of you to make an effort, Mister… Wilson,' the woman in the red catsuit said, consulting her notes on a piece of paper in front of her and unable to disguise the sarcasm in her voice.

'I beg your pardon,' a confused Wilson enquired.

'I mean it's good of you to dress up for us,' she elaborated. 'This is an interview for a job, isn't it? Anyway, never mind that. We'd better press on. I've just got a few questions to ask. What did you have for breakfast?'

The question caught Wilson slightly off guard, but he answered as best he could.

'What are your favourite television programmes?' she continued.

'I don't watch that much television,' Wilson replied honestly.

'He doesn't watch that much television,' the three men echoed in unison and with a definite tone of dismay and exasperation.

'Do you prefer beer or wine?' the lady interviewer enquired, moving swiftly on.

'I'm not a big drinker, but beer I think,' Wilson said.

'Beer, my goodness,' she repeated aghast, her eyes almost popping out of her head in utter disbelief.

Wilson couldn't avoid the overwhelming feeling things didn't appear to be going too well for him. He'd obviously come for the wrong job. He didn't know what he was being interviewed for, but surely it wasn't for the position of clerical assistant.

'I am in the right place,' he started to ask, but was interrupted before he could finish his sentence.

'Of course, now shut up,' the woman leading the interview stopped him. 'How often do you go to the toilet?'

It was getting too much and going too far for Wilson. A line was being crossed, he felt.

'That's a bit personal,' Wilson protested, wondering if he should just get up and leave.

'It's just another question,' she told him, as if it was the kind of thing he was asked every day.

Still, she had a kind of unfathomable authority in her voice like a stern headmistress that Wilson found difficult to refuse or disobey. He found himself hazarding a guess in reply, even though he really didn't want to and felt quite embarrassed in doing so.

'Has anyone else got any further questions?' she announced to the floor, apparently in the process of starting to wind the pointless interview up.

'Yes, I have a question,' said the man in the blue miniskirt. 'How often do you have sex?'

That was it. Enough was enough. These people were clearly pornographers or perverts of some sort. There was clearly no clerical job on offer.

'That's none of your business,' Wilson said firmly.

'Yes, I think it is, if you want to work in this office,' the lady interviewer insisted.

'So it is a clerical position you're seeking to fill?' Wilson asked with a note of caution in his voice, just seeking confirmation of why he was here in the first place.

'Of course,' she laughed. 'What do you think you're being interviewed for? Maybe a job as a porn star seeing how you're dressed,' she chuckled, with a mixture of amusement and outright distaste at Wilson's apparently unexpected state of dress and appearance. 'But that's not how we do things here. We're a bit more formal than that,' she declared.

Wilson was still as confused as he had been when he'd arrived, and no nearer understanding the situation he found himself in, but apparently the interview was over.

'You may go now,' he was told. 'We'll be in touch in due course to let you know. I think you can find your own way out.'

Wilson got up and left the room, still in a state of almost complete confusion. He had no idea what had just happened. He hadn't thought to ask more questions himself. He'd been too lost for words. He should have done, he realised, and now wished he had. He cursed himself for not doing so. It might have allowed him to make some sense of the excruciatingly awkward interview he'd just endured. It might have given him some inkling of explanation as to what had just gone on. As he was leaving, he still had none. At least it was something to tell his family and friends, he reflected. He just wasn't sure they'd believe him.

Once outside the interview room, Wilson found himself back in the waiting room, where he'd sat with that strange assortment of freaks and misfits. There was one door leading out and Wilson went through it without delay as quickly as he could. He shut the door behind him on the other side and started to walk off. He didn't look back. He should have, because if he had he would have noticed there were in fact two doors behind him where he'd originally gone in. Both had signs above them, but the ink was now cracked and faded, making them hard to read, but with a bit of effort they could both be deciphered. One said *Universe* and the other *Parallel Universe*. Wilson had just emerged from the second.

As he walked to the bus stop, Wilson looked at his watch. Funny, he thought. It was still saying the same time as when he'd first arrived for the interview. He was certain of that, because he remembered checking it to make sure he wasn't running late. A couple of hours at least must have passed since, but the hands hadn't moved on. The watch must have stopped. He'd better get a new battery, he thought. But he was mistaken. His watch wasn't wrong. It was still working. The hands were now moving again. Time had just stood still whilst he'd taken the wrong door and was walking, living and breathing in the parallel universe. It had only started again now he was out and back in a place he understood, where people wore normal clothing and where buses ran on time, at least sometimes.

As he made his way home, Wilson pondered whether he'd got the job or not. Something told him he probably hadn't on this occasion. The realisation hit him with a mixture of resignation, relief and even mild elation. He found himself smiling. There would be other, better jobs more to his liking, he was quite certain.

Printed in Dunstable, United Kingdom